D1474968

Whispering Trees

Lena Lyle

Published by Prominence Publishing.

ISBN: 978-1-988925-22-6

Acknowledgements

Maiden City Writers group for their support, great company and laughs.

Derry playhouse for the facility they provide to all creative artists.

David Gothard for his encouragement, direction and professional help in the early days.

Last but not least - Brenda McPherson, a kind and loyal friend, who shared many an adventure and a lot of laughs along the way.

Chapter I

"Aunt Letty said Granddad was a cruel auld brute. She said he cut Granny's diddies just cos they were festered."

Young Maggie Millar, standing on a stool at the kitchen table, was chattering to her mother as her small hands tried to rub the clay from the potatoes that were immersed in water in a tin basin. When a potato slipped from her grasp into the basin there was a splash of water that ran down her arms and dripped from her elbows. She didn't mind being wet for this was a fun job. She continued the chatter about her granny, unaware that her mother was no longer taking part in the conversation.

"Is that why she died? Was there a lot of auld pus and blood like the time I got a thorn in my finger?"

Through the words spoken by an inquisitive child Sarah Millar's past life flashed before her. It was a life she did not want to remember or want anyone to talk about. "Leave the rest of the potatoes and go outside and play."

"But there's only a wee wheen left," Maggie said, without lifting her gaze from the task.

"Go outside and play," Sarah shrieked and in a flash Maggie was off the stool and out the back door leaving her mother's mind peeling away the layers of time.

Sarah was thirteen and living in the village of Gleneely, County Donegal, when the news came that her half- sister Bella was ill. Bella had the dreaded tuberculosis and for the first time in her life Sarah was leaving home to go to Aghanloo, just outside Limavady, in CountyDerry. Her job was to look after Bella and baby Amy. While there with a sick woman and a young child she had time to think of the family that she belonged to. Her father died from cancer when she was eight. She remembered an old woman in the village declaring that cancer was a punishment sent from God for some terrible sin committed by the afflicted. She had no memory of her mother but from village whisperings in her childhood she sensed that her mother's death was shrouded in mystery. As she grew older she wanted to draw a veil over it and keep it hidden.

In her new situation she washed clothes, cooked, looked after Amy and kept her innermost thoughts to herself. Bella's sister- in- law, Peggy Fletcher, kept a little shop in the front room of her father's house close to Bella's home. Every morning she came to wash Bella and make her comfortable. It was during these calls that Sarah saw Bella's frail body wasting away. Her coughing penetrated the stillness of the night as this awful disease, like a battering ram, wracked her defenseless body. Every night Sarah shuddered underneath the quilt and listened to Harry Fletcher's footsteps as he tended his dying wife. One morning as she crossed the hall she saw him, sitting at the kitchen table with his head buried in his hands and his shoulders heaving as long deep sobs rose from the pit of his belly. She wished death would come soon to end Bella's agony.

At the end of her first week Sarah was traumatised. Her mind was filled with the fear of diseases that came like a whirlwind and snatched life away. By the middle of her second week the fear gave way to panic. As she fed Amy the spoon in her hand shook and there was no one to notice that she herself needed help. At the end of her second week she packed her bag, took the few shillings Harry had given her and waited for Peggy's arrival. Peggy was aghast to hear that Sarah was leaving and no amount of persuasion could make her change her mind. Despairing at the sudden turn of events, Peggy sent urgent news to Annie, the half- sister who had reared Sarah since she was two years old. The telegram read – 'Sarah left. Can you help? Peggy.' Shaking and tearful Sarah reached home in the afternoon. Before she got a chance to explain how she felt, a furious Annie was waiting for her. "So, feel proud of yourself do you, walking out on a dying woman and her bit of a wean?" Sarah whimpered, "You don't know what it was like. I had to…." But her words were drowned by Annie's fury. She was not by nature a volatile person but her frustration, locked away for years, now erupted. "Sit down," she roared and Sarah sat. Towering over Sarah threateningly, Annie continued. "I was the same age as you are now when your mother died. Do you forget who brought you up? Where would you be if I had just walked out? I watched six coffins carried out of this house so don't tell me I don't understand what it was like."

"I just couldn't face it," Sarah sobbed.

"Well you can get your apron and take over here. Maybe you can face that."

In the morning Annie set off for Aghanloo, telling her siblings she had no idea when she'd be back. Sarah was left to do the housekeeping. It was a miserable time for her. She tried her best but every meal had a starter of harsh words. There were constant accusations and bickering, sometimes about the food but more often about her desertion of Bella. Three weeks later Johnny, the elder brother, got the telegram and set off to attend Bella's funeral. When Annie and Johnny returned normal life went on for everyone, except for Sarah. She imagined that the neighbours thought it despicable that she had abandoned a dying woman and was sure that Harry's family and neighbours thought likewise. As her guilt grew she wanted to be where no one knew her.

The teenage rivalry of the young sisters was like a seesaw, swinging between friendship and war. Dora, the eldest of the three, became ostracized regardless of the moods of Sarah or Letty. When they quarreled she was expected to take sides and when they were friendly she was excluded. Soon the walls of their home could not contain the continual friction. Johnny and young Andy, working hard on the land, felt it was time the girls were doing more to contribute to their keep and Annie agreed with them. Dora got a job as a housemaid in Derry and after some months met James Harrison, a cattle drover. Annie invited him to visit and meet the family. For Dora the visit was a disaster. While she was talking to Annie, Sarah and Letty were showing James around the homestead and the nearby lake. Very subtly Letty hinted that Dora had a string of men friends in the village. Later while talking to Dora, Letty said, "Are you sure it's you he really wants? When you were in the house talking to Annie he asked me to go to the barn with him. You'll need to keep a tether on that boy. Ask Sarah, she'll tell you." Sarah nodded in agreement. Dora was silent. This was the last straw. For years she had put up with their hassle. They had rifled through her belongings, read her simple diaries and sniggered at what she had written in them. In short they had poisoned any friendships she had ever made. Tearfully she confided in Annie.

"I thought they had learned their lesson when they were told they were no longer welcome at the church socials. They tried the same sort of thing there, but leave it with me. I'll deal with it." When Dora told James how angry she was at their behaviour, she was horrified at what they had told him. "Would you wait here? I want to have a quick word with our neighbour, Mrs. McLaughlin." She sped off to a nearby stone cottage and on her return said, "James would you mind if we went back on an earlier bus?"

He appeared not to hear her. He stood looking out towards the lake. Through the trees that grew near the lake's edge the sun sent streaks of light that winked and blinked on the glassy surface of the water. Such colours, such beauty, such peace, he could not find words to fit the scene. He could only feel it. This was to be a day of hope for him. He had been offered a steady job as a shepherd on a hill farm in County Antrim and planned to ask Dora to marry him. For the rest of his life he would cherish the memory of her saying 'yes' beside this dreamlike lake. But what now? He kept staring at the lake as though the water was showing him what lay ahead, the two sisters visiting them and their nastiness causing rifts between him and Dora. He knew the damage a vile tongue could cause. His family knew more than most just how damaging that could be. His gaze was still held by the water but he wasn't seeing water.

He was reliving the evening his cousin Lizzy lay on her kitchen floor; sudden death delivered by a shot from her husband's gun. Matt was a gamekeeper and Lizzy supplemented their income by going to the houses of the more affluent to do their ironing. The odd job man of the village had been caught poaching pheasants and after he was prosecuted he vowed he'd get even with Matt. He poisoned his dog, broke fences and when he'd had a skin full in the pub, resorted to passing defamatory remarks about Matt's family. His mother, father, sisters, were all meat for this man's taunts and when Matt married, his young bride was added to the avenger's list. Lizzy kept telling

Matt to ignore him but Matt found this increasingly difficult to do. What started off as resentment had become a vendetta. The avenger's latest taunt was, 'You're a real civil man Matt, real civil, ready to rear somebody else's bastard…could even be mine.' When Matt returned home he found Lizzy putting on the rose pink lipstick that she'd bought from some of her earnings. He told her of the latest remark that had been thrown at him. She laughed and said, "You're one silly man to let that scoundrel bother you."

Something snapped in Matt's brain. Civil, silly, civil, silly… the words exploded in his head. He raised the gun. She fell. The shot ripped the air. The lipstick tube rolled across the floor. The second shot left Matt beside his wife. Pandemonium followed as neighbours, family and police rushed to the scene. The tragedy tore the village apart. They found a cardboard box containing a few pence, a receipt from the wool shop, a matinee coat and a piece of knitting still on the needles. A sweater for Matt.

Five years on it was history, with as many conjectures as there were dogs in the village. But for Matt and Lizzy's families the wound was still raw. As for James, the bible commandment, 'You shall not give false testimony against your neighbour,' was the only one etched on his mind. Matt was his best friend and since the terrible incident he refused to acknowledge anyone who made aspersions against others. Until now he found this easy to do. He loved Dora but how would he cope with her sisters. Since Dora had spoken he was silent, almost trance like. She touched him and waited. He turned his gaze from the shimmering lake water and looked at her.

"Would you mind if we went back on an earlier bus?" she asked again.

"Aye, might as well," he replied.

While they were outside Annie was both angry and busy. She made Sarah and Letty wash the dinner dishes and then set the table for tea. "Just three places," she said. At the kitchen dresser she cut the wheaten farls, sliced the cake and put the butter and jam into glass dishes that were only used when she had visitors. Then with a gesture of the hand she pointed to the bedroom. "You two, up to the room, I have something to say." They shuffled to the bedroom, sat on the edge of one of the beds and waited for her anger to explode. "How dare you insult any guest I invite to this house. It's impossible to put manners in either of you."

"I didn't say anything," complained Sarah.

"Maybe you didn't but you went along with it, didn't you?"

"Don't know what the fuss is about," Letty said with a defiant look. "It was only a bit of fun."

"Fun! I'll give you fun," said Annie. She took a key from her pocket, left the room and locked the door. As Dora and James entered the kitchen the kettle was singing as it hung on the crane over the glowing turf embers and the table was set. Dora noticed the three place settings. "Have those two gone out?" she asked.

"Not exactly, but sit down both of you and I'll wet the tea." They didn't have the heart to mention the early bus. As they sat having tea Dora asked Annie when she was due to take her next trip to Derry. When Bella was alive and in good health she used her crochet hook and knitting needles to make some extra money for her household. She crocheted woolen shawls and with cotton thread made fancy edgings for pillowcases, bedcovers and christening robes. She knitted sweaters and caps in thick Aran wool. After her death Annie took over Bella's place in this little cottage industry. She thought of how long it would take her to finish her present consignment.

"It will be three weeks before I go to Derry and when I deliver this order I was thinking of going on to Aghanloo for a few days to see Peggy and wee Amy."

"Do you think you could leave here on a Saturday? I'd like to spend some time with you but I can't get off on a week day." As the young couple left it was arranged that three weeks later Annie and Dora would meet. On the journey back to Derry James and Dora were quiet, each mulling over their own thoughts but when they got off the bus Dora said, "I have something to tell you. I won't be going back to Gleneely while my two sisters are there. This afternoon I made up my mind that I don't want to see them ever again. I know you'll think I'm a terrible person to do something like this but you don't know what it's like to put up with their lies and slander." She looked directly at him waiting for a comment. Was that a tear trickling down his face? Surely not she thought. She had never seen him cry before. In fact she had never seen any man cry.

"Did I ever tell you about my cousin Lizzy?"

"No, I don't remember you mentioning her."

They walked hand in hand across the street and on towards the bank of the River Foyle. He was trying to find a quiet place where he could talk to her and she was wondering what was wrong with him. When they found a grassy spot they sat down and James, this time looking out at the dark waters of the river, poured out all his pent up feelings about the death of Matt and Lizzy and the anguish Lizzy's mother felt at the loss of a grandchild she'd never know. He started to sob sorely. With her arms around him Dora held him close. Time stopped for them. Neither heard the noise from the city nor felt the whip of the wind that blew across the water onto their faces. James felt exhausted but strangely relieved. He never knew till now that crying could wash away so much of the burden he was carrying.

"Now I have something I want to tell you," he said as he wiped a tear stained face. "I have been offered a job as a shepherd on a hill farm in CountyAntrim."

"So that means we won't see each other again," she said as she thought of how alone she was going to be after he left.

"We could see each other every day if you'd marry me." She let the words sink into her head, then leaned towards him and kissed him. "Does that mean a yes?" With a smile she whispered, "Yes, oh yes."

He went on to tell her that the present shepherd had reached retirement age and would be giving up work in three months time. There was a small cottage that went with the job but there was no electricity or running water. Dora reckoned that if it was dry inside they could make it comfortable.

Annie and Dora met three weeks later and sitting at a corner table of a small tea shop Dora explained why she did not want to see her sisters again. It left both women facing the same dilemma. What values did they put on the cord of life-events that bound them? When things got tough should they cut it and move away into isolation or carefully untie the knots, examine what they found and determine to learn from it? It was clear what Dora wanted to do but the older and more experienced Annie was sad. She had always believed in hope and did not see people as all bad or all good. But on reflection she considered that Dora's way might be right. After all, don't horses in the wild isolate a misbehaving foal until it learns to live within the rules of the group? She was thinking about the situation when Dora spoke again. "James and I are getting married and I don't want those two to be told about the wedding."

"Dora, are you sure you're not making a hasty decision?"

"This is not a hasty decision. James is a respectable hard working man. We'll be moving to CountyAntrim and I'll write to you but I'll be sending the letters to Mrs. McLaughlin. You can tell Johnny but ask him to keep it to himself." A few months later Annie returned from Derry as the brothers were having their evening meal. She poured a cup of tea and joined them. "Sarah, there might be a job for you in Derry. It's Dora's old job. She moved away from Derry when she got married." Sarah and Letty looked at her, their mouths open at the shock of this news.

"Did she have to get married; I mean is she going to have a wean?" asked Letty.

At this comment Johnny was on his feet. He grabbed Letty by the collar of her jumper and shook her violently. "I should have scrubbed your mouth with soap a long time ago. Do you want to know why there was no wedding here? Dora wants nothing to do with you two and she'll never be back here. And no, she didn't have to get married but wait till it's your turn. We'll see what kind of wedding you have." His rage intensified and the hand that held the clothing at her neck tightened as he lifted her off the floor. "And while I'm at it, what did you tell Alice Reid about me, you filthy minded wee shite?" He threw her across the floor and she landed heavily on the wooden settle bed. "You're not even worth hitting," he spat, and went back to the table. "One of these days…"he muttered between mouthfuls of food.

Taking over Dora's old job gave Sarah a glimpse of how life was lived among the upper classes but her new position brought a strange kind of homesickness. Lack of companionship with her family made her visit home quite often. She felt unsettled, wanted more from life but didn't know exactly what. There were no letters or contact of any kind from Dora yet when neighbours asked Annie or Johnny about her the general reply was, 'She's doing fine.' Sarah began to think that these answers were a cover up. Maybe none of them knew where she was. If she could only talk to Dora she might be able to voice these feelings of unease that took all the joy from her life. There was no point in talking to Letty. Sure, she'd listen but at the first opportunity she'd use any confidences as ammunition. She talked to Annie about visiting Dora and got the reply, 'You'll have to wait till you're invited.' She asked Johnny if he knew why Dora never got in touch with them. He looked at her with disdain. "You hadn't a good word to say to her when she was here so why do you want to know where she is now?" His reply left her deflated. She found it so difficult to make friends or communicate with people outside her family circle. It felt like she was now living in a verbal desert.

Young Frank Millar, son of a well to do farmer, had taken a shine to Sarah. Accepting his marriage proposal would set her a notch above her compatriots. It would not get her out of her home village but it would get her out of the trap of being seen as an orphan. According to her people looked down on orphans. It was a badge she never wanted to wear. Annie warned her that Frank's reputation for drinking might not lead to a bed of roses but Sarah felt that moving into a higher strata of society meant people would look up to her. Besides she would see to it that if he married her he would give up the drinking. She acccepted the diamond and sapphire ring and almost immediately Letty was able to take the wind out of her sails.

"You must be easy to please. Who would wear a ring with auld blue stones?"

So devastated was she at this remark that she believed it was an inferior ring. She asked Frank to change it for one with red stones. The diamond and ruby ring was on her finger a short time when as if by a miracle to her thinking, events took a turn that promised an even better life. News came that her bachelor uncle, James Cowper, who worked for most of his life in America, had died, leaving all he owned to her father's family. Sarah's share was enough to raise her sights beyond a farmer's son. Her cousin Charlotte was planning to join her husband in America as soon as he found suitable accommodation. Sarah decided to go with her. Her excuse to Frank for ending the engagement was that she did not like his drinking.

With all the buzz of this new life in Brooklyn she was sure to find happiness. She would marry someone rich and no longer be a nobody. Sarah opened her eyes and seeing her pained reflection mirrored in the tin basin, said to herself, "I should have stayed in America."

Chapter 2

When Frank Millar saw his young daughter run out of the house in a tearful state he crossed the yard to find out what was wrong. "I was just 'washin' the spuds and Mammy told me to get out," she blubbered. He looked down at her, wet sleeves rolled up to her elbows and face smirched with damp clay and tears. In her he saw himself as a small boy in the midst of a turbulent household. And like her he didn't know the cause of all the friction. Long before his birth William and Agnes Fisher owned the land he now stood on. They had two sons, Tom and Robert and two daughters, Ellen and Rebecca. Agnes had a long and difficult delivery at Robert's birth. The local midwife, or handy woman as she'd have been called in those days, could deal with a birth provided it was straightforward but in this case mother and child were in great distress and a doctor had to be rushed to the scene. Robert was a loving and delightful child but his parents soon realised that he was somewhat mentally slow. Agnes believed it was caused by the effects of his long and harrowing birth and was very protective of him. Then one day their three year old daughter Rebecca wandered into the boiler house where a pot of gruel was left on the floor to cool. She slipped and partially fell into the gruel. Her death left the whole family in anguish. The 'if only' and 'we should have' phrases and the memories of her screams left her parents with so much guilt. Pneumonia took William's life some years later leaving Agnes and her elder son struggling to run the farm. Tom and his sister Ellen became more adept at handling the work and finances of the farm and eventually life was on a more even keel.

Then Agnes met Stephen Millar, a ruggedly handsome man five years her junior. He had come from CountyDerry to work at the local mill. To him, widows with land were catches not to be sneezed at and Agnes Fisher was flattered by his charms. She missed the close love and companionship she had known with her quiet adoring husband. This affable gentleman seemed to offer her a second chance of happiness. A year after the marriage their son Frank was born and soon the first rumblings of discontent came when Stephen Millar made it clear to Tom that he no longer had a say in the administration of farm affairs.

Young Tom became more and more disgruntled. He felt he was being squeezed out of the home and farm that he regarded as his inheritance and talked to his mother about his concerns. Agnes found the situation intolerable. Even King Solomon could not have made a judgment in her case. She felt that Tom, her eldest son, had a right to benefit from the farm he was reared on. Had she not married Stephen Millar, Tom would now be the rightful owner. But she had to think of her youngest son too and to compound matters her retarded son had a right to be looked after. No thought was given to young Ellen for it was assumed that when she married her husband would provide a home for her. The farmhouse, a large two-storey building, was already adapted into two separate areas, for years ago one end of the house had been taken over as a rural police station. Agnes suggested that the farm was big enough to support two families. When they married Tom and Frank could have separate homes and in the meantime Tom should have an equal say in the running of the farm. Discontent grew as Tom realised that eventually his young half- brother could inherit everything. He could no longer put up with taking orders from his step- father.

"I think it's time I put a headstone over my father and Rebecca's grave before they're both forgotten," he announced. The statement, calmly made, cut Agnes to the quick. He had a white marble headstone erected and some weeks later approached his mother again. "If I'm to work here and take orders from your husband I think it's only right that I should be paid a fair wage. Will you speak to him about it?"

"But Tom, you mustn't regard yourself as a farm hand. This is your home and if there's anything you need you know you only have to ask and you'll get it."

"Mother, I'm not a child looking for a new toy. I'm looking for a fair wage for a fair day's work and if I can't get it here there are other farms in the area where I can get work." Despair flooded Agnes' life. Her once sunny disposition was ebbing away and with it the love and respect of her beloved eldest son. She could not bear the thought of him working on a neighbouring farm. When she spoke to Stephen about it he saw no problem. He was sure it was the tantrums of youth but if a weekly wage gave Tom a feeling of independence he would agree to it. Four months passed with Tom playing the part of the obedient farm hand. He did however spend more time than usual with his best friend but no one paid any heed nor did they know that Tom's mail was being sent to his friend's home. Agnes began to feel that harmony was returning to the household for Tom was now working quite amicably with his step- father. But one evening when Tom was taking the horses into the stable he said to Stephen, "I need to tell you that I'll be quitting the job here. Would two weeks notice be enough?"

"Look here young fella, as head of this house I'm working as hard as any of you to keep a home for all of us. I suppose you're looking for a raise in wages."

"Naw, you'd be wrong there."

"Well you know you'll break your mother's heart if you go to work on another farm. Before I married her I promised her I would look after her and her family so I think I've a right to know where you're going." Tom had tried to keep his plans secret and to keep a cool head but this man's audacity was riling him. He hid his anger with a laugh.

"You know sir, when you married my father's land and took my mother to the weddin' it didn't mean I was part of the bargain. As for your promise to look after Robert and Ellen, I'd say you'd be wise to carry it out for I might come back and maybe blow your friggin' brains out."

Stephen stood rigid in shock. The gauntlet had been thrown down and he didn't know how to handle it. Tom went to find Ellen who was getting the hens shut in for the night. He gave a great sigh as he said, "Ellen, I need to talk to you. I've been in touch with Uncle Tom and he has offered to give me work on his ranch in Virginia."

"You're going to America. Have you told Mother yet?"

"Naw, I'm going in now to tell her but I want to ask you to do your best to look after Robert. You know it was our father's dying wish that we would take care of him. I never wanted things to be this way but I just can't go on taking orders from a stranger in what is our home."

Tom dreaded this meeting with his mother but it had to be done. When he told her his news she put her hand to her forehead and in a feeble voice said, "Tom, I didn't realise that you were so unhappy. Is there anything that will make you change your mind?"

"Mother, there's no point in talking like that. I'll slip away quietly and I'll write to you when I get settled. And just incase life doesn't turn out the way you'd hoped, here's something for you to look at." He took a piece of paper from his pocket, an account from a Dublin newspaper of the change in the law regarding married women's property. He told her to keep it in a safe place and read it when she got a quiet moment. In the yard Stephen had time to mull over what this upstart of a step- son had said to him but he had to be careful what he said to Agnes. He asked her if Tom had told her about his intentions to leave the farm.

"Aye, he did."

"Surely he must see that we can't have everybody here making decisions. If I knew the farmer that's taking him on I'd go and talk to him."

"Stephen, he's not going to a local farm. He's going to America and if you had been less harsh, talked to him about plans for the farm instead of barking orders at him, he'd have stayed here where he belongs." Stephen tried to hide his delight. A confrontation had been avoided and it looked like everything was going his way until a thought struck him. Was Tom expecting to be paid half the value of the farm? He decided to ruffle no feathers and try to keep the goodwill of his neighbours.

With a sinking heart Agnes went with Robert and Ellen to Moville, where Tom and a few other emigrants waited to be taken in a small boat out into the channel to board the ocean liner. Tom hugged his mother, told her not to fret about him, hugged Ellen and said, "You'll look after Robert, won't you?"

Then he wrapped Robert in his arms. "You look after the animals while I'm away." Robert's answer came in a smile and a nod as a tear rolled down his cheek. Reluctantly he released his hold of Tom's sleeve. They all stood till the little boat was a speck on the water and then watched from a high bank as the liner steamed out of Lough Foyle. Later Agnes read the newspaper cutting. She reread it and wondered what she should do. Stephen worked hard enough but it was his overbearing attitude that incensed her. Her first husband had never behaved in such a manner. If Ellen married she wondered who would look after Robert when she passed on. She told Stephen she wanted to set up a financial trust for Robert's future.

"There's no need for that. He'll stay on the farm and young Frank or Ellen will take responsibility for him in due course."

A few years passed during which time Agnes began to feel the same frustration that Tom had experienced and arguments between her and Stephen increased. Leaving Ellen to look after young Frank she decided to spend a short time at her family home in the hope that her brother and sister could give her advice. She showed them the newspaper cutting and her brother got a solicitor to check it out. Finding that it was correct her mind was eased but her physical energy and zest for life were waning.

"What do you want to do about this?" her brother asked.

"I think I should get the land registered in my name and then make a will leaving it equally between Tom and Frank. But they'd have to agree to take care of Robert. When that's done I'll write and ask Tom to come back. At the minute I feel so weak it could be the spring before I mend."

She never saw the spring. Before her death her brother knew that she had pleaded with Tom to return and from his letters knew that Tom had no intention of coming back to the situation he had left. He was married with a year old son, was happy and would never expect his wife to leave her native Virginia. Agnes was buried in her parents' grave and after her funeral her brother showed Stephen the newspaper cutting, told him about Agnes' last wishes and said, "You know Stephen if this has to go to court it could be a costly and messy case. I've written to Tom and I think we should wait till I get a reply from him."

Stephen waited, every day thinking of how he could hold on to the farm for himself and his son. When Agnes' brother got the reply it was brief. The letter stated, 'I can offer no suggestions about the farm. It would be advisable to seek legal advice for it is Robert's home and his welfare will have to be assured.' He called with Stephen, showed him the letter and said, "Well now it's up to you but I'll keep this letter in case it's ever needed." Stephen did nothing and hoped Tom would never open this can of worms. He hired Mick O'Brien as a farm hand and soon discovered he had another situation to worry about. Mick and Ellen announced that they were getting married. Mick was under pressure at home. His family had no objections to him marrying a farmer's daughter but if he had any notions of changing his religion they would disown him. Stephen tried his strict disciplinarian tactics on Ellen as he had done with Tom.

"I'm having none of it. That man has no prospects and he's Catholic. You can marry one of your own kind provided he can give you a home."

"And what prospects did you have before you married my mother? As for a home, I have a home. It's right here and after we're married we'll be moving to the other half of the house.

If you don't want to employ Mick he can work somewhere else."

Stephen, having worried for years as to what his entitlement was, did not want to make any legal enquiries and more than anything did not want to lose the goodwill of his neighbours, for the Fisher family were highly respected in the village. He decided that occupation was tantamount to ownership and so life went on until in his late fifties he died from a sudden heart attack. Frank assumed that he would inherit the farm but he had never had to take much responsibility for anything for Ellen had inherited from her father good managerial skills. With her at the helm he was more than happy to let her continue keeping the farm's financial state healthy while he went with two friends to New York. All three thought of this as a great adventure and all three had contacts in Brooklyn. They planned to get jobs and see something of the country and if that failed or they got bored they knew they could come home.

Just over a year after his arrival in Brooklyn Frank met Sarah again. She was working as a nanny and her dream of meeting someone rich had so far not materialized. In the following year they married and on the occasions when Frank drank too much Sarah went into a moody silence. His answer was to shower her with gifts. Once it was a beautiful beige coat with a fox fur collar. On another occasion it was a silver tea service but this gift came through an unusual channel. A friend of Frank's worked in the Waldorf Astoria Hotel and one week he lost all his wages at the gambling tables. In exchange for a few dollars one of the hotel's tea services was Frank's gift to Sarah. She cherished this gift that she believed came from an expensive New York store. But for the Wall Street crash they might have settled there for Sarah liked New York. It took a little time for the full impact of the financial crash to take affect. Businesses went bankrupt, banks closed leaving many people with the loss of their savings and work of any kind was extremely difficult to find. With the birth of their baby daughter Frank and Sarah were living on one wage and every day the newspapers brought more dire news of the country's situation. Frank's adventure had turned sour and he yearned for the security of his home in Gleneely. Reluctantly Sarah and her child boarded the RMS Athenia and sailed for home while Frank sorted out their affairs and followed a few weeks later.

Having a child in the house made them all feel young. Robert wanted to carry her around the yard and let her stroke the sheepdog. Ellen took every opportunity to bob her up and down on her knee and teach her singing rhymes. As Mick played his fiddle he watched her tiny feet trying to keep in step with the music. Frank was relieved to be back with his horses and stepping out on soft earth again. Sarah was the only one who was unhappy so it didn't take long for dissention to rear its head. She objected to Ellen having financial control of the farm. Surely, she declared, that should be left to her and Frank. Her position in this family was not as she had imagined it should be but Frank saw no reason to change the present arrangements.

Before Sarah left for America her sister Letty had run off with the philandering son of a mill owner. It was very mysterious at the time and caused quite a stir. The mill owner was none too pleased for he had hopes that his son would marry into money. He vowed that whether his son returned or not he would cut him off without a penny. Now Letty had returned with her son Arthur but without the mill owner's son and she was filling Maggie's head with family history Sarah did not want mentioned. Filled with rage Sarah left her daughter Maggie in Ellen's care and set off to her old homestead to confront Letty.

"Why are you telling Maggie such lies about our father?"

"Oh, you think they're lies. Well if you think he was a bloody saint ask any of the neighbours. They can't all be wrong. Anyway Maggie asked me why she didn't have grannies like all the other weans and I told her they were dead. She wanted to know what happened to them so I told her that too." Annie had given up any thoughts of marriage when she took on the task of rearing her young siblings, but quite by accident she met her childhood sweetheart and married him. When the quarrelling women appealed to her for support she looked at them and said, "I can see nothing has changed. Don't look to me for an opinion for I'm no longer responsible for either of you."

Sarah started badgering Frank about moving away from the village. Once again she used Annie as a sounding board. Didn't Frank have the right to sell the farm without consulting Ellen? Wasn't it legally his property? "And what would happen to Ellen and Mick and Robert? Have you thought about where they would go?" asked Annie.

"Well, they could rent a house and Mick could get a job. After all he had nothing before he married Ellen." Annie raised her shoulders and gave Sarah a long searching look as she asked her what she had before she married Frank. It seemed there was no one on Sarah's side and after weeks of wrangling Frank finally decided that a move was the only thing that would bring peace. He said nothing to Ellen but contacted an auctioneer and asked him if he could find a buyer without advertising it in the paper. At this stage he wanted it kept quiet. The first document needed was the title deed and the search for it began. Sarah, in her exuberance about getting out of the village she detested, could not contain her excitement. Maggie watched her mother wrap gaudy cushion covers, brightly painted ornaments, vases and the shiny silver tea service and put them into the wooden trunk. Her eyes were wide in wonderment. Her tiny hand reached out for a figure of the Statue of Liberty. "A dolly," she said and smiled.

"No you can't have that. That's not a doll." Then in a lowered voice she continued, "We're going to move to a nice new house and then I'll get you a real dolly but don't tell anybody about the new house." This meant nothing to Maggie for all she wanted was a doll. While Sarah was putting things into boxes Frank's solicitor was taking things out of boxes in his search for the elusive title deed. In those days many title deeds could not be found for lands passed from father to son without any written documentation being made and this farm had been in the Fisher family for many generations. Sorting out Frank's entitlement to it would take some time for a prospective buyer had to be assured that there were no loopholes. In this case there seemed to be no other strong claimants. Tom was settled in Virginia. Robert was retarded. Ellen had three points against any entitlement. She was a woman. She had no children. She was now Catholic. Secrets are often housed like sand in a sieve. Coming from mass one Sunday a neighbour could not resist telling Ellen and Mick the news he had heard.

"The farm up for sale! Where did you hear that?" Ellen asked.

"I heard a whimper of it in Carndonagh the other day. You wait and see, there's something going on, but don't say I told you." On Monday morning Ellen called at Frank's side of the house and asked him to call with her. When he entered the kitchen she came straight to the point. "I heard a rumour that you're selling the farm. If it's true I must say I expected better of you. I thought you'd tell me before going to the auctioneer." Taken completely aback and her eyes looking straight into his face, Frank was lost for words. His head dropped and he sighed. When he raised his head the eyes were still looking at him, demanding an answer.

"Well, with the way things are at the minute I thought the best thing for all of us was for me to move out."

"Aye, you could be right. The back biting that's been going on since you came home is not the way we used to live. Maybe it's time there was a parting of the waves." Frank returned to his end of the house, telling Sarah that someone must have leaked the news of the sale for Ellen knew all about it. Wondering who might have told her he went off to the stable to harness the horses but Sarah was certain it was Maggie who told their secret. How else, she reckoned, could Ellen have found out. To have her plans thwarted at this stage was unbearable. She lost control. Grabbing the child by the shoulders she shook her and uttered indecipherable sounds from behind clenched teeth. After the shaking she gave Maggie a push that sent her stumbling across the floor where she fell against the edge of a chair. This was Maggie's first experience of real fear. Like a wounded animal she fled to her Aunt Ellen. When Ellen asked what happened she got no answer for she was looking at a child screaming hysterically as blood streamed down her face. While she was trying to pacify her and find the cut Sarah came in. "She will race around like a mad thing no matter what I tell her," said Sarah. After washing her face they found the cut, a gash on her right eyebrow. Ellen had disturbing thoughts about the incident when she noticed that Maggie was reluctant to go back home with her mother. She quickly dismissed them. She had her own problems to think about and anyway children will have accidents.

It took many weeks for a form of entitlement to be sorted, during which time Ellen pondered her situation. She finally decided not to take any legal action, believing that the ruling would go against her. For this reason she agreed to accept Frank's offer of a small amount for her and Robert. At the parish church where the Fisher family had worshiped all their lives, there was a small house usually occupied by the church caretaker. When Ellen was offered the job of caretaker it was like a light at the end of a long tunnel. Now the three of them could settle down to a peaceful life again.

Frank bought a farm in CountyDerry and when the sale was finalised Sarah, with great glee, told Annie that they'd be moving soon and gave her the new address. Annie, recognising the area, lost no time in writing to Peggy Fletcher who opened the letter and read, 'You'll soon have Frank and Sarah as neighbours for they've bought a farm close to your place.' She read the rest of the letter, folded it and put it in the box with all the papers and invoices relating to the shop. "Well this will be an interesting turn of events," she said aloud, then passed the news on to her father and her brother Harry.

As Ellen was packing for the move to her new home Frank came in with a money order for her share from the farm sale and told her that he would be taking Robert with him. She was furious. "I thought it was you and your family that were so keen to get away from this village. Now you want to take my brother and his share of the money with you. Do you realise you'll be taking him from his home village and all the people he knows?" Frank argued that there would be more scope for him on a farm and he'd be with the animals he loved. She had to admit that there was no way she'd be able to keep animals at her new home. There would be room for a few hens in the garden but nothing else. Her mind went back to the day beside the hen house when Tom asked her to look after Robert. She looked at Frank and said, "I hope you understand that you'll be responsible for taking care of him and don't ever forget that if Tom hadn't left and Robert hadn't been retarded you wouldn't have what you have now."

"Don't worry. He'll be fine and I'll bring him for a visit next time I'm back."

"You could leave him with me for a couple of months every year and if he's not happy in the new place you must bring him home." It did not cross the minds of either of them to ask Robert what he wanted to do.

Chapter 3

M oving day did not start smoothly. A long stool was set behind the driver's seat to provide seating for Frank and Robert and the furniture was stacked tightly against it. Sarah and Maggie were to sit in the passenger seat. Never having been in a confined space the dog displayed great resistance to being hemmed in and jumped all over the furniture till he got to the open back door of the van where he bounded out and raced to the yard. Frank went after him, calling 'Flash, Flash, good dog,' but as soon as he got close to him, the dog bounded off towards one of the fields. Back at the house Maggie was kicking up a fuss. She wasn't going to the new house. She was staying with Flash. Frank looked at Robert and said, "Would you go and coax him back?" The wagons carrying the animals had already left and Frank was getting exasperated with the delay. Eventually Robert returned with Flash and Frank rearranged the seating arrangements. He and Sarah sat on the long stool and Robert sat in the passenger seat with Maggie on his knee and Flash on the floor, nuzzling his face at Robert's feet.

From Gleneely to Moville Maggie was alert, looking at all the houses and the animals grazing in the fields. Somewhere on the road to Derry she fell asleep and didn't waken till they were near Limavady. "Are we nearly there yet?" she asked. Frank and Sarah were so preoccupied with Maggie's further questions about how far they had to go, that on the road from Limavady ghanloo Sarah was not aware that they were passing Bella's old home where she had spent two weeks in her youth. From behind her lace curtains Peggy Fletcher watched the vehicles slow down and turn right but Sarah paid no heed for she had never been as far as the shop all those years ago. As they passed a neat government cottage Frank said, "It's the next turning on the right and there's a wee shop back there at the crossroads. It'll be handy for odds and ends."

The first items to be taken off the van were Maggie's tricycle with its tiny wicker basket tied to the handlebars and her doll's pram. Frank told her to go and play while the furniture was being taken inside but she complained that she didn't have a doll to put in the pram. She steered the tricycle around the yard, putting bits of turf and dock leaves in the basket and delivering these groceries to imaginary customers. Next day it was raining so she played house under the kitchen table. She poured imaginary tea, talked to imaginary people and introduced them to her baby, which was a rolled up towel tied with string. "We'll need to be careful what we say in front of her," said Sarah.

"Why, what do you mean?" Frank asked, with a questioning frown.

"Just listen to her. She picks up everything and you know the bother she got us into with her chattering. How do you think Ellen got to know about the sale of the farm? And what about all the money you had to pay to get the deed sorted out?" When Frank got angry his lips elongated into thin lines. The thin lines appeared and Sarah knew she had touched a raw nerve. There was a brief moment of silence. "The deed! I told you that should have been sorted out long before I was born. And if it had been I wouldn't have got the farm. Oh I know you never liked Ellen but don't bloody well blame her for that. As for blaming Maggie, what kind of mind have you got?" He left the kitchen, slamming the door behind him.

On the third day in the new home Sarah decided to go to the shop. She was delighted that she had finally escaped from the village where she imagined everyone was still whispering about her father. But this was a fresh start, a new place where no one knew her. She put on her beige coat with the fox fur collar and strode out. The door bell tinkled as she entered and in a moment Peggy Fletcher was behind the counter.

"Ah Sarah, Annie told me you were coming. I meant to get down yesterday to welcome you to Drumaderry but I couldn't get away. I hope you'll be very happy here. You'll find the neighbours are very friendly." Stunned, Sarah found herself unable to reply as Peggy chattered on. After getting her groceries she hastily left. On the way home she may have been geographically disorientated but it was nothing to her feelings of living so near to someone who knew her in the past. Circumstances had cheated her again. Without telling Frank that she already knew Peggy Fletcher, Sarah said, "I thought this place was called Aghanloo. The woman in the shop called it Drumaderry."

"Aghanloo is the name of the whole area. Drumaderry is just a small part of it."

"Well the woman that runs the shop knew Annie years ago and it seems they still write to each other. Sounds like a place where no body can mind their own business."

Frank gave a chuckle and said, "You'll be thinking of moving again?"

Robert had just spread fresh straw for the sow and her new litter when Maggie came along to see the piglets. She giggled with delight and asked, "Can me hold one?" In his large gentle hands he took a piglet and let her stroke it. "Me hold it, me hold it." He put the tiny creature into her cupped hands but it wriggled so much that he took it from her and put it back with the others. She went back towards the house, meeting her mother on the way. Full of excitement and holding her forefingers a short distance apart she described the pig.

"Wee pink piggie, this size. Unca Ober let me hold it. Can me take one home?"

"No, you're not taking a pig into the house."

"Unca Ober would help me look…."

"He's only your half- uncle." This remark came with such ferocity that Maggie sensed she'd done something to displease her mother. The two were silent as Sarah thought she had been an idiot to agree to have Robert live with them. His presence blighted her idea of the perfect family. Maggie was trying to figure out what a half really meant. She'd had half an apple and half a slice of bread but half of her Uncle Robert left her completely confused.

"Mammy, how do you get half of Unca Ober?" The answer came with a cold stare and a screech.

"Because I say so and how dare you cheek me up, you wee bitch. Get into the house. I'll soon put manners in you." Her glee at stroking the piglet was quickly replaced with fear. She dashed indoors, trying to keep as quiet as possible and out of her mother's way. Even at this young age her life was either an ocean of thundering crashing waves or the quiet lapping of exhausted waters. Frank was her safe sandy beach but sands can shift and shift they did in time. Her Uncle Robert became her sheltered bay. In her childish way she tried to harness the storms of life and now called him Ober.

One morning she woke to find something wonderful had happened. She had a new doll. It moved. It wriggled. It cried and gurgled. She heard them call it he, Thomas, Tommy, the wee man or the wee wean, but her only concern was whether or not it would fit into her doll's pram. She wanted to hold it and cuddle it. It was the best doll she had ever seen. Sarah got the milking stool and let her sit at the turf fire with the baby on her lap. "Now mind you don't drop him," Sarah said as she went to the bedroom. What a thing to say, Maggie thought. Of course she wouldn't drop him. She held him snugly in her arms. Then she traced her forefinger over the tiny hands and feet. He had real fingernails and he felt soft - not hairy soft like the wee pig, but a smooth soft. He was so much better than her tricycle and heaps better than her towel doll. Was it the heat from the fire or was she holding him too tight? He began to whimper and then to bawl. She tried to control the writhing bundle in her arms and rise from the stool at the same time, but she could not get herself balanced properly. She felt the bundle slithering away from the shawl. Her mouth opened and the piercing yell of Maaammy brought Sarah dashing into the kitchen. She snatched the baby and screeched, "You wee bitch, what did you do to him?"

Maggie did what she always did in answer to these outbursts, fled to a safe place. Her safe place on this occasion was the turf shed which stood a few feet from the back door of the farmhouse. The lower portion was built of grey stone and the top part was stout wooden posts to which the tin roof was nailed. At the back of the shed was the black turf that was dug every year from the bog. Regardless of how much of it there was, or what other implements shared the space, this building was always called the turf shed. Maggie was huddled in a corner beside the stacked turf when Frank, hearing the screaming, dashed into the kitchen. As the verbal onslaught in the kitchen got louder, she crept to the shed entrance and listened.

"She nearly let him fall in the fire. I caught her just in time. She was trying to stick his feet in the ashes."

"And how did she do that?"

"She wanted to nurse him and I let her hold him for a minute while I…"

"So you let her sit in front of an open fire with an infant and now you tell me it was her fault. It could never be your fault, don't I know it. Nothing is ever your fault."

"Oh that's you all right. She can do no wrong in your eyes." When the outburst died down Maggie crept into the kitchen but there was no one there. She went out again to the turf shed, muttering, "I didn't put his feet in the ashes. He just slid a wee bit." Later Sarah and Frank came out to look for her and found her pacing around a circle of turf sods as she quietly sang, "Ring a ring a Rosy, I'm a little bitch. Hush a, hush a, we all fall down. Ring a ring a Rosy, I'm a little bitch."

"What are you doing?" Sarah asked.

"Nothin'," said Maggie.

"Did you hear what she was saying?" Sarah said, looking directly at Frank.

"She's only playing," he answered.

"And what if someone was passing and heard her, what would they think? This is all Ellen's fault, learnin' her them stupid rhymes."

"She may have learned her rhymes but I've never heard her call Maggie a bitch," Frank snapped. He took Maggie by the hand and they walked across the lane that separated the farmhouse and turf shed from the row of outhouses that comprised byre, stable, corn stores and the big barn. Along the side of one of these outhouses was a row of strong hooks from which hung most of the horses' harness and at the opposite side was a workbench. A window in the back wall overlooked a hedge that needed cutting. This and the many cobwebs gave a very dim light. Pointing to the bench, Maggie said, "What's that thing?"

"It's a swing. Come with me and I'll put it in the orchard for you."

As she played every day with her toys she didn't notice anything different about her mother but Frank found it difficult to cope with the bouts of weeping interspersed with shouting at him and Robert. Postnatal depression was a concept alien to Frank. He did recall a neighbour once saying, 'that woman of mine has gone a bit off her head since the last wean was born,' but he had no idea how his neighbour's wife behaved and didn't like to ask. One morning Sarah was in a tearful state and couldn't cope with anything. She stayed in bed while Frank made breakfast. Some eggs were boiling in a saucepan that sat on top of the glowing turf embers. He was cutting a loaf of bread into thick wedges while Maggie skipped round and round the table. He told her to stop running so close to the fire but she ignored him. He went on slicing the bread and she went on skipping. As she passed the fire for the umpteenth time her foot touched the saucepan handle and boiling water and spluttering ashes hit the top of her foot as she screeched in agony. Immediately Frank dashed to the milk churn and returned with a pan of buttermilk. He plunged her foot into it just as Sarah appeared at the kitchen door.

"I can't leave you to do anything right. Go and get somebody," she yelled. Frank kept splashing the cold buttermilk on the burn. The skin began ballooning into a large blister as Maggie's screaming and Sarah's ranting went on and on, both to a seemingly higher pitch. "If all you can do is stand there raving you'd better go back to bed," Frank roared. Sarah retreated and slammed the door so hard that the walls appeared to shake and when Robert came in with a bucket of water Frank told him to go for Mrs. Brennan. Robert looked mesmerized. It dawned on Frank that since coming here Robert had never been outside the farm. "Go to the bottom of the stack garden, you know where the corn stacks are built. Climb over the low fence, cross the road and the cottage is right in front of you." Robert left and returned with Bridie Brennan who took Maggie to the waterspout and held her foot under the cold flowing water until the pain subsided. Then she carried her indoors, put a piece of lint on the burn and bandaged her foot with strips of cloth torn from a flour bag. When she left Frank made tea, buttered some bread, put it on a tray and took it to the bedroom. In moments he was back with a stern face and untouched food. He put some milk in a cup, cut a slice of bread in strips, set Maggie at the table and told her to eat it. Despite all his coaxing she refused to eat and in sheer desperation he lifted her from the chair, smacked her bottom, planked her on the chair again and said, "Well you'll sit there till you do eat it." Defiance told her not to eat it and fear told her she'd better eat some of it. She toyed with the bread then ate some of it and drank the milk. As she hobbled around the kitchen she thought of Tommy's feet. Did they really touch the hot ashes? When no one was looking she went to the pram, pulled down the blanket and lifted each foot in turn to look for blisters. She couldn't find any. His skin was white and smooth. She was in the act of replacing the blanket when Sarah appeared in the doorway.

"What are you at, you wee brat? Get away from that pram and don't ever go near it again." She couldn't run away this time. Wearing one shoe and the other foot heavily bandaged, she slithered out the back door and when out of everyone's earshot muttered, "I hate her and I don't want that Tommy anymore."

When her foot healed she was outside looking for things to play with and taking notice of her surroundings. The house had a thatched roof, windows with little panes and at both sides of the front door climbing roses and honeysuckle competed for space against the whitewashed walls. The front door was seldom opened. It faced the lane that was a right-of-way to a row of labourers' cottages. Once they had all been occupied by farm workers but now all except one was vacant. She went to the orchard and sat on the swing, pushing backwards with her feet till she'd got the rhythm going. Tiring of that activity she decided to explore. Apple trees stood in rows and behind them were three pear trees and some gooseberry bushes. To her they were all big trees and little trees. She put her hand out to touch one of the gooseberry branches and a thorn pricked her finger. Beating a hasty retreat she headed for the other side of the orchard. On this side was a high mound of earth and grass with a hedge sprouting from the top of it. When she managed to climb up the steep slope she could see the lane with its two tracks, hard packed and brown, with tufts of grass between them like a monster caterpillar crawling along, eating the foliage as it went. On the other side of the lane was a dense thorny hedge. She felt as though the lane was moving and wondered where it was going.

An old man and his dog made their way along the rough track. The waft of smoke from his pipe smelled like her daddy's. She watched him and the dog as they got smaller and smaller and finally disappeared around a corner in the lane. Some moments later a woman came along. Her hair, like dirty straw, was wound into a ball at the back of her neck. She was even slower than the man. Carrying a cloth shopping bag in one hand and a hessian sack in the other, the weight of both pulled her shoulders forward. Her tent- like coat, the same colour as her hair, made her look like a melting snowman. She muttered to herself as she plodded along and Maggie couldn't decide whether she was angry or sad. Like the old man the woman faded out of view, leaving Maggie to sit and listen to the sounds around her. There was the twitter of a bird, the distant bleating of sheep but the overriding sound was of the water in the fast flowing stream. Like a metronome she moved her head and shoulders to the clash and gush of water falling on rocks, until cheerful laughter drew her attention to the lane again. A young couple walked along hand in hand. Then they stopped and clung together like ivy groping a tree. Craning her neck to get a better view she willed them to do their little dance again. She was in this stretched position when the yell of, "Maggie, get in here," unbalanced her thoughts and her feet. She toppled from the top of the mound and slid to the bottom, leaving her dress and socks smirched with damp earth. She raced inside for it was time for tea. Sarah glared at her and shouted, "Look at the state of you, and that dress only clean on you this morning." Two sharp slaps on the legs, her muddy shoes and socks pulled off and the soiled hem of her dress tucked into her knickers, she was roughly lifted on to a chair. In her childish way she wondered why every great adventure had a price to pay.

One evening Ned Bolin, the man Maggie had seen walking along the lane, came to the back door. He wanted to let Frank know that he was available for any odd jobs that needed doing. Frank invited him in and immediately Ned was talking about the hiring fares. The hiring fare in Limavady was known as The

Gallop and Ned was explaining in considerable detail how two of his lads and one of his girls were hired in the big houses. In answer to Frank's question as to where they were hired Ned replied, "Damn it Sir, I couldney tell ye, for ye see I canny read or write but the wife could tell ye. She can read the books." Without seeming to take a breath he went on to tell how big the houses were. Any place with more than two rooms and a half loft was a big house to Ned.

"Were you ever hired yourself?" Frank asked. A local resident would never have asked that question for half an hour later Ned was relaying every detail of his young days, working in the fields in his bare feet, sleeping in barns and not getting much to eat. With a great guffaw he boasted that he never found himself in real hunger for he'd suck a few raw eggs when he got the chance. At the sight of Sarah bringing in a basin of eggs from the hen house he launched into a new subject, how good he was at making wire coops to keep the fox or the hawks from getting the hens. Then the kitchen door opened and his wife Molly put her head round the corner.

"Ned, are you going to sit there all night and keep these folks out of their bed?"

Ned, small in stature, wiry and lean as a greyhound, rose, yanking up his trousers as he did so. "Quare good stuff in them," he said, rubbing the material with his fingers. "Molly got them last week in the second hand shop. Last a life time they will." The trousers were at least two sizes too big for him and Frank offered him a leather belt, telling him it would be better than the binder twine he was using. Ned and Molly became casual workers on the farm when extra hands were needed. Gradually, either at the farmers' market or at the pub, Frank got to know more of his neighbours. One day a blond teenager called, carrying a bucket. She said her grandfather sent her for corn for the pony. It puzzled Sarah that Frank seemed to know her. She grasped the bucket of corn and held it to her chest.

"Now you'll ruin your nice cardigan, carrying it like that," said Frank.

"I don't want to do that. This is my best one. My Aunt Dora knitted it."

"Look I'll give you half a bucket now and I'll leave the rest at the shop this evening." When she left Frank looked at Sarah and asked why she hadn't a word to say to her niece.

"You mean that's Bella's wee girl."

"That's her." Frank's friendship with the Fletcher family left Sarah uneasy. Then she had a letter from Annie telling her that Letty, having been refused help from the mill owner, had gone back to England. She became more uneasy when Annie's letters never mentioned Dora, yet it was obvious that Peggy was in touch with her.

Frank surveyed the many leaks in the thatched roof and closely examined the crumbling walls of his home and decided that building a new house would be less expensive in the long run. During heavy rain they had to put buckets and basins under the drips. Maggie discovered that the raindrops hitting the basin and those hitting the floor made a different sound. She moved the basin backwards and forward but soon her attention was drawn to the bleating of sheep. Dashing outside she watched the flock being moved to new pasture and when Sarah got back to the house the floor was flooded. While soaking up the water with rags and towels she noticed that there was very little water in the basin.

"Did you move that basin?" she snapped at Maggie.

"Only a wee bit," Maggie said. As soon as Sarah's shouting started Maggie was off like a hare and speeding to the stable where Robert lifted her on to the straw in the manger. To Sarah's question as to whether or not he had seen her, Robert said, "Naw, didn't," and went on shoveling the horse manure into the wheelbarrow. When Maggie heard Frank's voice she climbed out of the manger, intent on following him, but Robert stopped her. He pulled all the clinging strands of straw from her clothes and hair and said, "Don't go into the house for a wee while." She hid in the turf shed till she thought it was safe to return.

Frank's second decision was to buy a car and with its arrival his social life became more like the one he enjoyed in his bachelor days. Sarah did not like the idea of him entertaining strangers in the home and when any of them mentioned locations in Donegal such as Culdaff or Carndonagh she became almost paranoid, believing that they were all talking about her family background. She put all the blame for her unfounded notions on Peggy Fletcher.

Often in the courtship stakes there were verbal labels attached to young women. The speed at which their relationships developed was also linked to their social status. The upper class young lady, perceived to have the highest standards in manners and morals was walking out with her young man. Running around with, was the term for the middle class girl. But the lass at the bottom of society's heap and deemed to have neither manners nor sexual morals was openly declared to be 'galloping about with' the object of her affections. Peggy Fletcher was not thinking of these labels on the day that she set out to accept Sarah's invitation to tea. Peggy always dressed in black, usually a Victorian style dress that seldom allowed a glimpse of ankle. For special occasions the only accessory was a sparkling broach or a coloured scarf. She kept her long hair in a roll that was secured with hairpins and she walked with a straight back and head held high. On this day she wore her plain black attire. The tea and scones were on the table awaiting her arrival, but when she was seated she soon realised that this was no social event. Sarah launched in with her accusations, believing that attack was the best form of defense.

"You've been talking about me behind my back, telling people around here that I came from Gleneely and got the orphan money when I was a wean. And when Bella was sick didn't you say the consumption ran in our family?"

"It's quite possible I mentioned that you came from Gleneely but most people around here know that anyway," said the shocked Peggy, but a further attack was on its way.

"Well maybe some of us did have TB but at least we didn't do what Harry did, galloping about with that tramp before his wife was cold in her grave."

"Now Sarah, you're going too far, that's slander you know."

"Oh you think so, well don't forget I was there, I know what time he came home at, and another thing, you keep it quiet that Dora sends Amy knitted jumpers. Can he not put clothes on the wean's back?" Peggy got up from the table.

"I don't have to listen to this nonsense, but I'd be careful with my tongue if I were you. Harry and Helen were married two years after Bella died and it can be proved that Helen came from Scotland to live in this area six months after Bella's death. It's true that Dora knits jumpers for Amy but that isn't any of your business. And if she doesn't keep in touch with you, that's none of my business, but you could mention to Frank that I need to have a word with him."

Peggy retraced her steps, shocked but not surprised, having had some insight from Annie about the behaviour of the Cowper girls. Sarah's adrenaline levels had risen during the encounter. Now she had to deal with the aftermath. Would she try to get Frank on her side or deny what she said and hope that the episode would fade in time? These were the tactics she and Letty used in the past. That evening after work Frank cycled to the shop for an ounce of tobacco.

"So Sarah gave you my message," said a solemn faced Peggy.

"No, I got no message. She likely forgot. Why, what was the message?"

"Oh she didn't forget and the statements she made were well planned." After telling Frank about her encounter with Sarah, Peggy voiced her own opinions on the matter. If she were to pass on to Harry what Sarah alleged, there could be a court case for slander. If her father heard the gossip he would not agree to build the new house. She had kept her shop for many years and did not need Sarah's custom to survive. While Peggy was expressing her views the thin lines on Frank's face became thinner than usual. "Frank, I don't need to tell you that when you live in the country and especially when you're farming you need the goodwill of your neighbours. People round here are friendly and helpful but that doesn't mean they can be walked over. If this sort of thing continues you'll have nobody to call on when you need help."

"I've been through this before and nothing I say makes a damned bit of difference."

"Well I'll wait for a week before I decide whether or not to tell the family and you can make up your mind what you're going to do."

A new Frank was emerging, one who'd have to keep his hand on the tiller of his own household. But how would he deal with the shadows in Sarah's life? He cycled home thinking of a different approach to this problem. In the past arguing with her had only exacerbated the situation. He told Sarah that he had to go to Carndonagh and since the town's fair was the next day they should all go. Robert and Ned Bolin were left to look after the animals and in the morning they set off. Sarah was bedecked in her beige coat with the fox fur collar, Frank in tweed jacket, grey trousers and trilby hat and the children in their finery. They got out of the car and mingled with the crowd, attracting glances from those in less affluent attire. To placate the children Sarah gave them money for the lucky dip stall. Tommy got a little mirror that kept him amused as he looked at himself and pulled faces. Maggie got a porcelain figure of The Virgin Mary which to her was the most beautiful doll in the world. When the vendor wrapped it in brown paper and handed it to her she clutched it to her chest, delighted that at last she had a doll of her own. As the family sat in a crowded tea room Sarah asked Frank why he needed to come to Carndonagh. He dropped his bombshell.

"I'm looking round here to see if there are any farms coming on the market for if the Fletchers go ahead with a case against you for slander, I'd have to move. You can't run a farm or any business if all the neighbours are against you. And there's no way John Fletcher would build the new house. I think I'd be better in a place where everybody already knows us."

"You're going to stick up for that Fletcher woman and sell because of her."

"I can't take anybody's side. Sure I don't know the details of what went on years ago when you were in Aghanloo but I'm sure a good solicitor will dig up all the facts."

Suddenly Sarah lost her appetite. She couldn't bear the thought of coming back to the place she fought so hard to leave. But a court case, with everyone reading of it in the paper, was at this moment an even heavier burden. They left the fair and Frank drove to the house beside the church where Ellen and Mick lived.

"Come in, come in," said Ellen, sweeping Maggie into her arms. "Let me have a look at you. Oh my goodness you have grown." She set her on the floor again and stroked Tommy's head. "What's his name?" she asked.

'Tommy," said Frank. A tear rolled down her round pink face as she sighed and turned towards the fire, wiping her face with the hem of her apron. As she prepared tea she talked to Frank of neighbours and friends they both knew. Mick O'Brien cycled into the yard and as he propped his bicycle against the wall Ellen went to the door and said, "Mick, you'll never guess who's here." He entered the kitchen, nodded a greeting to Frank and Sarah and looked at the children.

"Well if it isn't Maggie, tell me do you still dance?" She looked at him, trying to remember who he was, but couldn't. He went to the old gramophone in the corner and put on a record. "When we played music you used to dance and twirl round the floor." She smiled and gave a little giggle. Whether she remembered or not Mick was sure that she did.

Frank's next destination was Sarah's childhood home where the children, tired from their activities, were soon asleep. He parked the car at the side of the house and went off along a narrow lane that was a shortcut to the village. In the pub he had a few drinks with some of the locals. As he sat at the bar he determined to give Sarah plenty of time to think about what he said. When he left the pub he looked across the road at his own childhood home. Leaving it had not brought the contentment he had envisaged and he was adamant that he would not give in to Sarah again. He would stay in CountyDerry but for now he would let her think otherwise. He made his way back to Ellen's house where she was anxious to know how Robert was getting on and expressed her disappointment that he wasn't with them. Frank said they had to leave him to look after the cows but promised he would bring him on a visit as soon as he could. She had her reservations for she knew him too well to put much faith in his promises. To her he would always be like the seed that fell on stony ground. The smell of alcohol on his breath reminded her of his poteen drinking days and secretly she worried for Robert and the children if he fell into his old habits again.

"I've got these two photographs of mother and your father. I'd like you to have them. It will be good for Robert to have a reminder of his mother." As Frank watched her wrap them in brown paper his conscience was stabbing him as he recalled how much work this woman had put into the farm and the shabby way he had treated her. Meanwhile Annie sat with Sarah who cast her eyes at the cases, all packed and ready.

"When do you leave?" Sarah asked.

"We sail on Friday. I'll give you our new address for I expect I'll be so busy settling in that I won't have time to write for a while." With Annie and her family about to settle in England, Sarah had an overwhelming feeling of abandonment. She hadn't a sibling she could talk to apart from her brother Andy, and like his father, he had taken to stilling illicit poteen. She did not want to be associated with him. The drive home next day was in silence except for the chattering of the children. Frank waited for some comment from Sarah about the Fletcher incident but none was forthcoming. He hammered two nails in the wall to hang the photographs. In their black and glitzy frames they added a touch of class to the otherwise bare wall. Tommy kept looking into his mirror, pulling faces and laughing at himself. Maggie was preoccupied with her new doll. She called it Pink and wheeled it around in her pram. On the pretext of cutting thistles Frank set off with the billhook to one of the fields, slipped through the hedge and went to the shop to share his secret plan with Peggy. "Frank, I don't want any nastiness over this but I have been giving it some thought. If I ignore it I'd be a traitor to my own family so I wrote to Annie to ask for her advice."

"But she's moving to England on Friday."

"I know. I wrote to her new address. It should be there when she arrives."

That night Sarah asked Frank what he was going to do about the Fletchers. He shrugged and told her he had no control over what might happen. He had never met Helen Fletcher and had no idea how her family would react. For days Sarah lived in a state of panic and when no official letter came she began to relax. Then a registered letter arrived from Annie. It read, 'Sarah, regarding your slander of the Fletcher family, I was in their house for some weeks before Bella died so I will return to give evidence should they decide to sue you. As an adult woman I thought you had put this type of behaviour behind you but it's your life, live it as you please. Like Dora I am cutting all ties with you. Annie.' Sarah put her hand to her mouth and began to cry. She had to get herself out of this situation. What, she thought, would everyone think of her if she ended up in court? Saying sorry was something Sarah had never done but she was fighting for her reputation. She went to the shop and when Peggy answered the bell she said, "That day you were up I don't know what came over me."

"I don't know what came over you either. And I don't want to talk about it for it's out of my hands now."

Sarah burst into tears and fled from the shop. Some days later the solicitor's letter arrived. It was not a summons but a copy of Annie's letter and a warning that if anything like it happened again a summons would follow and the details of the present situation would be taken into account. She felt she had to show Frank the letter.

"I doubt if you'll get off as easy next time," he said.

Chapter 4

Sarah didn't know how much of her recent encounter with Peggy was known to others in the area so she tended to be wary of her and stayed indoors as much as possible when casual workers came to dig the foundations for the new house. But Maggie was talking to anyone who would listen to her laments about the loss of her doll Pink. No one felt the need or had the foresight to explain to her that a statue of The Virgin Mary is not a doll. "It's not the sort of thing for you so we gave it to Josie Brennan but we'll get you a real doll," Sarah assured her. Josie was the teenage daughter of John Brennan or John the Post as the locals called him and Maggie grew to hate her. Sarah bought a real doll but Maggie hated it too. When the loss of her doll Pink crossed her mind she treated the new doll badly, pulling out its hair and twisting its legs. Its life as a doll was a short lived one and still she cried for Pink. No one but Johnny Spin a Yarn, the village comedian, could console her. Taking a few stalks from a sheaf of corn he made a corn dolly and brought it to her, putting it in the palm of her hand.

"See this Maggie, a golden dolly."

"Where did you get it?" she asked and his storytelling mind didn't have to think.

"You see Maggie, at night when the moon shines down on the cornfield it plays wonderful music and when the stooks of corn hear the music they dance. They twirl and twirl, round and round, and make golden dollies. Sometimes when I lie very still in bed and listen I can hear the music. Then in the morning I get up early and go to the cornfield and what do you know – there's another golden dolly. It's magic," he said with a twinkle in his eye.

Maggie was fascinated with the corn dolly and even more fascinated with the story. She wanted more of these dollies and kept Johnny Spin a Yarn busy for a while. On the days he came to work without one he'd say, "I'm sorry Maggie, there was no moon out last night." At night she lay still, listening, but was soon fast asleep. During the day she put the corn dollies in her pram, wheeled them to the turf shed where she lined them up against the wall. Then she danced and skipped round and round in a circle. In her mind she was sure she heard the magical music and even believed the dollies were dancing.

As the farming activities of autumn slowed down a Halloween soiree was suggested. The idea was warmly welcomed and Frank agreed to it being held in his barn. Two old wooden doors were set on bales of straw to act as a table and local women brought a variety of their home baking. Large pots of tea, jugs of punch made from homemade wines and a crate of Guinness provided the liquid refreshments. More bales were used for seating. As dancing feet added to the rhythm of jigs and reels played on a fiddle and an accordion, the old barn was transformed into a place of jollity. Liveliest of the lot was Ned Bolin. His feet were jigging up and down like a well wound mechanical toy. Molly turned to the woman sitting beside her and said, "Would ye look at that man o' mine. No matter how much I feed him he still has an arse on him like a whin root."

Robert had been left in the farmhouse to stoke the fire so that hot water would be on hand to refill the big teapots. When Josie Brennan and one of her friends were sent for the kettles of water she persuaded Robert to join them for the dancing. Since joining this household he had learned that life was slightly easier if he did exactly what he was told. He was wearing Frank's cast off clothing – old boots with streaks of pig manure sticking to them, worn shirt and being taller than Frank, the trousers were too short. Like an obedient lamb he followed the two teenagers to the barn. Always ready for a bit of fun Josie dragged him on to the floor. The laughing and glib remarks heightened at the sight of this odd couple, Josie's lithe young body moving sensually to the music and Robert look-ing completely bewildered. Maggie was sitting on Molly Bolin's knee when the loud clapping and cheering started.

"Go on man, give her a squeeze," shouted someone in the crowd. Anger gripped Maggie. Robert was her sheltered bay, her protector when she was in trouble and now they were all laughing at him. Bolting from Molly's knee she darted across the floor and stamped with all her might on Josie's foot.

"Leave him alone, you auld bitch," she screamed. "I hope you fall off your bike and break your neck and I want my doll back." Consternation, a brief moment of silence, and then came the whispered mutterings. Josie, in floods of tears ran to her mother and Sarah too, trying to control her intense rage, went to Bridie Brennan. "Bridie, I'm sorry about that brat of mine," she said and looking at Frank, who by now was so drunk that he was unaware that there had been a commotion, she added, "It's well seen who she takes that behaviour from but I'll soon knock it out of her."

"Now just keep calm, I think I know what all this is about. We'll talk about it later," said Bridie. Sarah took the children by the hand and nodding to Robert all four left the barn. Once in the house she roared at Robert. "Didn't I tell you not to leave the kitchen," and shaking Maggie, she went on, "Don't you ever show me up like that again." They woke late the next morning to discover that Maggie was not the only one to cause disruptions. Josie and her friend had doctored one of the punch jugs with jalap, leaving many of the dancers with a sudden bout of diarrhoea. On the grassy patch at the rear of the barn were many little middens, topped with dock leaves. But it was the artistic flair of some young lads from the nearby Stanton Estate that really angered Frank. He heard the agitated bleating of the sheep and going to investigate found some of them with red and blue paint on their fleeces while others were decorated in green and yellow. As the turpentine in the paint seeped through to the skin the animals became more and more distressed. The protestant farmer and the catholic postman spent the rest of the day shearing the fleece and treating the affected skin. Very few homes had a wireless so the area at the crossroads beside Peggy's shop was a meeting place for shared information and a venue for the games of the youth. They played marbles, threw horseshoes and played football with a pig's bladder. One evening Frank strolled along to the shop for his usual supply of pipe tobacco.

"How's the sheep?" asked one young lad.

Tilting his hat, Frank said, "It's hard to say, but if you were to sit for a while in a bath of turpentine you'd have a damn good idea how they are. And I was just thinking that the boys that put their flags on my sheep could have saved their paint, for yon sheep of mine were never bigoted."

At last the new house was finished but John Fletcher showed no delight for he had a new problem on his mind. When he bought the pony he leased a patch of grazing land from the neighbouring farmer but now this man had sold his farm and the new owner wanted all the land for growing crops. Without his pony and cart John's livelihood would be in jeopardy. He carted the turf home, collected timber and building materials for his work and his grandchildren, Harry's daughter and two sons rode the pony on the patch of land where it grazed. He was grateful when Frank offered to let him stable and graze Lily on the farm. Both men agreed that Frank could use the pony for light work and Harry and his two boys would come regularly to clean out the stable. Sarah did not like the idea of the Fletcher family calling so often but she feared that any objections on her part might open up old wounds, so she kept quiet.

Although Maggie and Tommy had boundless energy and ate well Sarah thought they looked too pale and thin. She was sure they had worms and had visions of threadworms, roundworms and tapeworms eating at their insides. She started her attack on the worms by administering soapy enemas every morning and evening. Maggie, though she hated and dreaded the ordeals, seemed more able to cope with them than Tommy. He often fainted and Sarah would lay him on the sofa while she eagerly prodded the faeces with a stick, absolutely convinced that she saw the worms crawling around. One morning as Bridie Brennan approached the farmhouse to collect her can of milk she heard crying. On the concrete floor the two children were lying, obviously in distress. Sarah was warning them not to move until she told them or they'd get another dose. In the ensuing conversation Bridie heard that the doctor had ordered the treatment twice a day. Bridie, horrified at the sight before her, suggested that maybe worm powders would be less severe. After leaving the milk in her kitchen she immediately went to the shop.

"You'll never guess what I saw this morning," she said to Peggy and related her morning's discovery.

"Nothing that woman does would surprise me. She's obsessed with illness and the fear of illness, TB, cancer, scarlet fever, any illness and she goes berserk, and of course believes that she knows all the cures."

"I can't get the sight of them out of my head. Peggy I just can't ignore it. That sort of treatment twice a day could ruin their insides and you know what she's using – Sunlight washing soap and said the doctor ordered it twice a day. There was a packet of soda crystals on the table. Surely she wouldn't add that? Do you think I should mention it to Frank?"

"Tell him! He's never had to take responsibility for anything in his life, had everything handed to him on a plate. He wouldn't have the gumption to ask a doctor. He'd just believe her and let her get on with it. No, leave it with me and I'll find a way of letting the doctor know what's going on."

"Aye, right then, you'll know what to do and if she takes the hump I can always get my milk at Nesbitt's, even it is a bit further away." It was common knowledge that many people came to Peggy for help and advice but this situation was something she'd have to deal with on her own. In the surgery she told the doctor she had a friend whose children were badly bothered with worms and knowing that he had told Mrs. Millar to give her children enemas twice a day, her friend wanted to know how much Sunlight soap and washing soda she should use. The doctor swallowed and frowned. He knew this woman was in good physical health but he wondered about her mental health.

"Tell me, Miss Fletcher, how are you keeping yourself?"

"I'm worried. I know other people's children are none of my concern and my neighbour feels the same way, but what do we do about children who can't speak up for themselves?"

"And this imaginary friend?" said the doctor. Peggy sighed and the doctor went on, "Don't worry about it. Sometimes an imaginary friend can be useful. Now leave this matter with me and I'll deal with it." Peggy left the surgery thinking of going window shopping. Then she remembered that her father was minding the shop and he didn't like being left too long in it. She bought an ice cream cone and waited for the next bus home.

"I'd say the enemas have stopped," Bridie reported on her next visit to the shop, "but the atmosphere is like the milk, it's strained."

Frank's trips in the car became less frequent when Sarah announced that she would accompany him and leave Robert to look after the children. Her first trial run did nothing for marital relationships and her second spelled disaster for the car. Sarah, who had no experience of driving, did her best to steer the car in first gear all the way from Limavady. Approaching the sharp corner at the entrance to the yard, the car plunged into the midden. Maggie and Tommy watched in horror as Frank, Sarah and two men struggled to get out of the car and plough their way through the pig manure. When they reached hard ground the two men sloped off down the lane. This was the first time Maggie had seen her father staggering and she thought he was sick. Robert was ordered to get a bucket of water to wash the offending shoes. In the morning Frank and Robert harnessed the horse to the car and pulled it out of the midden. During the week, much to Sarah's annoyance, several locals called to stare and give advice, none of which worked.

"I think the pig shit has done for her. She'll never be any good," Johnny Spin a Yarn declared and later the car was towed away while Sarah raved and lamented to Frank about his drinking. But when her next visitor arrived she had to rely on Frank for help. One night as the children were ready for bed a man they had never seen before came to the house. He and Sarah were soon deep in conversation. Next morning Sarah took the children to the pantry and said, "Now we have to go to town and if anyone calls you're to say there's nobody here but you and Robert." She then went to the byre and gave Robert the same warning before she and Frank left to get the bus. The stranger took a bottle of lemonade from his pocket and said to the children, "See what your Uncle Andy has brought you. Come on, get some cups and we'll all have a drink." They put four cups on the table and called to Robert to come and share the treat. When the bottle was empty Robert returned to his work and Andy took the children for a walk along the lane beside the orchard. He put some pebbles in the bottle, replaced the stopper and shaking the bottle started to dance and clown around in the lane. With his encouragement both children had a turn at this crazy dancing. Then Andy gave the bottle to Tommy who took it upstairs and hid it under his pillow. That evening shortly after it got dark Andy left and next morning Sarah, looking out the window, saw Tommy dancing around with his newly acquired musical toy. When she asked where he got it, Maggie said, "Uncle Andy made it for him." For a moment there was silence. It was as though Maggie had just divulged state secrets. "Did he tell you that's who he was?" Sarah inquired and Maggie nodded. "Don't you ever mention to a soul he was here. If ever I hear you telling anybody, I'll give you a good hiding. Do you understand?" and she shook Maggie's shoulders as she said it.

Maggie didn't understand but she feared her mother when she was in one of these moods. Sarah's attempts to hide her family's secrets were in vain for Annie, in a letter to Peggy, told her that her brother Andy had been arrested by the gardai for making poteen. He was out on bail and his case was due in court soon. Annie was angry for she had begged him many times to give up the poteen stilling. Now he planned to get over the border between CountyDonegal and CountyDerry and go to England. He had written to her asking if she would put him up till he got a job and somewhere to live. When Sarah next went to the shop Peggy remarked on the family resemblance and asked if Andy got away alright. Sarah froze, then regained her composure and replied, "Oh he was just here on a visit." She strode home, rigid with rage, barged into the house and confronted Frank.

"Did you tell her at the shop that we went to the town to get him a ticket?"

Frank looked at her and said, "Did I tell her? Not at all, he managed to do that himself, called with Harry and Helen and then called at the shop. It seems he was quite pleased at how he could taunt the law. A chip off the old block, I'd say."

Sarah was still doing her utmost to present her family in the best possible light but felt that she was being thwarted at every turn. Thinking of her father, she'd wake up at night thinking of all the things she'd heard about him and the more she tried to forget them the more they came into her mind to haunt her. Now her brother had brought disgrace to the family and he didn't seem to care. She went to the hall to hang up her coat and muttered, "Well damn him, I'll never lift a finger to help him again,"

While she was still smarting over Andy's betrayal two problems had to be dealt with. She had given birth to her third child at a time when the financial situation on the farm was not healthy. Because Maggie was born in New York her name was not on the local register of births and the school attendance officer had called to see her birth certificate. He said she should have started school the previous year. Frank's only way out of his present financial difficulties was to get work in England for a spell. Unlike his adventure to America this one was a necessity. Andy owed him a favour, so he'd stay with him and with Robert doing the milking and John Brennan keeping a wary eye on affairs he set off. It never crossed his mind that his farm might not be run as smoothly as Ellen had managed.

It was while he was away that Maggie witnessed something she had never seen before. There was angry shouting outside the byre door and when she ran out to investigate her mother was flailing Robert about the head and shoulders with a stick while he was shielding his head with his hands. Maggie froze at the sight. Her first thought was why Robert did not defend himself or run away or hit her back. Then she wondered what he had done to deserve such a beating. She thought of all the times he had saved her from a hiding and she was helpless now to save him. To her he was the gentlest person on earth. She had never known him to be rough even with the animals.

One evening Andy Cowper answered a knock at his door and there stood his sister Letty, rather bedraggled and down at heel. He recalled her going to England without leaving a forwarding address. Unlike her first disappearance few people passed any remarks. "Jasus Letty, where did you spring from?

I see you have another one since I last saw you and where is himself, your knight in shining armour?"

"Don't talk to me about that bastard." Andy invited them in and they sat on the old sofa that was communal seating during the day and Frank's bed at night. Here was a Letty who had no fiery remarks to make like she had in her youth and the once quiet Andy who had plenty to say. All she wanted was some money and Sarah's address and Andy provided both. When Sarah answered the knock at the door she was shocked to find Letty and the two children staring at her, all looking forlorn and exhausted. Thinking of the rows she and Letty had in the past, her first feeling was of satisfaction at seeing her sister in her present state. But after they had a meal and all the children were in bed the two women talked late into the night. Both were back on well trodden ground. Sarah ridiculed Frank and Annie and Dora. Letty ridiculed Annie and Dora and her husband Marcus, telling Sarah what a reprobate he turned out to be, abandoning her and the two weans. Now Sarah felt sorry for her.

"Of course I'll look after them till you get sorted out," Sarah offered.

In the next two days Letty made it her business to find out all she could about Marcus' father, old Arthur Henton-Gray. Then she returned to England and plotted her next move. She got a job as a live-in housekeeper and wrote to Sarah assuring her that she would soon be back for the children for old Henton-Gray had agreed to take them in. Subtly she suggested that they could both end up in the same boat for it looked like Frank was seeing other women. There wasn't a modicum of truth in either statement Letty had written but she planted the seeds and waited for them to germinate. While collecting the eggs the words in Letty's letter grew louder and louder in Sarah's head. "If I thought he was…and me slaving over here… I'd…" and her body tensed as anger swelled and she squashed the egg that was in her hand, leaving the yolk dripping on to her apron. Her letter of reply was better than Letty had expected. They exchanged places and with great gusto Letty took on the role of mothering five children.

Tommy still wet the bed at night and was used to having a rubber sheet placed under the cotton one. Letty was not prepared to wash a soiled sheet every day so she announced that from now on Tommy could get up and use the pot under the bed like the rest of them. Next morning Tommy's nightclothes and the mattress were soaked. Like a bolt out of the blue this affable and jovial woman turned into a monster. She pulled the wet clothes off him, reached for the pony's whip hanging on the back door and lashed out at him. "I'm not here to wash your pissed clothes," she roared. As the whip came down again and again his naked body writhed and rose from the floor like flailed corn and his screams filled the air. Her daughter Jenny stood frozen. Arthur's face turned deathly pale and Maggie couldn't believe what she was seeing. She sprang like a wild cat at Letty, pulling her hair and clawing at her face. As Letty dropped the whip Maggie grabbed a handful of her hair, twisted her hand round it and kicked at her shins. But Maggie was no match for a grown woman.

"I'll tell my daddy when he comes home," she spluttered.

"Your daddy my arse, he's not coming home. He doesn't give a damn about you lot. I'm in charge now and you'll not rule the roost here."

The blows to Maggie's head continued as Letty dragged her to what was known as the good room where she threw her in and slammed the door. This good room was meant to be a sitting room where the household could relax or entertain guests but this particular one never reached that status. John Brennan, with Ned Bolin's help had covered the floor with straw and put all the apples down to await collection by the grocery van. As Maggie lay crumpled on the floor the walls and the apples seemed to be spinning around her. When her head began to clear she had murder in her mind for her Aunt Letty. "So she's in charge. Well if I can't kill her I'll ruin everything she has." She took a bite out of each apple and spat it on the floor. When she got to the cooking apples they were too sour to bite so she thumped each one several times on the concrete floor and then sat with her back against the wall looking at the destruction. When Letty went to the bedroom to examine the mattress she found Arthur consoling a whimpering Tommy. Her eyes caught sight of the weal marks on his body and she realised she had completely lost control. She thought of Maggie and hurried to the sitting room where the sight before her sent her into a panic.

Her plan had been to wait a week and then ask one of Sarah's neighbours to look after the weans for an afternoon while she went to confront old Henton-Gray. Now she reckoned that it had to be done immediately and without prying neighbours coming near the house. As she was thinking about it Jake Rogers, a local farmer, came to the door. The neighbours put it very well when they described him as a man who had a talent for helping young widows and women on their own. His offer of help was accepted and in the morning after Bridie called for the milk he was there with his pony and trap to drive her to Limavady. From there she got a bus to Derry and a connection to Moville, certain that Robert and Arthur could hold the fort while she was away. During her bus journey she rehearsed what she wanted to say to old Henton-Gray. He had always been a harsh and domineering man in his own household, yet craved the adulation of his business associates. People close to him were unhappy about his rejection of his grandchildren and with this knowledge Letty was going to deliver a crushing blow. A wealthy business man living in the lap of luxury, while his fourteen year old grandson was homeless on the streets of an English city might make him take notice. But the evidence she had that his son Marcus had, not just abandoned his wife and children, but had recently committed bigamy and now called himself Marcus Gray, was news that a newspaper might pay her for. If this failed she would throw herself on Sarah's mercy and ask her to look after Arthur and Jenny while she'd return to England to earn some money. This plan, worked out before she left England, was her only hope of getting out of her dilemma but she had to make sure that her actions of the previous day were not discovered. Not only would she be in her present homeless state but she would lose the sympathy and credibility of those who heard of her plight. Nervously she approached the front door, less confident now that she could carry out her mission. A woman in the act of putting on her coat opened the door and looked at her.

"If you're looking for himself you may go on in. I only work here two hours a day." She stepped into the hall and had an eerie sensation when nobody appeared. All the doors leading from the hall were closed bar one. Quietly she entered and saw him sitting in an armchair, a shadow of the man she had confronted all those years ago. He didn't speak, just looked at her with sunken eyes. It was obvious he was a sick man. In his present state she doubted that he could take in what she had planned to say. She decided that by using another angle she could play a better hand.

"Marcus has left us without a home or any means of support and I wondered if you could give Arthur a job here. I'll go back to England and get a job and a room for Jenny and me. It would only be for a while till I could get a job for him over there."

"I don't know about that but I could get somebody to track Marcus down. He should be providing his family with a home." Opening her bag she took out a newspaper photograph of Marcus' recent wedding and handed it to him. Before he could reply she said, "And no, we're not divorced if that was what you were going to ask, so searching for him could lead him to prison." Gazing at the photograph he recognized his son and on reading the name Marcus Gray, tried to hide his anguish.

"I know it would please you to see my family's name dragged through the mud so why haven't you reported it?"

"If I was on my own I would, but how do you think my children would feel if they knew that I helped send their father to prison. As it is, with him changing his name, it could be years before he's found out." While old Arthur Henton-Gray saw all his dreams and ambitions for his family come to naught he realised that this woman had the only thing he wanted – the grandson who bore his name. Since there was no offer of a job for young Arthur, Letty realised that her plan, regardless of what hand she played, had also come to naught. She had to get back and face the situation she had left that morning. As she bade him goodbye he asked her if she would bring young Arthur to see him. She could feel anger welling up and tried to control it.

"I can't afford bus fares to go visiting. Every penny I can earn is for a roof over our heads. We'll all be going back to

England in two or three week's time so coming here is out of the question." He fumbled in his pocket and brought out a white five pound note. "Here take this. It will more than cover the fare. I would like to see the lad."

Feeling nothing but contempt for him she took the note and said, "I'll ask him if he wants to come and if he doesn't I'll post this back to you." She felt delight at the thought of returning his five pound note. But on her return she found that her son did want to meet his grandfather and reluctantly agreed to take him. Her mind was in overdrive as she thought of the destruction of the entire apple crop. The family was fed large portions of apple tarts, custard with stewed apples and baked apples with raisins. As she carried a bucketful of them to the pigs Robert told her that too many apples would give the pigs 'the scour'. She couldn't risk any more disasters so she told him to take the rest of the apples and put them in the midden. Maggie's sullen moods and refusal to speak concerned her. She couldn't trust this child so she kept her from school and from going to the shop to ensure nothing would be told.

One night as Maggie felt herself drifting off to sleep she heard a loud creaky noise from outside. In a moment she was alert. Tommy and Jenny were asleep but Arthur was standing at the side of the window. "What is it?" she whispered. He turned his head and said softly, "It's nothing. Go back to sleep." She could not stay awake any longer. Her head sank into the pillow and her eyes closed, but Arthur kept peering out from behind the curtains. The following afternoon she was in the yard skipping with her new rope, the one with the tinkling bells. Jenny wanted to skip and Letty suggested that Maggie might give her a turn when she was finished. With a stony expression Maggie dropped the rope on the ground and walked away. She remembered the day she got it. Her daddy brought it home and two days later he left. Next day Jenny was skipping when Letty told her to give Maggie a turn, but Maggie didn't want the rope. She sat moodily watching Jenny skip then got up and went to find Robert. As Robert did his chores she followed him around, still thinking of her skipping rope. She didn't want the tinkling rope ever again. She'd get her own rope and she knew exactly where to find it. In the barn there were rolls of rope used to tie down the corn stacks. Later in the evening, when all the children were sitting round the fire after supper, she got Robert's razor and put it into her pocket. Quietly she slipped outside, up the steps to the barn and was about to go in when she stopped. She saw the soles of a pair of shoes. Bewildered, she crinkled up her eyes and stared, recognizing Letty's legs. "And Jake," she mouthed. She looked again. He was on top of her with his arms round her neck and they were both thrashing and moaning. She dared not breathe or make a sound. "Good, he's killing her," she whispered to herself. Turning quietly she went down the steps, keeping away from the railing in case it would creak. Back in the kitchen she put the razor on the cabinet shelf. "When she's found dead I'll never say Jake was here," she told herself. Then she joined the others at the fireside, hardly able to contain her glee. When Robert came in after foddering the cows he warmed his hands at the fire and then sat at the table. Arthur poured him a cup of tea and buttered slices of the raisin loaf. Maggie felt that she could sit all night at the warm glow of the fire. She had never known such delight. Then the door opened and Letty came in. Maggie swallowed and felt herself go cold and sweaty.

"What's wrong with you? Anybody would think you'd seen a ghost," Letty said.

Maggie could hear her heart pounding. The colour drained from her face and she felt as though she was sliding off the chair. Recalling the scene in the barn and using all her powers of reasoning she concluded that Letty had killed Jake.

"You're sitting too near the fire. Go out and get a breath of fresh air," Letty said.

She went out and thought of going to the barn. If she found him she would run to John Brennan and he'd get the police and they would hang her. Her heart started pounding again as she timidly climbed the steps. Peering in she could see nothing but straw and suddenly she got scared. Certain that he was there she decided to wait till the next time Robert went for straw. Her ultimate devastation came next day when Jake strolled into the yard.

Letty started packing her belongings. Her new plan was to write to Sarah and ask her to return. Then she would turn up at Andy's flat. Surely he would let them stay till she and Arthur got jobs and could afford to rent rooms of their own. These last weeks had been a disaster for her. She was still thinking of a plausible story to explain the loss of the apples and how to curb Maggie's tongue. On the Friday morning Robert was told to heat the stew for their dinner. Jake was there again with the pony and trap to take Letty and Arthur to Limavady to start the journey to Moville. Old Henton-Gray looked at his grandson and saw a mirror image of himself when he was young. His legs were more wobbly than usual as he hobbled on a stick to show the lad round the mill. Letty refused to go with them and sat on a low wall waiting till they returned.

"Do you think you'd like to work here?" the old man said. Young Arthur frowned and tried to explain that he liked the place alright but he couldn't take a job here for they were returning to England in two weeks. "Maybe if I talked to your mother she'd let you stay."

"No she couldn't. It will take both of us working to pay rent and then there's Jenny." The old man was crestfallen at the thought that he might never see his grandson again. He asked Letty if he could have a private word with her. What a difference, she thought, to the visit she made years ago when he chased her from his door. She listened to what he had to say and snorted in disgust. Then she laughed.

"You want to take us in and make a will leaving the mill to Arthur. You must think I'm really stupid. Anybody could make a will today and change it tomorrow. I've worked as a housekeeper and but for my youngsters could get a live-in job anytime. I didn't come here to beg."

"Well I could give you a job as a housekeeper. I think the lad wants to stay."

Letty thought of Andy. He really had no room for the three of them but she did not show her desperation. She wanted the terms of their employment clearly stated and given to her in writing. It was agreed that she would start work as soon as her sister returned. Old Arthur said they could take whatever rooms they wanted.

"We'll use the servants' rooms at the back and there's your change from the fiver. Now we must go. We've three bus journeys before we get back and I don't want to miss the last bus from Limavady." Letty felt completely relaxed until she stepped into the kitchen of the Millar house.

Chapter 5

During Letty's time at the Millar farm she paid little attention to baby Louise. Out of her pram she was left to crawl on the concrete floor in a sodden nappy and in her pram Maggie or Jenny was sent to hold a bottle of milk to her mouth. When Lettie left Robert as housekeeper she gave no thought to the fact that he had a full time job looking after the animals. After mucking out the pigsty he heated some milk for Louise's bottle and approaching her pram to feed her he noticed her eyes were odd and when he touched her skin, it was burning hot. He panicked, sure that if anything was wrong with her he would be blamed. Dashing through the stack garden and over the low fence he rushed to Bridie Brennan's house, shouting as he went.

As soon as Bridie looked into the pram everything that followed was done at break neck speed. She scribbled a note and sent Robert on the bicycle to Peggy's shop and then lifted the child and wiped her face with a cold cloth. On getting the note Peggy rushed to the post office to get a message to the doctor and then went to her brother's house to ask her sister- in- law Helen to come and mind the shop. She was out of breath when she got to the Millar farm. The doctor looked at the child. "Why wasn't I sent for sooner?" As he examined the child Bridie explained that she was just a neighbour. "And where are the parents?"

"They're in England and Mrs. Millar's sister is looking after the family but she doesn't seem to be in," Peggy said, exasperation in her voice.

Letty and Arthur's absence was a mystery to both women but before they could make a comment the doctor took Peggy aside. "Miss Fletcher, this child is very ill. I've given her an injection but she may not make it through the night. I need your help to get her to hospital and the parents need to be informed." Peggy wrapped Louise in a blanket, followed the doctor to his car and over her shoulder said to Bridie, "Get a telegram off to Frank." In a moment the car sped off leaving Bridie with staring and frightened children. She tried to console them as she thought of what to do next. "An address," she said aloud. "We don't have their address but where am I going to find it in this house? Robert, would you dash over to Molly Bolin's place and ask her to come and look after the weans for a while?"

"But…but, I don't know where she lives."

"Oh I never thought of that. Would you look after them and I'll go and get her? I'll only be a minute or two."

When the two women returned Molly wasted no time in telling the children that she was going to make pancakes and they could help her. Bridie hurried off to her own cottage to leave a note for John and then went to the shop but the only address Helen could find was Annie's.

"As far as I know Annie lives quite near to her brother Andy," Helen said.

"Well I may send word to her and hope she can contact them."

Bridie returned to the Millar home to find the children helping Molly with the pancakes. Molly agreed to stay till Bridie went home to make John's dinner. When John came home she told him of the day's happenings, getting angrier by the minute at being put in this situation. She put some stew in a bowl and they both went to the Millar home. There was a stack of pancakes on the wire tray and Bridie insisted that Molly take some home with her. "Poor weans, they don't know what's going on," said John, as he surveyed the situation. He surmised that Letty was off somewhere with Jake Rogers but that did not fit in with Arthur's absence. Then he noticed that all the apples were gone and assumed that Letty had sold them. He decided to cycle to the post office and ring the hospital to ask if he could speak to Peggy. She told him that Louise was still not out of the woods and she was planning to sit with her. Back at the house Bridie was upstairs putting the children to bed when Letty and Arthur entered the kitchen. Letty was surprised to find Bridie coming down the stairs.

"What are you doing here?" she asked.

Bridie, filled with rage, looked her straight in the eye and said, "You could say I'm doing what you should have been here to do. We didn't have an address for Frank so the telegram was sent to your sister Annie and I don't know whether the baby is alive or dead or if Frank got the telegram." Suddenly Letty was in shock. Her voice was barely audible as she kept asking what had happened to Louise. Offering no sympathy Bridie continued, "I'm no doctor so I don't know what's wrong with her but I'm sure you'll find out soon enough and since there's nothing more I can do here I'll get off home." She put on her coat and left. Letty questioned Robert but could make no sense of what he was saying. She swore at him and rushed to the shop. It was closed but her hammering at the kitchen window brought John Fletcher to the back door. He could only pass on what the doctor said and told her that Peggy was sitting with the baby in the hospital.

Whether the child lived or died Letty knew she could not face Frank and Sarah. Back in the house she packed all her belongings, listened to every noise and creak and as soon as it was light she wakened Arthur and Jenny. All three boarded the early morning bus to Limavady. On Peggy's return from the hospital she was relaying the news to her father when Bridie arrived. "You'll never believe this. When I went for the milk that woman has gone again and taken her weans with her. Robert knows nothing. He's standing at the table hacking at a loaf of bread to make the weans something to eat."

John Fletcher, Peggy and Bridie discussed the dilemma, wondering if Annie got a message to Frank and trying to work out how long it would take them to get home. Bridie suggested that she take the two weans to her house. With the lack of sleep Peggy was in a foul mood. "To hell with this, I'm not putting in another day like yesterday." She went to the phone box and rang the doctor to explain their situation. "None of us are related to this family but what are we supposed to do, knowing that a retarded man is left to look after two young children and feed all the animals on the farm?"

"Miss Fletcher, I know you're upset. Leave it with me and I'll pass this information to the police and they'll be able to deal with it."

In the meantime Bridie was having no success in taking the two children with her for they were adamant that they wanted to stay with Robert. On her way home she decided she'd boil some extra potatoes and when she and John had their dinner she'd take some food to Robert and the weans. As she entered the Millar home there were two policemen talking to Robert and Maggie while Tommy cowered in a corner.

"Oh Jasus, it's the wean. Don't tell me she's passed away," said Bridie.

The policemen assured her that the baby was alive but they were sent to assess the welfare of the children and asked her if she could throw any light on how long they has been left in their present state. She set the food on the table and had no sooner started to tell them what she knew when the door opened and Frank and Sarah walked in. For a moment there was silence as faces looked at faces. Sarah sat on the settee with her head buried in her hands. Frank stood like a zombie as the older officer went on to say that his instructions were to remove the two children if he found they were not in the care of a sensible adult.

"You know with that turf fire there should always be someone sensible around to look after the children," he added. Bridie, whose anger of the previous day had not abated, was like an incendiary bomb that had just hit its target.

"What the hell do you mean? Are you suggesting that Robert hadn't the common sense to look after them? Only for him the wean would have been dead in the pram by the time Letty got back last night. If she had spent less time with Jake Rogers and more with the weans she was supposed to be watching, you wouldn't be sitting there scribbling your notes. And who do you think made them their breakfast this morning?" Almost immediately she regretted her action for John had warned her to say nothing of what they knew about Jake and Letty. As she left she knew she'd have to go home and tell him how she had lost her temper. The elder policeman turned to Frank and said, "I'm sure you both have a lot to do so we won't take up any more of your time." Both officers took their leave. Frank and Sarah went to the hospital taking Maggie and Tommy with them, but the fall out from Bridie's verbal bomb left debris that would cause friction for many days. The full impact of how near to death Louise had been hit them as the matron gave them details of the child's case. Each mulling over their thoughts, they were silent until they got home.

"I don't know what took you to England anyway," Frank said.

"Did you think I was going to be a slave here while you galloped around with other women?" Frank looked at her in disbelief but she continued. "You needn't deny it for Letty wrote and told me." Frank jumped to his feet in rage.

"If you're so quick to believe her maybe I should have believed what she said about you. If you ask me you're two of a kind, only happy when you're spreading filthy lies about other people." Sarah's anger now turned to Letty but Frank was not prepared to listen. "Sarah, I'm telling you once more, I don't want to hear that woman's name mentioned or what she did when you were young and if you must talk about her, find another listener." As he was delivering his ultimatum the door opened and Jake Rogers was about to step in.

"Ah, you're back. I was just...I thought I'd... call and check on the calf."

Frank stepped outside and facing Jake said, "I'll be able to check on the calf and anything else round here that needs checking." A sudden fist caught Jake on the jaw followed by another punch to his nose. He lay sprawled on his back as blood trickled down his face. "Get to your feet, you sleekit bastard and don't ever set foot here again." Frank stood with gritted teeth and clenched fists, glaring at Jake as he skulked away.

Louise was improving but daily visits to the hospital were taking their toll on Sarah and the guilt she felt was draining her energy. When Louise was discharged Frank resolved to try and curb his drinking and get someone to help Sarah in the house. He went to the hiring fair and returned with Jane Thornton. Not as tall as Sarah, she had long dark hair, parted in the centre and tied at the back in a ponytail. The coat, much too big for her, may have been a hand me down from someone else. When she took it off they saw the rough tweed skirt and the brown woolly jumper with patches on the elbows. Maggie took an instant liking to the voice and gentle laugh of this girl. She slept in the bed with Maggie, who loved to watch her brushing her hair, intrigued at how she tied the bow at the back. Every evening when Maggie got home she enjoyed telling Jane all about school and the games they played in the playground. Jane told Maggie about her brother who worked on the Stanton Estate.

"Maggie, do you know where the Stanton Estate is?"

"Naw, but I can soon fine out. We can ask Peggy at the shop. She knows everything." When Maggie and Tommy went to the shop, Jane was sent with them. Peggy was pleased to see a bright sparkle return to the faces of the two children. Maggie, full of chat like she used to be, proudly introduced Jane.

"She wants to know where the Stanton Estate is. Do you know where it is?" Jane told Peggy that her brother Sam had just got a job on the estate and she wondered how she could get in touch with him. It was the first time for both of them to be away from home. Peggy told her that her brother Harry did odd jobs at the estate and could deliver a note for her. Jane returned with the children, more than glad that she might soon see her brother. Every evening after her work was done and the children were in bed Jane strolled to the shop in the hope that Sam would be there. When they finally met neither could stop talking. Sam was more homesick than Jane was and since they didn't get wages till their contract was complete they couldn't go into the shop to buy anything. They exchanged details of their work place, talked of their folks at home and arranged when they would next meet. With great delight Jane told Sarah how the woman Peggy in the shop had helped her get in touch with her brother. She found Sarah's reaction rather strange.

"You should be very careful what you tell that woman for you never know where she would spread your business." But Jane felt she had nothing to hide. She was used to lots of talking and laughing with her family at home and found this household a bit odd in that there was little or no pleasant conversation. She went to see Peggy most evenings after work just to find someone to talk to. Five weeks after Jane's arrival Sarah's workload was lessened but she was not satisfied with the new worker.

"She's been out nearly every evening since she came here and we all know what that means," she said to Frank.

"Doesn't she do all the jobs she's given, helps with the milking and she's good with the weans. Her free time's her own. What more do you want?"

"I know she's at the shop and hanging about the cross roads at night and how do we know what she gets up to?"

"Ah, I can see where this is comin' from. You don't want her talking to Peggy Fletcher. You'd do well to remember that it was Peggy that got the wean to the hospital and sat with her all night when she nearly died. But go ahead; get rid of her for you'll do it anyway no matter what I say."

Jane, with a few shillings and her fare home, started crying. She despaired of getting another job and knew her mother would be depending on her earnings. Peggy was surprised to see Jane come to the shop in such a state and tell her that Mrs.

Millar said she didn't need her anymore. As Peggy tried to comfort the crying girl she was thinking of a solution. "Jane, would you stay here overnight? I'll make a few enquiries and see if we can get you another job."

Jane stayed that night and the next night and the following evening Harry Fletcher delivered a letter to Peggy. She smiled when she read it. Harry was working on a job where extra stables were being built and the owners were prepared to give Jane a job on a month's trial. Peggy warned her that mucking out stables would be hard work and at times she might have to work long hours. Jane was delighted; glad to get work so that her mother didn't have to worry. Helen Fletcher took Jane to her new job the next day.

On the day that Jane had to leave the Millar house Maggie came home from school and finding her missing asked her mother where she was.

"We had to send her away," Sarah said.

"But why?" asked Maggie.

"Oh she was galloping about at night with a lot of men and if anything happened your Daddy would get the blame and it would cost us a lot of money."

Maggie couldn't wait to tell Tommy this strange news. She found him in the turf shed, building a little enclosure with turf sods.

"I know something you don't know."

"What?" he said, looking up at her from inside his newly built den.

"I know why Jane's away. At night she turns into a horse along with a whole lot of men, and they gallop all over the fields and destroy the corn and potatoes and then Daddy will have to pay for them."

"But how do they turn into horses? I never saw them."

"They just do, when it gets dark. I heard them last night neighing in the field."

"Well I never heard them."

"You were sleeping, stupid, how would you hear them?"

Within a short time young Jane Thornton was replaced by Maurice Jackson, a lad of sixteen. Tall and pale as paper he was painfully thin. There was no way he'd get work at the hiring fare. A friend of Frank's asked him if he would take the lad on for six months, for his mother was a widow and times were tough for them. Sarah felt sorry for him. She made him drinks of raw eggs and milk, always gave him second helpings of dinner and commented to Frank that his mother had no idea how to feed a strapping lad of his age. He slept with Tommy and when he'd been at the farm for a month he woke up one night with sweat on his body and with the smell in the room and the hormones racing through him, he was overcome with a powerful sensation. He got out of bed and quietly went to the bed where Maggie and Louise lay sleeping. Carefully he pulled back the blankets and stroked his hand on Maggie's leg from her knee to the top of her thigh. She woke with a jolt and clawed at his arm. "Don't you dare take our blanket, you thieving git," she said, glaring at him. He had not expected her to waken. All he wanted was to touch one of them, he told himself. Fast as a ferret he was back in bed worrying about what would happen in the morning. As for Maggie, she was going to fight for what was hers and the blanket was for her and Louise, but along with her anger came fear - a fear she could not understand. She did not want him in the room. In the morning she said to her mother, "Maurice came to our bed last night and tried to take our blanket. Can he not sleep in Robert's room? I'm scared of him."

"Don't be stupid, how can he sleep in Robert's room? There's only a single bed in there. You can't always get your own way."

When Maurice came into the kitchen for his mid-morning tea Sarah asked him if he was warm enough at night and suggested that he might want another blanket. With face reddening and heart beating he assured her he was warm enough and waited for the real accusation to come. He need not have worried, for it would not have dawned on Sarah that there was anything risky in having a lad of sixteen in the same room as the young girls. Her mind went immediately to the quilt she was making. It was nearly big enough to cover a bed. She would finish it and line it with a flannelette sheet for his bed and when his six months with them were up she'd see to it that he went home well nourished. Yet regardless of how well she fed him he didn't gain any weight or get any stronger. Out in the fields he took weak turns, coughed a lot and twice he passed out in a faint. Rather than being a help to Frank he was a liability so he took him home to his mother and explained to her that if he took a turn or fainted near any of the animals or moving machinery, it could be dangerous. He gave her some money and a bag of potatoes.

With no help in the house since Jane left Sarah was feeling the strain of the extra work. One evening she was in the pantry holding the large sieve, while Robert brought in a bucket of milk. As he lifted the bucket on to the shelf he spilled a little of the milk which splashed on to the wooden slats. She threw down the sieve, lifted the wooden potato masher and delivered blow upon blow on the head and shoulders of this docile man. It seemed any excuse or no excuse at all was enough to bring on one of her attacks. Usually she pinned him in a corner when she delivered her blows and he stood shielding his head with his hands until the furore was over but this time he ran outside, screaming. She ran after him, indignant that he had the cheek to run away from her. Frank and John Brennan had just returned from the bog with a load of dried turf when they heard the noise. Frank quickly climbed the fence, took the short cut through the stack garden and was in his own yard to witness the continued assault.

"What the hell do you think you're doing?"

"He's worse than useless, spilling milk that I'll have to clean up. He only makes work for me."

"So he spilled a drop of milk. I suppose you never make a mistake. Well you do the milking if he's that useless. Every other woman round here does the milking but you're scared of your arse to go near an animal but you won't admit it. You should be damned glad he's here to milk the cows." The battle of words went on till both ran out of saliva and Frank was sure it would never happen again but the following afternoon when the carts were once again carting home the turf Sarah delivered another flailing.

"That's for running out yesterday and shouting your head off." Her hatred of this man knew no bounds and physically abusing him was no longer enough. Maggie had often watched her mother baking, putting the flour in the tin basin, measuring out a little baking soda in the palm of her hand and rubbing it with her thumb to break up any lumps before mixing it into the flour. One day she ran into the kitchen to tell her mother about the hen's nest she had found in a sheltered corner of the orchard. Sarah had the flour in the basin and was in the act of throwing a big handful of baking soda into it.

"Oops, that's too much," said Maggie.

"This is for Robert. He likes it this way," said Sarah, but when she wiped her floured hands on her apron she glared at Maggie, saying, "Don't you ever mention this to anyone or I'll give you a trouncing that'll keep your mouth shut."

This threat left Maggie feeling that there was something strange going on. If Robert really liked this kind of bread why was her mother trying to keep it a secret? Then one day at harvest time when several neighbours came to help with the cutting of the corn Maggie was sent to the cornfield with a tin can of tea and a basket filled with bread. One parcel of bread was wrapped on its own. "Make sure you give this one to Robert," Sarah insisted. She knew this must be the bread with a lot of baking soda and she planned to watch and see if Robert enjoyed eating it. The harvesters were in a jolly mood when she got to the field. Instead of letting her hand out the bread Frank took the basket from her and all she could do was say, in a feeble voice, "Mammy says I'm to give this one to Robert." But with all the laughing and joking no one heard her. Frank started handing out the bread and Mary Conner poured the tea into the mugs. Mary's sister Lily got the bread that was meant for Robert. As she took the first bite her stomach heaved and pieces of bread spewed from her mouth. She took a quick sip of tea, rinsed it round her mouth and spat it out. "Jasus Frank, are you trying to poison us?"

Frank took a piece of the offending bread, put it in his mouth and just as quickly as Lily Conner had done he spat it out. He snatched the offending bread and stormed off to the house with Maggie in hot pursuit. He slammed the bread on the table and roared. "What the hell do you mean by sending bread like this to the field? There's more soda in it than flour. So who was it meant for, me or Robert?" It all happened so quickly that Sarah was taken by surprise, never having imagined that she'd be found out. She thought that Robert was so scared of her that he would never complain. With a little chuckle she looked at Frank as though she didn't know what he was talking about and this incensed him even more.

"Well if that's what you think take him back where he came from and stay yourself when you're at it."

"It might come to that quicker than you think. And if you want to know what people think of you, go out to the field and ask Lily Conner what she thinks of the poison you sent out for her to eat." As he was talking he took a few slices of bread and tasted a piece before buttering them and wrapping them in a tea towel.

"That's right, make sure it doesn't poison you," Sarah taunted.

In his fury he snatched a piece of the bread he'd brought from the field, reached for her and tried to force it down her throat. He was roaring. She was screaming and Maggie stood petrified, shouting, "Stop it, stop it." She had never seen her father in such a foul temper. As he left the kitchen he was muttering and swearing. Sarah, believing that Maggie had given one of the women the soda laden bread, was ranting and reeling out a list of woes and threats.

"Come over here you bloody wee tinker," she roared, and reaching for the stick she lashed out, seemingly unaware of where her blows fell. "Didn't I tell you to make sure he got that bread? Didn't I warn you?" Maggie did what Robert always did, shielded her head with her hands. When Sarah stopped she continued lamenting her hard lot in marrying a man like Frank. Maggie looked at her bruised hands, took a deep breath and said to herself, "Some day I'll kill her."

In the privacy of Sarah's home no one noticed her strange behaviour that showed itself on two opposing levels. Sometimes her mind was thrown into trance like states that only lasted for seconds. She'd mumble about things that had happened, and had anyone been listening they could not have made sense of it. Once they passed she was left trembling and terrified. The other level exhibited itself in outbursts of violence. When she hated anyone in a strong situation she thought of what she'd like to do to them and it got to the stage where she believed she had actually carried out her thoughts. But vulnerable people were easy prey.

When Maggie got outside she wandered aimlessly around trying to make sense of what had just happened. She could not make any connection between the bread and their talk about poison. The only poison she knew about was rat poison that was used in the farm buildings. She saw her mother butter the bread and was sure she had not used any rat poison. The harvesters finished work for the day and after Frank and Robert ate their evening meal in silence Frank went upstairs and came down with blankets over his arm, saying that he and Robert would be sleeping in the barn. Sarah sat quietly thinking. Had she said too much? She thought of Letty and did not want to end up like her. Frank brought the milk in, strained it and went out again. On Friday evenings the children were allowed to stay up a little later but on this particular evening it was much later than usual. When Sarah went out to bring them in Tommy and Louise were playing in the yardbut Maggie was nowhere to be seen. She fed Tommy and Louise and put them to bed, feeling sure that Maggie would stroll in any minute. Half an hour passed. An hour passed and soon it would be getting dark. She looked in all the outhouses, found Frank and Robert but they hadn't seen her. In a panic Frank told Robert to search all the outhouses again while he cycled to Brennan's cottage, then to the shop, but no one had seen her.

She was sitting beside the fast flowing stream deep in her own thoughts and oblivious of the voices of Frank and Robert calling her as they searched the fields. Her daddy and mammy would go away again and her Aunt Letty would come back and maybe kill Tommy and Louise and her. It was only when Frank touched her shoulder and spoke that she was aware of any sound. She flinched from his touch and went to Robert. She was still working out how best to deal with the tides in her life as she said to Frank, "When are you going back to England?"

"Why do you ask that? Do you want me to go back?"

"Naw, it's just….well if you go Aunt Letty will come back and Tommy and me…we'll have to run away with Louise and I don't know where to go. I ruined her apples the day she took the whip to Tommy. If she comes back she'll kill us."

The sight of her, as though all the spirit of life had been drained from her sent a dagger through his heart. He was filled with guilt and a burning anger at Lettie. He bent down to take her hand. She drew back, putting her hand in her pocket but not before he noticed the swollen bruises.

"OhJasusnaw" he whispered, but did not ask her anything. "Maggie, your Aunt Lettie will never be back here so don't worry about it."

After they got home and Maggie was in bed Frank sat at the table and said, "Sarah, I need to talk to you. I know a lot of this is my fault." She was gloating as she waited for the apology and the promises she had heard so many times before, but he went on to talk about the slump that farming was going through, prices falling and some farmers going bankrupt. Sarah saw that they could be in financial difficulties and her earlier feeling of triumph deserted her.

"Is there anything we can do?" she asked.

"This is not the worst problem I have to face. I want you to keep Maggie from school till her hands heal. I don't want the teacher reporting it to the school doctor and have them take all three of them from us. If they have to go to some kind of home I want to have a say in it."

"I never... did any...." But Frank kept on talking. "And for your own sake I want you to see the doctor. He should be able to find the kind of doctor who can help you. To lose your temper is one thing but going so far that you can't remember what you've done is another matter. I know you're not happy with me and that could be the problem. Many a time you've told folk that I followed you to America but you know that isn't true. You shouldn't have married me knowing that you wanted somebody else but if I can hang on here till prices rise you'll not be left penniless."

When he went out to join Robert in the barn Sarah filled the kettle and hung it on the crane but her mind was elsewhere. Although Frank had been in Brooklyn some time before she met him again, she couldn't help boasting that he had followed her for she desperately needed to be wanted. Now she needed to be needed. In the periods between her violent outbursts and her peculiar trances she was a hard working woman, doing everything she could to keep the house running smoothly. She knew what Frank meant by a special kind of doctor but the stigma of being sent to an asylum for what she called 'crazy' people sent shivers down her spine. She would avoid going to the doctor at all costs. Planning a future without Frank was a preferable option.

Chapter 6

All Sarah ever wanted was someone to lift her out of her perceived poverty to a position where she would be highly respected and giving her children as good an education as possible seemed at this moment a better option than depending on Frank. She asked him to fix their bicycles so that they could go to the school in town and found that he was quite keen on the idea, leaving her convinced that he fully intended to leave her but she asked no questions in case the subject of the doctor came up again.

The headmaster ushered her to his office and noted the children's names, ages and the class they were in at present. "You say the girl is in class three but for her age she should be two years ahead."

"Well there was only one teacher for the whole school so what do you expect?" She failed to mention that Maggie was late in starting school and had a very poor attendance record. The head assumed that he had just enrolled a very backward pupil or one who had no interest in learning. On the Sunday prior to starting at the new school Frank cycled to town with Maggie to show her the way and time the journey. Next day Maggie and Tommy started their new adventure, going to what they called, 'the big school in town.' Without any hassle the changeover was complete.

One morning John Brennan delivered a letter addressed to Frank. Sarah looked at the unfamiliar handwriting, convinced that Frank was planning something. She held the envelope over the steam from the kettle and carefully removed the letter. It was from Mick O Brien. Ellen was sick. Just as carefully she put the letter back in the envelope and tried to stick it again but not all of the flap would stick and pressing her hand on it left it grubby. She put it in a drawer with a pound weight from the kitchen scales on it and gave it to Frank the next day.

"There's a letter for you but I'm afraid it fell on to the ashes as I went to put it on the mantelpiece. Lucky I grabbed it before it got burned."

He tore open the letter and told her everything she already knew. There had been little communication between him and Ellen since she'd given him the two framed photographs. Now she was in CarndonaghHospital and asking to see him. He had promised to look after Robert and bring him back to visit her but had kept neither promise and now guilt overwhelmed him. When he got to the hospital a nurse informed him that Ellen had died in the early hours of that morning. The shock hit him like a boxer's left hook and when a doctor came to speak to him he couldn't take in a word the man was saying. In a faint whisper all he could say was, "She's dead, oh my God she's dead." The nurse took him to a little room and gave him a cup of tea. What he wanted was a drink but he knew he could not face Mick O Brien with the smell of whisky on his breath.

"So you got my letter," said Mick, as he opened the door.

"Aye, I did."

"She kept asking for you and Robert too, wondering how he was. Then yesterday she took a turn for the worse and passed away around two o'clock this morning."

Frank sat staring at the burning turf in the hearth and the blue-grey smoke being drawn up the chimney. Mick stood at the window staring at a crow perched on the stone wall. Both men were so deep in their own thoughts that they could not find any other words to say. A knock at the door broke the silence. Neighbours, hands held out. "Sorry for your trouble. She went quick. Ah she'll be sorely missed." Words from familiar voices brought both men back to reality as they started talking about the funeral. Then women from the village drifted in with little parcels of food for the wake. At one stage Frank went to the graveyard on the other side of the stone wall. He knew his father's grave was at the far end beside the boundary hedge. Not all graves had headstones but he eventually found it, marked with the name S. Millar on a piece of slate. With head bent he looked at it. After all these years he had not erected a headstone as he had intended. Then he gazed down the hill towards his old homestead and couldn't believe that his life had gone so badly wrong. He felt he was living life in a cage and mostly a cage of his own making. He wanted to cut the tether from the whisky but always came up with excuses. There was his need for stimulating conversation but he had to go out to find it. A drink helped him to forget his problems but one drink was never enough. Then he blamed Sarah. Her main concern was what people thought of her. She couldn't talk to him without casting blame and if he stayed he'd have to listen to the refrain, 'what will people think,' always playing as background noise. Even though he knew he'd been drinking too much long before he met her, it seemed that for both of them it was easier to have someone to blame.

As soon as he returned home he went to the yard to where Robert was slicing turnips on the old metal cutter. With solemn face he looked at him and said, "I have to tell you that Ellen's dead." He didn't wait for a reply but rushed to the orchard where he lay against the high grassy mound, the same mound where Maggie as a child had climbed to watch the people passing along the lane. There with the distant sound of water tumbling over the rocks, he wept alone. Robert, seemingly unconcerned, finished slicing the turnips and then took the bucket and went to the byre. He sat on the milking stool, pressed his head into the side of the cow and as he pulled the teats of the udder in rhythmic fashion his uncontrollable tears flowed into the bucket, mingling with the milk. He had lost the last of his true family and feeling utterly alone in his grief he wiped his face with the sleeve of his shirt and went to the house to get the milk strained. There was no one to offer a compassionate word to this man that the world had forgotten or chose to ignore. He was regarded as a simpleton who couldn't possibly have feelings yet ironically as the family sat round the table for the evening meal they drank his sorrows as they drank their tea.

Prior to Ellen's death Robert's share of his childhood home had been on Frank's mind. As soon as he could raise the money he planned to send him back to her, sell the farm and buy a small house in town for Sarah and the children. Often he would sit on a bale of straw thinking of his future. He would like to breed horses or get a job as a ploughman but in the meantime he could go to England to work for he was sure that Sarah would never be happy with him. Now all his plans were knocked on the head and like most of the struggling farmers he hardly knew where to turn to earn a living. Shortly after World War II was declared changes were taking place in this rural community. The building of a runway for the Aghanloo Aerodrome gave farmers work as they carted sand and gravel to the workmen. Farm produce was in great demand. Churns of milk set on wooden platforms at the entrances to the farms were collected every day. A general feeling of prosperity was in the air as Frank, like many others, benefited from all the extra work. One evening he answered a knock at the door and was faced by an army officer who informed him that the army would be using his farm for practice manoeuvres.

"Naw, I don't think I'll be agreeing to that," Frank replied.

"You'll see from this letter that you don't have a choice." It turned out to be a bizarre situation. The children's first introduction to the British Army came one afternoon on their way home from school as they pushed their bikes up the lane. Through a gap in the hedge they saw an odd shaped log and stopping to take a closer look found they were looking down the barrel of a gun. Hypnotized like a rabbit in a stoat's gaze they couldn't move till the camouflaged soldier broke the spell. "Go home," he said. Soon they were used to seeing soldiers darting from one hiding place to another while cows were taken to and from the field or sheep being herded to fresh pasture. One evening Tommy was sent for a basket of turf. As he lifted the turf his fingers were inches from two black boots and on lifting his head he looked into the eyes of a face splashed with dark patches. All fear of these strangely dressed men having gone by now, Tommy engaged in conversation with the soldier. "Why do you put that black stuff on your face?" This was answered with lips pursed in a circle like a fish taking food and emitting the faintest 'shush'. Amused at the contorted face Tommy started to laugh and asked if his mammy would beat him for putting dirt on his face. The soldier crouched and told him to go home but Tommy said he couldn't go back without the turf. Three soldiers with cocked rifles and suppressed giggles entered the shed. Their officer was not amused. He strode to the farm house and knocked on the door. "Mr. Millar, I have to insist that while we are here your family may go about their business in the normal way but on no account are they to speak to my men."

To Frank Millar this kind of antagonism was like a red rag to a bull. In his droll fashion he said, "Well now, I can see your point but there's nothing in your letter that says the army is in control of my family. The youngsters are not used to smoke screens and guns, but when you get back to your base tell your boss I'd like a word with him."

"There will be no need for that. I can deal with the situation."

"You tell him anyway and while you're here I'll have a word with you. You've seen the big Clydesdale. He's a nervous brute and I'm sure you don't want any of your men to get hurt, so I'd advise you to keep them well clear of the stable." The horse's previous owner had once led him to the stable without taking off the harness and the stable door being rather low, the hames on the collar got stuck in the crossbar of the door frame. Getting the animal free of his harness had caused such frenzy that he was reluctant to go through any doorway again. Any sudden noise or unusual movement was enough to start him bucking and flinging. Frank only discovered this trait after he bought him and realised why he got the horse for such a good price. The young officer, city bred and with little knowledge of rural life, had been thrown in at the deep end and was feeling the stress of his first time in command. But out in the yard the second in command was having more success with Tommy.

"Would you like to be in the army, son?"

"Would I get a gun and a helmet?"

"Well no, but you could be a special soldier. When we're here to-morrow don't say a word to us. Just pretend you don't see us and then in the evening you can play with my helmet and you might even get some chocolate. Do you think you could do that?"

"Is that what special soldiers do?"

"That's right son, that's what special soldiers do." Tommy took his new role very seriously, using the dog's bowl as a helmet while one of the soldiers put a few leafy twigs under the edge of it. As soon as he got home from school next day he put the dog's bowl on his head and walked around the yard ignoring everyone. The young commanding officer was learning fast. Providing there were no interruptions during the day he allowed the soldiers to converse with the family for a short time in the evening before they returned to barracks. During this spell of manoeuvres was the only time Robert had any social life to speak of. The townies among them got an education from him, with their questions about farm machinery, the harness for horses, milking cows and watching him let a young calf suck his fingers as he gently lowered his hand into the bucket of milk. He benefited too with their gifts of chocolate and sticky buns from the army mess. When the manoeuvres were finally over Robert missed the excitement. As the soldiers left one of them said, "Well mate, it was nice to meet you. Maybe we'll have a pint in town some evening." He had never been to town since he came to this farm many years ago and for him these soldiers sparked off a trail of memories. He recalled cousins and young men from his village wearing uniforms and going off to war. Many never returned and he had a sense of foreboding that he too would never see his childhood home again.

To the outside world this family was like any other, dealing with compulsory blackout on windows, food rationing and the carrying of gas masks. Like others they huddled outside their doors looking in dismay at the inferno of fire and shooting debris thrown into the night sky as yet another plane crashed into BenevenaghMountain. At the shop they heard the latest news that often never reached the newspapers.

"Wait till you hear this. They caught him," said Johnny Spin a Yarn.

"Caught who?" asked one of the customers.

"The bastard that was putting sugar in the aeroplane tanks." But they failed to find out what happened to him. All they knew was that he was whisked away by the military police. Before this news was stale Johnny came into the shop neighing and snorting. "What the hell's wrong with you?" someone asked.

"I'm putting in a bit of practice. Last night one of them soldiers on guard duty heard a noise and shouted 'Halt, who goes there?' All he got was a snort and this morning Hamilton's auld mare was found dead behind the hedge. You see boys, in times of war you need to know when to neigh and when to snort." Everyone was used to Johnny's yarns. They laughed and bantered with him but never believed a word he said. He knew that but this time he had to convince them it was true. "Sure as God, there's a couple of them army big knobs up at the farm and they've sent for the knacker's lorry. Come on up and see for yourself. And I'll tell you more, them weans coming home from school were caught climbing on the wings of one of the wee planes. I tell you boys, give them another day or two and they'll be flyin'. You'll find some of them spitfires missing from yon runway."

Security at the airfield was tightened, closing the road from the Orange Hall to the shop. The alternative route for the villagers was to go towards the hills and along the Murder Hole Road. When the village children were younger, Josie Brennan used to tell them stories of men being robbed and murdered on this road. Memories of the stories returned to haunt them but what they did not know was that these incidents happened in the previous century. But the young woman found stripped and tied to a tree was a recent happening and terrible news to the whole community. Not far from the Orange Hall was a rough track which over the years became a right of way. Locals called it The Loning and it shortened the journey to town by cutting off the steep hill to the Murder Hole Road. Only pedestrians or a careful driver with a small cart would venture on to it, such were the potholes, the overhanging hedges and the deep ditches. A farmer on his morning round of feeding his animals found the woman. For a few seconds he stood in shock not knowing if she was alive or dead. Awkwardly he untied her and laid her on the ground. He heard a low moan and rushed towards the farmhouse, shouting, "Martha, bring a blanket, quick." He was breathless by the time he got his wife to realise that they had something awful to deal with. Police and ambulance men were quickly at the scene. Just as quickly the news was spreading through the community, where several versions of the story could be heard long before it was reported in the newspaper, whose headline read, 'A young woman is being treated in hospital after being tied to a tree. A number of soldiers are helping police with their inquiries.' Conversation in the shop was subdued as Johnny Spin a Yarn said, "Ah, it's a bad business boys, a bad business."

With their income increasing farmers started to rear more livestock for the sale of animals was an important contribution to the household purse. Frank began to feel like he did in his bachelor days and as in those days he gave little thought to the bills that were due for payment. There were days when he did not have the milk churns ready for collection and eventually he lost the contract. After selling animals at the market he'd go to the pub and when he got home he would not have enough left to pay the household bills. Sarah made plans to thwart his drinking. On market days she told Maggie that she was to go to McFinn's pub after school and make sure that her daddy came home with her. Maggie pointed out that it was only men that went into pubs. "You'll bloody well do what I tell you. You can see how he's drinking. We could end up on the street. Is that what you want?" Used to letting her mother's ranting float over her head, Maggie now felt she was being pushed into the front line of this family battle. She had often heard her mother talking about the kind of women who sneaked into the pubs by the back door, loose women and trollops she had called them and thought that her parents should both go to town and leave her to keep house. Wasn't she kept at home most Fridays when her mother went shopping? But it was not an idea she felt she could voice at this time. On her first attempt at this new duty she crept with the look of a frightened animal into the pub. Drunk men swaying on unsteady limbs, the loud noise of their gutter language and the stench of tobacco smoke and beer in this unventilated room made her want to flee but flee she couldn't. The consequences of disobeying her mother she knew only too well. She sidled up to the stool where her father sat with a group of men.

"Mammy says you are to come home with me," she said in a half whisper. His look was one of anger and humiliation. "Give her a lemonade," he said to the bar man. She sipped the lemonade and then shuffled from foot to foot not knowing what to do next. Frank raised himself from the stool, took a handful of coins from his trouser pocket and gave her sixpence. "Go and get yourself an ice cream and then go on home." It was a relief to get out of that place. Since she had no success in her mission she was sure she would not be sent on a repeat performance. She pocketed the sixpence and went home but could not believe her mother's unreasonable attitude, asking her why her father would not come with her and did she really go into the pub or was she lying. As she slammed the sixpence on the table she said, "I'm not lying. He gave me this and told me to go home. You tell me one thing and he tells me another so who am I to listen to."

"Oh, sixpence, that'll feed us won't it," said Sarah, pacing from the pantry to the kitchen, banging lids on saucepans and plunging the long poker into the fire till a shower of sparks from the burning turf flew up the chimney. When Frank got home he slumped into a chair at the kitchen table and asked if there was any tea. After Sarah had finished giving him and his drinking companions their due pedigree, she slapped the sixpence in front of him. "Take that and give it to whoever entertained you all day and get them to make your tea." Usually he'd listen in silence to her outbursts but this time he got up clumsily and said, "Don't ever send her into a pub for me again." With a defiant stance Sarah replied, "While you keep on drinking I'll keep on sending her." In an instant his fist swiped every piece of delft to the floor and with both hands he upended the table. Gone were the days when Maggie thought of him as her safe sandy beach. Now there was turbulence as the sands between them shifted. She felt disgusted at his drunken behaviour, at the company he kept and at his nonchalant attitude to Robert who worked from dawn to dusk without ever complaining.

On his next trip to market Frank changed his usual routine, going to a different pub but tethering the horse in McFinn's back yard where there were two stalls and further down the yard a blacksmith's forge. Maggie, going from pub to pub was stopped by a policeman. "I've been watching you. This is the third pub you've been in. Don't you know you're too young to be in pubs?" Putting her hand to her face she tried to hold back the tears that would not be held back and answering his questions she told him she was Maggie Millar and she was looking for her daddy. His attitude softened. "Well now Maggie, you get along home and you know you should have a light on that bike when you're out at this time of night." Maggie opened the kitchen door and before Sarah could ask any questions or shout at her, she blurted out that she had been stopped by the police. "Jasus, as if I hadn't enough to deal with. What did you do now?" Maggie told her what happened and Sarah listened, quietly working out her plan. "When you get your homework finished I've something for you to do." Sarah had threatened that if she came home without her father she would send her straight back and Maggie knew there was no light for the bicycle. As she did the six sums in her exercise book she thought of what she would say if she met the policeman again. When she put her books into the school bag Sarah came to the table with notepad and pencil and said, "Write down what I tell you." Maggie took the pencil and waited for the words that Sarah dictated. 'Dear Sir, I am writing to say that if youse spent more time on the streets and in the pubs youse would see what is going on in this town.' Maggie stopped writing and asked who was getting this note and was told to keep on writing and stop asking questions that were none of her business. Again she wrote as the dictation flowed. 'I seen a girl from school in the pub and the pub owner should be fined for selling drink to ones underage.' Maggie put the pencil down.

"If this is about me, I'm not drinking in pubs. I don't even want to be there."

"I didn't say you were, but if I can't get him away from them tramps he drinks with, the police will. You just keep on writing till I tell you to stop." And again the dictation continued. "Are youse going to wait till something happens like that thing that happened to the girl on The Loning?"

"What happened to that girl?"

"Never you mind about things like that." Maggie knew to ask no more questions. When the strange letter was finished Sarah told her to write it out again but this time she was to try and change her writing. Then an envelope was pushed towards her. "Who will I address it to?" As directed Maggie wrote, The Police Station, Catherine Street, Limavady. Her brain raced, filling her with terror as to what would happen when it was discovered that she wrote this letter. "What if the police find out that I wrote this?" she asked. Sarah leaned forward, fixed her with a glassy stare and slowly said, "If you are ever asked about it, you just deny it and if I ever hear you mention this to anybody you'll have me to deal with." Feeling more afraid of her mother than she was of the police, she made one last attempt to get herself out of this situation. She offered to post it next day, having already decided to destroy it. Tearing up the first letter and throwing it in the fire, Sarah took the envelope and said, "No, I'll post it." For days after this incident Maggie watched the expressions on the faces of any policemen she met in the street and froze in her seat if anyone came to the classroom door to speak to the teacher.

With an ever- mounting bill at the grocery store Sarah went to see the auctioneer and asked him if the money orders for the sale of livestock could be made out to her. He was sympathetic but without Frank's agreement he couldn't do that. "I'm going to make a suggestion," he said. "There's not much that goes on around this town that I miss and if I were you I'd stop sending that young lassie into the pubs to coax him home. It's not very nice to hear your husband shouting, 'Go home you fecking wee hoor. Get on home you fecking wee bastard,' when she's left to get him into the cart after the spongers of this town have fleeced him. I suppose you know that she drives the cart home more often than he does." Sarah was completely stunned to find out that the ordinary decent people of the town knew her business and to think that they put any blame on her was more than she could bear. Why, she asked herself, did Maggie never tell her this, but the auctioneer was still speaking. "Could you not come in with him yourself, get the money here in the office and pay off some of the bills before he gets to the pub. You wouldn't be the first woman to do it." Sarah assured him she had no idea this was going on. He didn't believe her and his expression conveyed his thoughts more poignantly than any words.

Gone was Frank's idea of getting a house for Sarah while he went to England. He was now in an arena where the lions were out to get him. Sarah had humiliated him by going to the auctioneer. He could not leave the horse and cart in McFinn's yard if he no longer frequented the pub. The police kept hounding him for having the animal tied up for so long. He had a letter from the grocer telling him that no more groceries could be supplied till some effort was made to reduce the bill. And Sarah provided the harshest snarl of all. One evening as she put his dinner on the table she said, "Maggie's closing the hens in. Now that you're sober go out and call her the filthy names you call her when you're in the pub. And if you think I'm making it up, check with the auctioneer and everybody else that hears you." He left his dinner untouched and went outside. He met Maggie in the yard.

"Maggie, I need to talk to you."

"What about?"

"You know drink is a terrible curse. I don't remember what I said to you, but I didn't mean any of it." She closed her eyes and looked at the ground. From his pocket he took half a crown and handed it to her. Shaking her head violently she said, "I don't want your money." Suddenly she dashed off down the lane at the side of the orchard. He knew that another apology would make matters worse. The demon drink had claimed him, blinding him to the destruction he had caused and he didn't know how to deal with it. Sarah was still furious that the auctioneer had dared to suggest that she go to the market or the pub with Frank. A kind of misplaced pride had claimed her too, blinding her to the destruction she was causing. Children, with no experience of reality other than what they lived with, and a retarded man, were learning how to hold this family together.

Frank agreed to let the auctioneer hold back some money and pay it directly to the grocer, so tension at home began to ease but Sarah still insisted that Maggie go to the pub every Monday that Frank went to market. On the few occasions when he was willing to go home with her, she quite by accident discovered a means of keeping him in a good mood once he was in the cart. She would ask him about his time in America. On some of these night drives he talked about Brooklyn-Bridge, Madison Avenue, China Town, Long Island, Manhattan and The Statue of Liberty. On one particular evening talk of New York only lasted till they got to the Orange Hall. That

day Frank had taken the big cart to hold the turf he was selling. Instead of going straight on towards the Murder Hole
Road he turned left and was abruptly stopped by the barrier at
the entrance to the airfield. As the heavy wooden pole hit the
horse's neck Frank urged him on. Charlie Boy neighed, bucked
upright leaving the cart at an angle. Maggie screamed in terror.
Frank swore and using the whip still tried to get the horse to
move forward. Then soldiers appeared and there was shouting
from every quarter.

"Get that horse out of here," boomed a loud voice. Frank
was swearing that no one would stop him getting through and
Maggie was pleading with him to stop. A sharp order, obviously from someone in command, shouted, "Get Corporal
Davies out here." A soldier came running over the grass, put
his foot on the hub of the wheel and in an instant was in the
cart. "Good night sir. Heading home are you? A Clydesdale,
lovely big animals they are. My father worked with Clydesdales
for years on the dray carts." He didn't give Frank a chance to
reply, just kept on talking as he took the reins, got out of the
cart, manoeuvred it backwards and turned it on the road. As
they continued their journey Frank became more and more
incensed that he could not get through the airfield. "Bastards,
I helped to build the damn place," he muttered and started
to use the whip on the horse again and to Maggie's horror he
turned into The Loning. She panicked and for a few moments
thought of jumping out of the cart. Before she could make any
decision the near side wheel dropped into the ditch and strong
as the horse was he could not pull it out. This was worse than
the episode at the barrier for there was no one around to help.
She started shouting. "Leave the bloody horse alone. You're in
the ditch." At the start of their journey home she was cold and

hungry but now a mixture of fear and anger left sweat pouring down her face. Grabbing the whip from his hands she got out of the cart, looked at the mess and flung the whip over the hedge. She got into the cart and eased the bicycle over the tailgate and let it drop on to the ground. Frank sat muttering to himself, head bent and body slumped forward. She took the reins out of his hands and threw them over the horse's back. In a fit of rage she pushed him off the running board and as he fell in a heap she said, "You can lie there till I get back." Mutterimg, "Useless bastard," she cycled home to raise the alarm. John Brennan was wakened yet again and he and Robert, with shovel, spade and a torch, set off to The Loning. When they got to the scene Frank and the horse were just as she left them. The reins had dropped from the horse's back and were tangled around one of his back legs. Maggie held the torch as John Brennan got them sorted out and then the digging started. When the track was partially cleared John told Maggie to hold the reins in case the horse took a plunge forward when the track was clear.

"John, I'm terrified of that animal. If he leapt forward I'd drop the reins and run. Would you hold him and I'll help Robert to shovel the rest of the clay?"

When they got the cart out on the lane Maggie went ahead with the torch, calling out directions – keep him to the right a bit, there's a big pothole coming up, watch this branch, if it hits his head he'll go crazy. Finally they got to the road and back home.

"Now we have another problem. How do we get him into the stable?"

"I was just thinking that myself. Your father is the only one who can lead him in without a fuss."

"Sure he always makes a fuss, stands swaying and shaking, puts his nose in the door and then takes a mad dive. The only thing is you never know exactly when he's going to make the leap and you could be under his feet before you had time to get out of his way." As the postman removed the harness Robert said, "Could you put a meal bag over his head then he wouldn't see where he was goin'?"

"Well it might work or it could make him even worse," said John. Robert got some corn and a bucket of water, fed the horse and John got the meal bag ready. The first attempt brought no success. Then John led him to the yard behind the old thatched house, into the turf shed, out of the turf shed, down the yard, up the yard, in the big barn door and out again and into the stable. "The poor brute is so confused he doesn't know where he is," he said with a sigh. "Now we need to get Frank out of the cart."

"We can lower the tailgate, upend the shafts and he'll slide out," said Maggie.

Robert and John got Frank upstairs, took his boots off and put him into the bed. Sarah had a pot of tea and soda farls on the table. As they ate she turned to Maggie and said, "You'd need to get off to bed for you've school in the morning." Sarah's remark made Maggie want to scream. Usually she bottled up all her anger but at that moment she was tired and hungry and felt that nothing in her life was fair.

"Does anybody in this house know that I haven't had a bite to eat since lunchtime? I could eat more than a bloody farl and I have no homework done so I'm not going to school tomorrow." Sarah gave her one of those glassy stares and she knew that as soon as John Brennan went home she would meet the consequences of her outburst. In a fury she got up and stormed out the door and just as quickly John Brennan dashed after her.

He tried to persuade her to come in but all she kept saying was, "Damn, I wish I could run away somewhere. I can't stick any more of this." As he continued to plead with her to go home she poured out all her woes, telling him about the letter her mother made her write and how scared she was that the police would find out. "I'm sick of him swearing at me when I go into the pub to bring him home and I'm sick of her swearing at me if I come home without him. Anyway I'm not going in till they're all in bed for I know what I'll get as soon as you leave." From his past experiences John Brennan knew more about the Millar household than anybody else and like Peggy Fletcher he debated with himself as to whether or not to interfere.

"You stay there a minute and I'll go back to the house." In the kitchen he faced Sarah. "Listen Sarah, she's not coming in till you're all in bed and I know why but I'm not going to say, at least not yet. It could be you're putting too many burdens on young shoulders. And I'm going to sit here till you go to bed before I call her in. But maybe you'll order me out of your home and of course I'll go." He sat on a chair and Sarah, without a word went upstairs telling herself she'd question Maggie later. She was furious with the postman but knew that she dare not fall out with him. He and Frank were close friends and besides he was the only one she had to call on when Frank was in a drunken stupor. In the morning the house was eerily still as Sarah went downstairs to get Tommy ready for school. When Frank woke, still wearing his coat and trousers, he went to the yard to find that the horse was in the stable, the cart in the yard but he could not remember how he got home. Indoors again he sat down to have a cup of tea and some bread. Maggie came into the kitchen.

"What's wrong that you're not at school?"

"The usual," she said with a shrug.

Chapter 7

After much consideration the idea of having a house in town was not as ideal as Sarah first thought. Living without a husband would be viewed with disfavour. And what if Frank went off to England and disappeared like Letty's husband? And then there was Robert. She had no intention of taking him with her. She put the idea out of her head and determined to soldier on. Frank put more effort into working on the farm and for a while life was quite pleasant. He bought small bottles of whisky and hid them in nooks and crannies in the barn. Every evening he went to the barn and took a swig from one of the bottles but it was not as satisfying as drinking with companions.

Very late on a raw January night Sarah went into labour. Frank rose and cycled to the phone box a short distance past the shop. "I'll be waiting with the hurricane lamp at the end of the lane," he told the doctor. While he stood sentry waiting to wave the lamp at the first sign of car headlights the rest of the household was asleep. Maggie woke to the sound of groaning and her Mother's voice calling her. She went to the bedroom and stood in shock at the scene before her. Her mother was lying on the bed, speechless and her face void of expression. At the bottom of the bed the blankets were pulled up and there was a pool of blood and what looked like guts. "Oh my God! What's he done? He has burst her stomach and run off." Then she saw the heap move. It was a baby. The room and everything in it began to sway and her mother's voice saying 'Stay here' was like an echo coming to her from a far distance. Suddenly the doctor was in the room. "Get out of here. This is no place for you," he said. His voice was stern as she rushed to her room. Turning to Sarah he said, "You should have sent for a neighbour woman. What did you expect a child like her to do for you? Get a neighbour woman to bring her into the surgery as soon as you can and don't let her witness this again."

Maggie had often looked at her mother's swollen belly and wondered how a baby got out. She concluded that the navel opened like a flower in bloom and the baby crawled out. All illusions were shattered that night. She lay on the bed, every limb shaking uncontrollably, as sleep eluded her until the early dawn brought exhausted slumber. In the morning she was more or less ignored as Frank went for a neighbour, the local handy woman to attend to Sarah and cook the food. The shock of the previous night gave Maggie nightmares. She saw scenes of people with their innards spilling out on the roads and the fields and she'd waken up screaming. Frank would come to pacify her but Sarah's comment was, "Don't you start that screaming to-night again and waken the whole house." Sarah's periods in labour were always very short and in less than two years Maggie witnessed the birth of the next two siblings but Sarah made sure that Maggie was out of the room before the doctor got up the stairs.

With an ever growing family Frank tried to settle down to work and there were Mondays when there were no animals to take to market, leaving Maggie delighted. When a pub crawling Monday came she always felt famished with hunger for she had long ago decided that she would not try to coax him home. Asking her mother if she could get something from the bakery brought the reply, "Tell him you're hungry and he'll come home the sooner." At school she dreaded these Mondays, her mind constantly thinking of what the evening would bring. If only there was a sensible adult she could confide in but no one ever noticed her. She decided to change her tactics. She stole some money from her mother's purse and after school sat in the window seat of the tea shop on Linenhall Street hoping someone who knew her would report it. Spending as much time as possible having a cup of tea and a scone, she waited till she thought her father was inebriated enough to come home without a fuss.

When she entered the back yard of the pub the pony stood in the stall. She couldn't risk leaving her father to gallop the poor animal home for old Lily was special. A drunken argument was going on as she entered the pub and not only her father but his foul mouthed companions were telling her to get out. She went outside but from the row going on inside she sensed that her father was in danger. Part of her didn't really care for there were times when she actually wanted him dead. She used to picture it, maybe a night like the one on The Loning when big Charlie Boy would upend the cart, tip him out and break his neck. A wave of guilt at her evil thoughts swept over her. She thought of home, the mounting bills and her mother shouting, "Do you want us all to end up on the street?" Then there was Robert. Without her father her mother would have free rein to treat him any way she wanted. She decided to give it another try. With a stride of boldness she certainly did not feel she entered the pub again and went to where her father stood at a tilted angle up against the high counter. "Give me some money to take home and you can stay here as long as you like." His glazed expression ignored her as he went on arguing with the men around him. She pushed her way out again into the yard where her trapped feeling gave way to relief and gave her time to think. She had often heard her mother say that she would not 'lower herself' to go into a pub, so what was she expected to do in her present situation? She despised both her parents. Had it been the big Clydesdale in the stall she would have left him there and cycled home. Now her plan was to put the bicycle in the cart, reverse it out of the stall and take the pony home. Two men in mud stained trousers and ragged jackets came staggering out to the yard. Probably out to pee up against the wall, she thought. She had parked the bicycle against the outside wall of the stall and was leaning forward to grip the handlebars when she noticed one of them right behind her.

"Come ere you wee fucker. You're askin' for it," he slurred and in the split second it took her to turn her head she saw the arm holding the iron bar. He lunged it between her legs. She froze, felt warm liquid run down her legs as the second blow landed on her shoulder. Stunned, she fell to her knees and passed out. Earlier that day Frank took a litter of pigs to sell and decided he would avoid the auctioneer and make a private sale. After a few drinks the sale was agreed and before he realised it the litter of pigs was whisked away, but when he found that the buyer did not have the cash to pay for the pigs, a row broke out. After several more drinks and more arguments Frank was persuaded to do an exchange of two calves for the pigs. A drover in the pub, hanging around for the chance to earn a few shillings, was sent with Frank to pick up the calves. When they got to the address everything was in darkness. Two guard dogs in an enclosed yard started barking and after banging on the front door a burly man appeared and confirmed that he was

Bill Gregson, the man they were looking for. "Calves! What are you talking about? I'm an arable farmer. The only animals round here is them dogs in the yard guarding the machinery." The drover realised that the men who sent him on a wild goose chase had no intention of paying him. He drove the cart to some grass at the side of the road and vanished into the night.

How long Maggie lay in a semiconscious state she didn't know but when she tried to move, her head was fuzzy, like she'd been in a terrible crash where the details are a complete blank. She tried to remember why she was here but nothing made any sense. She got to her feet and gripped the handlebars of the bicycle and like a zombie wheeled it out to the street. Dark and quiet, with no one around, it was frighteningly eerie. Walking slowly and leaning on the handlebars she started the long walk home, stopping to rest when she felt her legs go wobbly.

At home Sarah was frantic with worry, saying to herself, "Maybe I shouldn't have sent her out, but what else could I do?" She thought of all the things that might have happened. "Oh my God, that letter. I know Maggie would break down if the police quizzed her about it and Frank would find out." She thought of the many times he told her not to send Maggie to the pubs and the number of times she'd told him she'd keep on sending her as long as he kept on drinking. She went down the lane, looked up and down the road and listened but the night showed nothing but dark shadows. Back in the house she stoked the fire to make some tea, convinced that in the morning she was going to get some terrible news for Maggie had never been out as late as this. As she drank the tea with shaking hands, streaks of light were already brushing away the shadows of the night. By now she had seven children and with an ever increasing grocery bill and constant demands for payment she didn't know where to turn. She thought of what would happen if the grocer refused to give her any more food. Utterly exhausted she dozed off on the settee. When the dog, curled up at the side of the fire, gave a low bark she sat up with a jerk. She went down the lane again but there was no one in sight. Another hour passed before she heard a noise. Maggie stumbled into the kitchen and in a feeble voice said, "I'm bleeding. A man at the pub…" but Sarah wasn't listening and interrupted with, "Oh, you'll take that every month or so. I'll get you some rags and you can pin one to your knickers." Sarah was certain it was the start of what she called, that monthly sickness and Maggie was certain that her mother was insane. It would explain her odd behaviour years ago when she talked in a quiet strange way. Maggie dragged herself up the stairs and exhausted lay on the bed. Sarah, following her with a rag and two safety pins, sat on the edge of the bed, looking for answers to all her questions - Did you see him? Where did he go? What kept you out so late? Maggie looked up with eyes barely open as snatches of the previous evening were coming to her but in such a jumbled way that her mind was completely confused.

"I don't know. I don't remember. I just want to sleep." Sarah's agitation erupted. "Waken up and listen to me. Have you any idea what I went through last night?" Instead of listening to her mother's ranting like she used to, Maggie sat up on the bed. "No, I have no idea what you went through for I wasn't here. Next market day you can go looking for him for I'd rather throw myself in the river than go into that pub." Sarah's only way of defending herself had always been to attack. "I'm doing the best I can for youse all, but if that's how you feel then go ahead and jump in the river. You're not the only one suffering over him drinking." These words slipped into Maggie's sub-conscious mind and like a neap tide resurfaced at odd times throughout her life. She was firmly convinced that she was, like Robert, of no use to anyone.

In this house, as in many others, home cures were the norm. Earache was treated with warm olive oil and the ear hole plugged with cotton wool. Constipation warranted a dose of syrup of figs or the cheaper caster oil. Robert's continued toothache was eased with a swig of poteen gargled in the mouth or a sock con-taining warm salt held to the jaw. Maggie, gritting her teeth, tried to heal her injury by washing away the horrible discharge with disinfectant and warm water as though it was a cut knee.

The Fletcher boys called to ride the pony but the poor beast was sick. On the evening that Frank was conned into parting with his pigs he'd spent the night in a drunken stupor on the floor of the cart and in the morning, still hazy from the drink, he galloped the pony all the way home. Robert unyoked it, rubbed it down with a meal bag and led it to the old thatched house. He made a warm mash and tried to get her to eat but he knew she was dying. The ordeal of standing for so long with-out food or water and then being galloped all the way home was too much for the old pony. It broke his heart to watch animals being badly treated but in this house there was nothing he could say. He tended her like an old friend and on the day that she got worse he went to the kitchen and said to Frank, "She's down. Ye better come and look." A fog of sadness enveloped everyone in the house and the Fletcher boys were broken hearted. Everyone except Frank and Robert thought she had died of old age.

Maggie was in the last term at the primary school and Sarah wanted to ask the headmaster about her future. After primary school Amy Fletcher and her half- sister Maureen had gone to the technical college, followed by a spell at a secretarial college and now both were working as secretaries. Often Sarah saw them when they'd come home for the weekend and she didn't fail to notice their clothes, outfits she'd never seen in the shops in town. She couldn't bear it if Maggie could not become a secretary too, but thought that her late start at school would be a barrier. Decked out in the beige coat with the fox fur collar that was kept for special occasions, though these days special occasions were non existent, she went off to the school.

There are times when half a picture is worse than no picture at all. The headmaster knew that Maggie came from a farming family and from the look of this woman sitting in his office he assumed that her family was as affluent as all the other farmers and business men in the area. The qualifying test had not yet come into effect and some of these wealthier families sent their children to the grammar school regardless of their academic ability. Some stayed a short time and went into the family business. A few were sent to a college or a university. They had the choices that bright children from poor homes did not have. The headmaster sat at his desk and gave a glowing report of Maggie's work and boasted that in spite of being so far behind her age level when she came to his school, he had managed to get her into the top stream of her class.

"With these results she can get to the technical college but I'd say that it would be worth your while sending her to the grammar school." Generally this was the advice he gave to most wealthy parents but Sarah completely misread the situation. She thought he was telling her that Maggie was a genius. It may have been true that she was above average in her grades but only because steeping herself in school work compensated for the kind of life she had to lead. He elaborated on the variety of careers that an education in a school like this could bring and the time scale each was likely to take. Not a word of what he was saying sank into Sarah's head. If Maggie was as smart as this man said she was, then surely the rest of her children would be just as smart. She told him she would think about it and come back and see him. The mould Sarah had created for her life with Frank was completely shattered and she could see that he was not the one who would help her attain her dream. Maggie was the new mould that would be a stepping stone to help her educate all the family and bring her the accolade she desired. On her way home she could not resist telling Peggy Fletcher her latest news and went into the shop on the pretext of needing a loaf of bread.

"I've just been to see Maggie's headmaster and he says Maggie is so smart that I should send her to that grammar school. She'll get a really good job from there."

"She probably could Sarah, but it would take about eight years before she'd be earning anything and there's all the money you'll need for fees and books. What does Maggie think about it? You know she could do just as well at the technical college."

Sarah, still on a high from the headmaster's news took her loaf of bread and as she left smiled and said, "We'll see." Later that evening Helen called for some groceries and Peggy told her of the odd conversation she had with Sarah. "I wonder when she's going to let her youngsters grow up in a normal way. You know some of my customers talk about the way Maggie hangs about the pub trying to get her father to come home and Sarah thinks nobody around here knows about it. If she's not careful she'll have a rebel on her hands but you couldn't reason with her."

"Well after the bother we had with her years ago, I certainly won't get involved." As they talked a bit more Peggy was of the opinion that Sarah should let the children have a bit of fun and mix with other youngsters of their own age. Helen advised her not to interfere.

On the bough of a tree in the orchard Maggie sat contemplating her life after she left school. She knew she would be offered a place at the technical college and knew all the subjects that were taught there. Two more years, she thought, was a long time but if she worked hard there was bound to be a job she could do. She was aware that she had grown up without the normal social graces of her peers. There were opportunities to make friends but taking advantage of them was always a problem. To the questions, who did you see, what did you say to them, what did they say to you, she would no longer have to give answers nor face the consequences of bringing a friend home. Were she not to be sent to the technical college she saw her prospects as equally bright. A job of any kind away from home would be ideal. One where she had to stay at home would still be acceptable till she saved enough money to escape. "I'll buy a pink dress like Josie Brennan's and a pair of white sandals," she said, and jumped down from the bough.

Such was the dire state of Frank's finances that he went to a loan shark. The pub spongers and the whisky may have taken several years to bring him to his knees but the loan shark finished him off in a short time. He could not pay the exorbitant interest let alone pay off any of the capital and the inevitable was just round the corner. So Frank and Sarah dealt with their problem, the final decision that the farm had to be sold. With no stock to take to market, Frank once again looked back to his younger days, the big farm, the accolade of winning cups at the ploughing matches and the general easy going way of life. He stayed away from the pubs in town, drank from his store of bottles in the barn and tried to concentrate on the loan shark's demands for payment.

"When the farm is sold I'm going to keep aside enough money to pay Maggie's school fees at that grammar school for a couple of years. She can get a good job and help to educate the rest of them. I can see no other way out for by the time you have squandered everything we've got, we'll have to depend on the weans to keep a roof over our heads."

As she made her intentions clear, Frank bore the salt in the wound with silence. Twice he went for a drink to the local watering hole, a quarter of a mile away and came home at a reasonable hour. On the third occasion he left much earlier and by milking time had not returned. Sarah seemed to have a complete breakdown. She told Robert that Frank would milk the two cows when he got home. As time passed the cows became more and more stressed and agitated but still she would not allow them to be milked. The youngest child, a baby of six months lay crying in his pram. Robert could not contain his anguish. There was no way he would even attempt to reason with this woman but he felt he could not stand idly by. Quietly he slipped out past the pig sheds, into the stack garden and through the hedge bringing him to John Brennan's cottage.

"It's the cows, an' the wean - there's somethin' ong way the wee wan," he said as he gestured with his hands and uttered more and more unintelligible words.

"Robert, would you calm down, you're talking so fast I can't make out what you're saying," said the exasperated postman.

"Ye hifte come," Robert spluttered, as he gasped for breath.

John Brennan accompanied him to the house as he tried to explain that the cows hadn't been milked since early morning. John was angry at the number of times he had been called to this house and he was not in the mood to pussy foot around but did not want to get Robert into further trouble.

"What's wrong with the cows? I can hear them bellowing from my place."

"He's away and when he gets home I want him to see that his weans are starving with hunger while he's out enjoying himself," said Sarah.

"So you're going to let that youngster scream its head off and the cows stand in agony in the byre till he gets home. If he was here this minute he'd be too drunk to know he had a wife, weans or cows. Now I'm going to get a bucket and help Robert milk them cows."

"You'll not go near the byre. I want the whole countryside to see what he's doing." This attitude was foreign to Sarah. In the past she would put on a brave face in public, denying, sometimes even to herself, that her circumstances could not be much worse. The normally placid postman had had all he could take.

"Fair enough, you leave me no choice. I'll phone the police and tell them to get a vet out here right away. Then you'll likely be hearing from the cruelty to animals folk. And if that youngster cries itself into a fit of convulsions nobody will be able to say I stood by and did nothing. Right, I'm off."

"Wait. Wait a minute," said Sarah. She got up and went to the pantry for the milk bucket, saying, "Just wait till he gets home from that town."

"But he's not in the town. He's been in the local pub all evening." John stayed till the two cows were milked and things

seemed normal again. When he left Sarah told Maggie to cycle
to the Roe Bar and see if he was there. The very mention of
a pub made her shudder. She was already having nightmares
about her last ordeal. "I'm going to no pub. I don't care if he
never comes back. Why don't you go and I'll stay and keep the
house. You can ride a bike as well as I can." Without her usual
ranting Sarah tried to persuade Maggie that he was more likely
to come home for her. Maggie was not taken in by the quiet
persuasive tones but she knew that the situation had the poten-
tial to develop into a blazing row and they would all suffer.
She reckoned it would be easier to cycle along the road, come
back and say she didn't see him. Wasn't she a thief when she
took that money from her mother's purse? She could be a liar
as well if it got her out of the pub crawling missions she hated
so much. She set off, pedalling at an easy pace and stopped at
a quiet spot where a grey stone wall encircled an old graveyard.
She had not been on this road since she moved to the school in
town and memories of those early days flooded her mind. The
graveyard was on a raised area some eight feet above the road
level and back then she feared passing it for it was so still and
eerie. But now it intrigued her and leaving the bicycle against
the wall she went to the entrance, an iron gate about fifty yards
up a rough gravel lane. Gazing through the bars of the gate
she looked at the rows of graves, caretakers of the dust of the
dead and the many headstones, keepers of the memories of
the living. It set her thinking. What kind of life did they live?
How long did they live? How long were they dead? Had they
any family still living in the area? She had never heard of a
burial taking place here and wondered if all the space was used
up. Leaning on the gate, watching the clouds drift by she felt a
sense of peace as she remembered the old school at Bellarena

and the masses of bluebells in Moody's Meadow. They had fascinated her since those early days at BellarenaSchool and smiling she recalled her thoughts of hiding in their midst to get away from her Aunt Letty. "I'll go a little further and then I'll go home," she said aloud. Dusk was falling and everything was quiet and beautiful as she cycled a little further round the bend in the road.

Her countenance changed when she spied her father slumped on the grassy bank. Glaring at him gave her a feeling of nausea. "Damn," she said. Much as she despised him she could not leave him there and cycle home and lie as she had intended. Now there was no horse and cart to deal with, the old fear she used to have of him when he was in a drunken stupor melted away to be replaced by seething anger. She caught the lapel of his coat and shook him. He was in such a state that dragging him home and wheeling the bicycle was out of the question. Setting the bicycle against the grassy bank she yanked him to his feet. He clung to her to steady himself and as she dragged him along he kept mumbling about his horses and his trophies at the ploughing matches as though he was back in his youth. Her rage seemed to give her renewed strength as she shouted, "Shut up about your bloody ploughing matches and just keep on walking."

At the shop neither of them saw Peggy Fletcher looking through her garden hedge as they passed. "Oh dear, things don't look good for that house," she said. When Maggie finally got her father home her rage was boiling over. Sarah told her to get him to the sofa and go for John Brennan. "I'm going for no John Brennan. He's going up these stairs should I drag him up by the feet." Going up backwards she grabbed the shoulders of his coat and hauled him roughly up the stairs, with Sarah behind him, lifting his feet one at a time from step to step. When she got him to the bedroom she threw him across the bed as though he was a bag of wet chaff and bounded down the stairs. Sarah was going to make him tea, saying he must not have eaten for hours. Maggie was outraged.

"Make him tea! I'd let him lie there till he rots. I'm the one that dragged him home and there's no mention of me needing tea. Now I have to go back again for the bike."

"Did you not bring it with you?" said Sarah, as though it was the easiest thing in the world to do. Maggie looked at her in disbelief. Teeth gritted, sweat pouring off her from the exhaustion, her anger exploded. "Tell me, could you drag that heap of shit the same distance that I did and take a bicycle as well? I should go up and choke the bastard." The tirade of foul language, the same type of language that he had shouted at her not so long ago, poured from her lips like an overflowing gutter. Sarah was shocked. She had never heard Maggie swear like this. Realising that she was no longer dealing with a child that she could shake into submission like she used to, she tried to calm the situation.

"Oh, I never thought of that. I'll get Robert to go for the bike." Sarah's remark had the opposite effect for Maggie now turned to bitter sarcasm. "What a bright idea," Maggie said. "And a man who has never been further than the shop, too ashamed to let him be seen, you're going to send him to find my bicycle." She stormed off and once out of sight of the house slowed her pace to a leisurely walk. It alarmed her that she had lost her temper in such a violent way and if she was kept at home to work on the farm after she left school she feared that she might become even more violent. She had to act fast to avoid such a prison sentence. Next day she asked her mother if she would be allowed to go to the technical college or would she have to stay at home and work on the farm.

"I'm sending you to that grammar school." Of all the situations Maggie thought of, this one never entered her mind. Her heart sank as she made her case. "That school is for rich people and cost money, whereas the technical college is free and they teach the same subjects as well as typing and bookkeeping. After two years I can get a good job and start earning money." While she was thinking of something more to say in her defence Sarah interrupted. "After two years at this school you'll get an even better job and while you're under sixteen you'll do what you're told. It's all arranged and when you start work you'll use the money to educate all the rest of them." Maggie was silent, her brain seeking escape routes. "Were you listening to me? Did you hear what I said?" Sarah demanded.

"Aye, I heard you."

Chapter 8

Maggie could not get the words, 'while you're under sixteen' out of her head until other concerns loomed into her life. The <u>Farm For Sale</u> notice was in the paper and although she did not know about it, she knew something was afoot when two men along with the auctioneer came to the farm and went into all the outhouses and into the fields. When she asked what they were doing Sarah said, "We might be moving to another farm." The school had closed for the summer holidays and Maggie felt hemmed in for school was the only place where she could talk and laugh with her class mates.

"Maggie, to-morrow you and Tommy are going to take the weans to the beach for we have business to do in town." She put some small jam pots into the wicker basket and on a chair laid out fresh clothes for the younger children. "Go into the shop and get a big bottle of lemonade and a packet of plain biscuits. There's money here in the basket and don't lose the change." There was a lot of excitement next morning as the young children were dressed and told they were going out for the day. Tommy carried Brian, the youngest and Maggie with the basket, had Sam on her back with his hands clinging round her neck. The others, following behind, asked where they were going. "Downhill," said Tommy. The shop door belltinkled and Peggy appeared, surprised to see the tribe of children looking at her. "And where are you all going?" she said. Several voices chimed in with, "Downhill." Maggie asked for the lemonade and plain biscuits and set Sam on the floor as she got the money out of the basket. They all left, crossed the road and waited beside the bus stop. Peggy's next customer was Bridie Brennan.

"Peggy, where are all the Millar weans going? I see them standing over the road at the bus stop."

"Would you believe it? They are off to Downhill beach."

"What! On their own?"

"Aye, on their own and my heart'll be in my mouth till they get back."

For the younger ones this was their first trip outside the farm and they were like mesmerised mice as their eyes took in the unfolding countryside. A complete stop at Bellarena Station left them all agog as the long gate barred further travel. They heard the puff of the oncoming train and watched the spiral of smoke as the thundering beast sped past. At Downhill they spilled out of the bus and gazed around, straining their necks upward to the black jagged rocks. In a deep ravine a waterfall tumbled down, silvery white at the top, with its music of tinkling bells giving way to symbol clashes as the great volume of water smacked the rocks below. Wide eyed they stood looking at it until Maggie ushered them away from the road. The dry sand lay before them like a tanned sheet and further off they could hear the lullaby of the waves swishing in, wetting the sand at the water's edge.

Shoes and socks were taken off and left beside the wicker basket as they raced in circles, whooping and shouting over the sand. Scooping handfuls of sand they giggled as they watched it trickle through their fingers. Then they noticed tiny shells and pieces of seaweed and wanted to bring some home. "We should have brought a bucket," Maggie said. Tommy suggested using the jam pots after they had the picnic. They watched the waves with their foaming collars lunge towards them, and then as though all their energy was spent, lap gently round their feet. At first they were scared and ran backwards as each wave came in but gradually they inched forward until the water was up to their ankles and then to their knees. When they'd had enough of paddling they went back to the grassy patch near the road. Tommy lined up the jam pots and poured out the lemonade while Maggie doled out the biscuits. Picnic over, the older ones started to build a sandcastle but the dry sand kept sliding down the sides. Tommy went to the water's edge for two jam pots of water and with damper sand the building continued. Colin, the most excited, wanted to paddle. He pulled off his short trousers and jumper and sped towards the water. Carrying Brian in the crook of one arm and holding Sam by the hand Maggie followed. The three youngsters squealed with a mixture of fear and delight as each wave rolled in. Maggie's attention was fully absorbed with the two younger ones as they clung tightly to her. She glanced up briefly and saw Colin, water up to his waist and his arms splashing in the foam. "Don't go out too far," she shouted. The next wave of the incoming tide splashed in Sam's face and he started to cry. Maggie bent down, wiped his face with her hand and as she stood up she screamed, "Oh Jasus look where he is." All she could see was Colin's head bobbing on the surface. The spray of the next wave left him invisible and then his head appeared again. He shouted, "Yo ho, look at me." Panic gripped her. She tried to release the grasp of the small hands at her sides while yelling at Colin. In the seconds that followed she yelled to the older three on the sand and to a man in the distance walking his dog but the wind silenced her yells. "Stay there till I get him," she said to Sam and Brian but they clung to her legs as she tried to leave them. She pushed them roughly away and waded through the water with all the strength she could muster. The two abandoned children fell as they tried to crawl away from the water. In the next few seconds visions of three drowned siblings filled her mind with horror. When she reached Colin the water was up to her chest.

"It's great out here. I was waving to you," he said. She grabbed his arm and pulling him to her shouted, "Get in to the sand before I kill you." He looked at her, not understanding why she was so cross. Like his father this sibling was a natural swimmer. He slipped from her grip and like a fish cut through the water and was standing on the wet sand waiting for her to plough her way back. The contented sand castle builders and the gulls circling around the rocks were all invaded by Maggie's angry shouting and the crying children.

"How did you all get so wet? Tommy asked.

Looking at Colin, Maggie roared, "That stupid wee brat went out too far. Right, get your clothes on, we're going home." The two younger ones, with sand in their eyes and in their hair, were crying and clinging to her. Tommy put the jam pots and the empty bottle in the basket and helped Maggie to get them all safely across the road where they waited for the next bus going towards Limavady. When the bus stopped at the cross-roads Peggy Fletcher was waiting with her list of shop stuff she wanted sent from town. As she passed the list to the conductor she watched the forlorn children get out of the bus. Maggie's wet clothes stuck to her skin as she tried to carry Sam and Brian, both sobbing and soaked.

"God bless us weans, how did you get so wet?"

"It was Colin, he nearly got drowned," said Maggie. Peggy took them into her kitchen and stripped the clothes off the wet ones and wrapped them in towels. She put the clothes on the fender in front of the fire and soon a mist was rising from them. With some of them standing at the table and some sitting on the floor Peggy gave them milk and slices of buttered bread. When the bus from Limavady stopped at the shop Sarah and Frank alighted and Peggy ran out waving an arm and calling, "They're all in here." Sarah and Frank surveyed their brood and the clothes on the fender.

"What's wrong here," said Frank.

"Oh they had a bit of a mishap," said Peggy. As the story of the disastrous picnic unfolded Sarah tried to contain her fury. Yet again this auld maid, as she thought of her, had come to the rescue. Back home Sarah glared at Maggie and said, "Could you not have kept an eye on them? Can you do nothing right?" And Colin felt that Maggie had ruined the best adventure of his life.

A bid for the farm was accepted and the loan shark introduced Frank to a farm that was as unlike his present one as it could be. More suited to grazing hardy mountain sheep it was much further from town and had little arable land. The auction of farm machinery that would not be needed in the new home had been arranged and Sarah planned to sell some of the household items. She took the two glitzy frames that Ellen had given Frank and was removing the photographs when Maggie asked if she could keep them. "Don't be daft. Nobody would want auld faded stuff like that, but we might get something for the frames." As she spoke she tore each one in two, scrunched them up and threw them on the floor. They were the only contact Maggie ever had with her paternal grandparents and hung on the wall for as long as she could remember. She thought of Robert. A picture of his mother was the only tangible thing he had and now it lay in shreds. Frank was solemn as he looked up at BenevenaghMountain, remembering his early walks in its foothills. The black rocks lay sprawled out like a sleeping giant and when the lorry rumbled off on moving day Old Man Benevenagh looked down in silence as he had done on the day they arrived.

It was a jumbled lot that bedded down that night in the mountain side house. They were so tired they threw the mattresses on the floors and slept. Maggie rose the next morning, dressed, combed her hair and took a slice of bread and a glass of milk. The house was quiet as she set off on the bike to school, believing that this was what she was expected to do. It seemed easy enough to head towards the town for it was mostly downhill. On her way home the route was still easy enough, following the land marks she had noted on the way up the previous day, the house with the windmill and the one with the white washed wall around it. Then the road forked into three narrow roads. She stopped. They all looked the same, rough tarmac surfaces and hawthorn hedges. Never being a good navigator in any situation, she had no idea which one to take. She opted for the one to the left and after some time began to feel uneasy. An old shepherd, looking as rugged and thin as the sheep he tended saw her approach.

"If you don't mind me askin' where are ye headin'?" She told him she was going home. "Not up this way, lass. See yon cottage you passed, that's the last house on this road. After that it's just sheep and heather." He asked her where she lived. She told him she didn't know the name of the townland for they had only moved the day before. "Ah by jakers, I know now where you live. That's Brown's auld place. I'm afraid you're a brave wheen o' miles off your track." He gave her directions, interspersed every few words with, 'ye can't miss it'. It was after six o'clock when she reached home to a barrage of Sarah's questions.

"Where the hell were you to this time? And what made you go to school the day of all days? Didn't you know we needed help with getting the beds and stuff upstairs?"

As Maggie listened to the ranting she heated the stew in the pot and muttered to herself. "How am I going to stick this till I'm sixteen?" Frank came in, poured himself a cup of tea and sat at the table beside her. "I got lost coming home the day. You know the three forks on the road, where does that road to the left take you?"

"Ah, that takes you over the mountain to Slaughmanis. When you come to the three forks in the road, you take the middle one."

"And I saw a flock of the scraggiest looking sheep you ever saw."

"That'll be the mountain sheep. The kind of sheep we used to keep wouldn't survive the winters up there." Conversations with her father were rare but when they happened she felt that she could ask him anything. Her first year at the new school was a disaster. She felt isolated in a world where she did not belong. When she was invited to a birthday party or a trip to the cinema, Sarah's answer was always the same, a no, qualified with, 'you're there to learn, not to go to parties' and very soon no invitations came which in many ways was a relief. She would not have to explain why she could not invite anyone to her home. From the new home the cycle run to school was much longer and in wintry weather her hands were numb when she got there. Asking if she could get warm gloves brought an outburst she didn't expect.

"Do you know how much it's costing to send you to that school? Do you know we're doing without to send you there? You can get all them fancy things when you're earning your own money."

"And do you know that we're going over the same English and arithmetic that we did at the primary school and the ones at the college are on to new stuff. It's not too late for me to change over and with typing and shorthand I'd be earning money a lot sooner."

But arguing or reasoning with her mother never got results so Maggie planned to do no work and fail the end of term exams. There might still be a chance to join her old classmates at the technical college. On the other hand some of the pupils there regarded grammar school pupils as snobs. She was in no man's land. Added to this, farming in hill country was not working out for Frank and before the year was up he sold the farm and bought one with a smaller acreage and nearer to town. They were on the move again. One evening Maggie was reading a short essay before answering the list of questions on its content. "You should be doing homework instead of sitting there with your head in a book," Sarah said. It seemed useless to explain that what she was reading was her homework so she made no comment on the remark. In the end of year exam Maggie did not come first in her class in all subjects and doubts crept into Sarah's mind. That headmaster had as good as told her Maggie was a genius, but for now she would keep her thoughts to herself. She would see to it that Maggie worked harder next year. There would be no more slouching around reading books. The tug of war went on for another year with no obvious winners as Maggie counted the days and kept saying, "Sixteen, roll on sixteen".

Sarah was pregnant and in despair. She contacted a handy woman in the district who arrived one day and strode into the house like an autumn wind. She had a mass of grey curly hair that she kept flicking behind her ears with a finger and thumb. Her voice, loud and cackling, irritated Sarah who would have preferred that she talked in whispers. While having a cup of tea the visitor wrote a few words on the sheet of paper that Sarah had given her. Unaware of the visit Maggie was sent to the chemist shop with an envelope. "Don't go to the usual chemist. Go to that one on Main Street. They don't know me there."

"What difference does it make whether they know you or not?"

"Why do you have to be so bloody nosy? Just take it where I told you and stop asking questions." Maggie stood at the glass counter waiting her turn to be served. She handed over the envelope and the lady opened it, scanned it and then went to the back of the shop. After a short time she returned and told Maggie to wait a moment. She served the next customer and the next and still Maggie stood there. Then a man with his glasses perched on the end of his nose came from the back of the shop, peered at her over the rim of the glasses and said, "Who sent you in with this?"

"My mother."

"And your mother's name?" When all his questions had been answered he had Sarah's name, Maggie's name, her age and their address. He returned to the back of the shop, beckoning the assistant. She followed him and after another wait they both returned. Presenting her with a small piece of paper, he said, "Would you just sign your name there." He handed her a paper bag with string tied round it. "Take that home to your mother and the change is inside." Maggie did not tell her mother about the series of questions. Life was easier that way but she became suspicious about the contents of the bag and convinced herself that it was poison. A number of years had passed since that day in the cornfield when poison was mentioned and the memory of it came back to her.

"She still mumbles in a strange way. Maybe that old madness is coming back again. Is she going to poison Robert, or herself, or maybe my father?" In the days that followed she watched like a hawk for any tell tale signs. One day she got home from school and found that Robert was missing. When she asked where he was Sarah said that he and Frank were at Mullan's helping to get the corn in. At the first opportunity she looked in the wooden box known as the medicine cabinet but the brown bag wasn't there. She thought of going back to the chemist and confiding her fears in him. That might cause a stir and the news of it would get back to her mother. With her hand on her brow and looking at the ground she said, "What am I going to do? Surely if it was poison he wouldn't have handed it over to me." Fear and curiosity were getting the better of her and finally she asked her mother what was in the parcel from the chemist.

"I hope you weren't rummaging in that cabinet. Just keep your hands to yourself and don't ask questions that are none of your business." Since there were no signs of any one falling sick she put the incident out of her mind. Sarah's pregnancy was becoming apparent. Libby, the handy woman, called again, loud and brash as ever. "So it didn't work," she said. "Ah well, times it works and times it doesn't." The baby girl arrived in mid winter and by the autumn the loan shark was in control again. For Frank, life as a farmer was over and life as a farm labourer was about to begin for there was not enough money left to buy even a small farm so they bought a thatched cottage owned by the loan shark. Slimy Harry, as Maggie named him, had a buyer for Charlie Boy. "Not a great price for he's such a nervous brute not many would have him," he said.

Maggie was in the shed, mixing a feed of potatoes and meal for the last of the pigs when Harry Dowds slithered in the door. He had always been on her hate list and was about to be added to her hit list. Coming up behind her he put a hand on her hip as he said in a taunting voice, "I suppose you'll soon be looking at the boys." Something snapped in her mind. She saw the men from the pub and heard the noise. It felt like it was piercing her very skull. It wasn't that this man looked anything like those drunks but it was the way he walked towards her and the suddenness of it. She lashed out with the wooden potato masher and hit him on the shoulder. He stumbled on his way out and hit his head on the edge of the door. She stood rigid. "I'll get a quare hammering for this," she said to herself. After she fed the pigs she went to the kitchen, frantically thinking how she would explain her actions. There he was sitting at the table with a hankie pressed to the cut on the side of his head.

"Pour a cup of tea for Harry. He slipped coming out of the byre. I'll see if I can get a plaster," said Sarah. Under her breath Maggie muttered, "bloody liar" as she took the teapot from the range and approached the table, curbing the urge to throw it over him. "Here Mr. Dowds, have some tea, some bread, some jam, have every damn thing we've got for you'll take it all anyway, you slimy auld bastard." At this outburst he got up and headed for the door, saying he would go and see if Frank had the horse in the stable for the buyer would soon be here. Sarah came into the kitchen and glowered at Maggie.

"What has got into you, talking to him like that? Don't you know we owe him money? Only for him we'd have no where to go. I think it's time I put some manners in you," and reverting to her old time pattern she lifted a stick from the wood pile and just as quickly put it down again. Maggie stood facing her, filled with anger, hatred and revenge. At school she was hard working and obedient but at home she was becoming impossible to live with. As Sarah busied herself with clearing away the dishes, Maggie said, "Did you think I was going to stand here and let you batter the skull of me with that stick?" There was silence. "Well, did you? Maybe you'd like to come out to the stable and ask that heap of vermin what really happened to his head. But then he would deny it and you and my father would back him to the hilt because, we owe him a lot of money." Sarah sensed that something had happened but she could not deal with a crisis. She felt herself go stiff. Whatever it was it would be better left unmentioned.

There was no great drama about moving from this place. It was a case of sell, pack and on the road again. The drama came into play when they reached the new home. It was a semi-detached cottage with a thatched roof. An old man was living in one end and the two rooms in the other end were the only accommodation they had. Sarah had been led to believe they had bought the whole building and immediately inquired when the old man was going to move out. She soon discovered that he owned his side of the house. A woman calling at the door to welcome them to the village could not believe that so many people were crammed into this small space. Sarah, not known for telling her business to the world at large, was so incensed that she blurted out to this stranger how Mr. Dowds had deceived her.

"That doesn't surprise me. Round here we've often wondered does he tell the tax man how much he rakes in." These words were like a gift from the Gods. Sarah pounced into action and sent a message to Mr Dowds, asking him to call with her. When he arrived her anger knew no bounds. "But I thought you understood that you were only buying the one end of the house," he said.

"Like hell you did. If that was the case why did you say that we could make a door into the other end and have double the space?"

"Aye, I did say that, but I meant that when the old fellow next door died it wouldn't take much to buy that end and put a door through to this end."

"You're a lousy scheming liar but I'll tell you to your face what I'm going to do." She went to the door and shouted, "Maggie, come in here." Maggie was slow to respond and when she strolled into the kitchen Sarah was standing over a tin box that she had placed on the table. Looking at Maggie she said, "This box has all the papers about the loans we got, so sit down and write what I tell you to the tax man." Remembering the last time she was forced to write her mother's dictation, Maggie was indignant that she was still being treated as her mother's possession yet she relished the chance of taunting the loan shark. "Firstly, you do not refer to him as the tax man. He is an investigating officer for The Inland Revenue. Secondly, will the letter you want me to write contain a complaint or the reporting of vital information?"

Harry Dowds rose from the chair and left with fear on his mind but not fear of these two females. He had to find Frank and find him quickly. When both men met Harry agreed to pay back the money for the cottage and any solicitor's fees, find Frank a farm job with accommodation included, while Frank agreed to block the delivery of the letter for he knew from the outset that he was only buying one end of the cottage and Harry reminded him of this fact. In the cottage Sarah sat at one end of the table drinking tea and vowing that Harry Dowds would not know what hit him when she was finished with him. Maggie sat at the other end of the table drinking tea and methodically looking at the papers one by one, occasionally stopping to make silly notes in a jotter. Never having seen papers like these before she had no idea what they meant but she sensed that old Dowds would like to get his hands on them. When her mother went to the well for water she tore out the written notes from the jotter, put them in the box and placed one of the genuine papers on top. She pushed all the other papers under a mattress until she could decide where to hide them and thought about the letter.

Frank returned to a furious Sarah who was determined to make trouble for the loan shark. It took Frank some time to convince her that if Harry returned the money for the cottage and got him a job with accommodation included it would be better than antagonising him. Maggie listened to their conversation and when Frank went out Sarah took the tin box and put it back on the bottom shelf of the cupboard and told Maggie there would be no need to write the letter but Maggie had another letter on her mind. She was now sixteen and the fight for freedom was once again on her agenda. Every week she scanned the weekly paper for job applications and noticed that they were mostly for secretaries and bookkeeping which left her sighing. "Oh, if only I could type." Then one week she spied it, standing out like a beacon – Train to be a nurse at The Royal Victoria Hospital, Belfast. Out of the grocery money she bought a stamp and wrote for an application form. All she had to do was get on with the Junior Certificate exams and wait for the form. It was always midmorning when the postman delivered the mail and seeing the hospital name on the envelope, Sarah steamed it open and surveyed the contents. Then she closed the envelope and hid it in the drawer where she kept her underwear. She was furious that Maggie had gone behind her back to do this and determined to keep control of her. "Selfish little bitch, she should be grateful for everything I'm doing for her." But in her heart she had not lost sight of her grand plan. She could see that Maggie was champing at the bit to get off to work where she would spend her money on fancy clothes like the girls she'd seen in town. Frank was still going to the local pub at the weekends and she realised he was never going to give up the drink. Until Maggie got a well paid job she would make sure she had no fancy clothes or money to go anywhere.

At last Harry Dowds found a job for Frank with accommodation included and soon the family's possessions, so recently unpacked were packed again for another move to a two storey house with a lot more space than the cottage. Maggie made sure she was there to help dismantle the beds for the round metal tubes of the bed posts were the hiding places of Frank's loan statements from Mr. Dowds. With long pieces of string and a pencil she had turned them into tight cylindrical shapes, unscrewed the brass tops of the bed posts, took the pencil out, tied a knot on each piece of string and eased them into the cavities. As she screwed the brass tops on again she was sure no one would find them. But now as the beds were being dismantled she needed to keep a close eye on them. She had no immediate plans as to what to do with the papers but it gave her great satisfaction to know that she had something that could cause old Dowds stress in his financial world. When they settled into the new home Sarah waited for Maggie's exam results with glee and a certainty that they would bring a good job and a good wage. Maggie was in a dilemma for she had to get another stamp to write to the hospital giving her new address and to mention that she had not received the application form. Weeks had passed since she sent for it and she couldn't figure out why it was taking so long to arrive. The exam results came and Sarah watched Maggie open the envelope and look at the contents, showing no emotion and uttering not a word. Sarah's heart sank for she thought Maggie's lack of excitement meant she had failed. As Maggie looked at the paper in her hand she knew exactly what it meant – enough grades to do the Senior Certificate. To date her teenage years had floated past without her having had any involvement in the world around her. She had never been to a local dance, to the cinema or even met with other school mates for girlie chats. Was it any wonder, she thought, that they regarded her as being very odd? "Well, what does it say?" Sarah asked. As Maggie handed her the paper she said, "There it is and it will get me sweet nothing." Sarah looked at the paper but had no idea what it meant and Maggie had been so moody of late that she did not want a confrontation with her. If she had failed, Sarah thought, maybe now was the time to give her the letter she had kept hidden for so long but firstly she would go and see the headmaster. This time there was no beige coat with the fox fur collar. Already the coat was too tight for her and was showing signs of wear. She didn't possess a garment that merited a fox fur as an assessory but a picture of affluence was not what was needed on this occasion. She explained to the dignified and aloof man that she understood Maggie would get a well paid job after a couple of years at his school but Maggie seemed to think this certificate would not get her a job.

"Mrs. Millar, I have never given anyone the impression that one could walk into a well paid job with this certificate. It's a stepping stone to doing the Senior Certificate which entails another two years study. Had you wanted Maggie to start work at sixteen, the technical college would have been a better choice."

"I suppose it's too late for her to go there for a while."

"Yes it's too late. Now as I see it you have two choices. I'm not saying that these results are brilliant but they are good and depending on the results of her senior certificate she might be eligible for a scholarship. The other option is that she gets a job locally and studies at night school."

Only to herself would Sarah admit that her great plan was a mistake. She thought of the day Peggy Fletcher told her it could be eight years before Maggie earned a salary if she was sent to the grammar school and now this headmaster had confirmed it. But the thought of the Fletchers hearing that Maggie had to leave school without the prospects of a grand job was unthinkable. She had no idea what a scholarship was and did not want to ask this teacher. Whatever it was it sounded very impressive. Now that she had control of the money from the thatched cottage she left the school office with a steely determination that Peggy Fletcher would never be given the chance to say, 'I told you so.' "Well I'm damned if I'll give in now. Two more years and I'll show them."

Chapter 9

Maggie had written to the hospital to give her new address and to say that she had not yet received the application form she had requested. She was reading the hospital's reply when Sarah returned. "Who is the letter from?" she asked. "It's from a Belfast hospital about a form they sent to me in June but I didn't get it." Sarah stood still for a moment and then said, "Oh heavens, there was a letter and I forgot all about it." She went to the bedroom and returned with the letter. Maggie took it and noticed the postmark, 26th, June. She turned it over, saw that the flap was rather dirty and wrinkled, looked at her mother but said nothing. "With the moving I likely forgot about it," Sarah said. Maggie went upstairs to read the letter. The final date for the return of applications was already past. Her whole body slumped and then she gritted her teeth in anger and frustration. "I know she tampered with this letter but what's the point anyway. I haven't got clothes for an interview or the fare to Belfast." With the letter back in the envelope she put it in a drawer and went downstairs. Not having an outfit to wear or anywhere interesting to go was becoming a sore point with her. Sarah was expecting a confrontation about the letter so she could not figure out why Maggie said not a single word. She told her about the nice buns she got in the bakery and fussed around making a pot of tea and taking the buns out of the bag. Maggie sat watching but still said nothing. Sarah tried to make casual conversation with remarks about the bakery, the cake she was going to buy but thought the buns looked nicer. Then she said, "I saw the headmaster today and he thinks…"

"I don't want to hear what he thinks. What I want to know is why you insist I keep going to a school that I should never have been at in the first place and then you constantly complain to me about how much it costs you. If you had listened to me years ago and let me go to the tech I would be qualified to get a job right now and it wouldn't have cost you anything. Anyway I need to go and see the headmaster myself."

"But why do you need to see him?"

"It's personal. I need some advice." Sarah, like a purring cat, tried to assure her that two years would pass quickly and then she'd have a really good job, better than nursing or typing.

"What is this really good job you talk about? Most people I know start at the bottom rung of the ladder and work their way up regardless of what school they went to."

"Well it would be better than nursing or typing."

Maggie could listen no longer. Without eating any of the buns she went outside, walked aimlessly to the end of the yard and in a quiet corner leaned against the turf stack. The salty tears flowed down her face and her shoulders took on an involuntary shaking. After a few moments the shaking stopped and a noisy sigh came from the pit of her being. She wiped her eyes with the sleeve of her jumper, looked at the darned elbows and the threadbare skirt. "Look at me," she whispered to herself. "This and a school tunic that's too small is all I have and I'm questioned and grilled if I stop to talk to anyone. I'll never forgive her for what she did with that letter. I know with the grades I got I would have got into the nursing school." There she stood, Cinderella of the turf stack. She sighed again and wiped her nose on her sleeve. There was the sound of horses' hooves. Looking out to the road she could see her father and young Nat Bradley sitting on the running board of the cart. She may have felt trapped in her mother's cage but nothing could stop those feelings of womanhood that welled up in her breast. As he chatted to Frank young Nat Bradley did not know that his every movement was being watched. Maggie remembered the orchard in their home at Aghanloo, remembered the young couple entwined in each others's arms as she watched from the high mound. It was a funny dance to her then. Now it was a deep yearning. She wanted to be entwined in Nat Bradley's arms, run her fingers through his hair while he kissed her and moved his strong hands over her body but not in these rags and not in his rough trousers and greasy shirt. No, that repulsed her.

She went into fantasy mode as she did when things were bleak. He wore a shimmering white shirt, top three buttons open to reveal a bronzed chest with a slight feathering of dark hair. She had blond hair that tumbled on tanned shoulders and her dress was deep pink and silky. Their rendezvous varied, quiet woodland paths, warm sandy beaches or standing on the rocks at Downhill watching the waves buffet the coastline. Always they were lithe and gazelle like, skipping to meet each other and the strength and hardness of him blending with the softness of her while the music of the wind transported them to paradise. Then she'd change their outfits depending on how the tailor's dummies in the local drapery shop were dressed. Somehow these fantasies only made things worse. She plucked up the courage to go and see her headmaster and briefly told him of the situation she was in.

"But Maggie you worked so well and seemed to enjoy school."

"I love school. It has been the only life saver for me but my home situation is going to drive me over the edge. I want to know if you would give me a reference and could you suggest where I could get a live-in job. I may be able to continue my studies later at night school." The headmaster had never encountered a case like this. Satisfied that Maggie was serious about her studies he looked at her recent results and said he would write to the Department of Education to see if she could get a scholarship for the next two years. The reply was that even though this student has good results in the Junior Certificate she was outside the age limits and no scholarship could be awarded. Sarah got a letter from the school asking her to call in the office. She was informed of the Department's ruling and her talk with the headmaster left her in no doubt about two things. Maggie was keen to complete her education and she was determined to get a job and leave home. Maggie was back at school for the new term and Sarah felt that things were still going her way.

As the months passed Frank was getting exasperated for the more work he did the more was expected of him. Eventually he found another job on an estate near town. Moving was no trauma for any of them now. In fact it was almost expected. The new place turned out to be idyllic in many ways although this wasn't apparent on their arrival. The gate lodge had a certain romance about it, like a picture in a child's storybook. Nestled just inside the iron gates, a shawl of honeysuckle and wild roses embraced the small gate lodge. The long avenue leading to the estate house was bordered on one side with tall trees and masses of rhododendron bushes. The younger children gasped as the large house came into view. "Blimey! Are we going to live there?" said one of them. "No, we turn off to the right," said Frank and the lorry with its weak springs rumbled over a narrow lane, then turned left across the top of a ploughed field and into what was meant to be a garden. It was overgrown with tough grass, nettles, thistles and docks. Its walls had probably been whitened with lime many years ago and against one gable wall a lean-to shed made of corrugated tin stood like a dark open cavern. Near the opposite gable the outdoor toilet, no bigger than a telephone kiosk, looked apologetic with its rusty tin sides. From its dilapidated wooden door a well trodden path led to rough gravel outside the house. The hedge behind the toilet gave way to a low wooden fence from which the railway line could be seen at the bottom of the adjoining field.

After the lorry driver had gone everyone helped to carry the furniture and boxes into the house while Sarah decided where each item would go. Maggie offered to help with the beds but Sarah said Frank and Robert would do that job. "You go and get the range lit and take the kettle and cups out of that box." She knew she'd have to do something about the stash of papers for sooner or later her secret would come to light. The ash pan was filled to overflowing and when she opened the range door some of the ash tumbled on to the floor. Carefully she carried the ash pan outside and looked around to see where she would empty it. Behind the toilet looked as good a place as any so she tipped the ashes at the base of the hedge and a spray of dust enveloped her. Tommy and Louise carried turf and a few logs inside to get the fire lit. The younger ones were exploring. They expected to find a road at the front of the house but a tall hedge surrounded the entire front garden. At the far end of the back garden they found a huge hole and rushing indoors shouted, "Daddy come and see this hole. It must be a mile deep." Frank followed them and they all stood gaping at the hole.

"That's for putting the rubbish and ashes in. Now stay away from the edge of it for if you fall in there you'll get hurt."

"Daddy, where's the road out of here?" Colin asked.

"There isn't a road out. We get out the same way the lorry came in, across the top of the field and on to the avenue but to-morrow I'll show you a short way into the town."

Next day he took the four younger ones into the field that overlooked the railway line. Once at the bottom of this hilly field Frank opened the gate that took them on to the tow path. He stopped to give them instructions that they were never to leave the gate open or to go on to the railway line. It was a short walk from the gate to the wooden bridge over the River Roe where they stood gazing down at the swirling water. Further off were two men walking along the river bank with fishing rods. Once off the bridge they were beside the cattle trucks and two railway carriages parked on the sidings. Then they came to the railway station where Frank stopped to let them watch men wheel large cartons from a railway truck on to a dray cart. A big Clydesdale horse was yoked to the dray cart and as Frank looked at the horse he wondered where Big Charlie Boy was now. A little way along Main Street they stopped at a confectionery shop where Frank bought them cones of ice cream and licking them with relish they returned home.

There was so much to do that time seemed to fly. The outside walls were whitewashed, the inside ones were washed and painted and new hinges put on the toilet door. Everybody did what they could to dig up the weeds in the garden so that vegetables could be grown. Frank, with Robert's help, made a chicken coop for the rooster and two hens they had acquired. A young goat was next to arrive and even though it provided a little milk the downside was that it ate branches from the hedges and any greenery it could find. They tethered it in the front garden but it jumped up and chewed the clothes on the washing line so after a short sojourn it was sold. A local farmer's wife gave the boys two goslings. They kept them indoors in a cardboard box but when they got bigger they found an old barrel near the tow path, dragged it home and with some straw in the inside and a few bricks on the outside to keep it from rolling about, it made a cosy home for the geese at night. Like the bastions of Rome the two geese became the protectors of the Millar household. They hissed and nipped the ankles of anyone who approached. The children coming home from school could not get to the door without being chased. After suffering several nips on the legs and ankles the older ones worked out a defense strategy. Instead of running away they waited till the head of a goose was quite close and with the flat of their hand, whacked it on the head or neck.

Maggie's final year at school was punctuated with a count down of how many more months she had to go. It didn't matter that her school tunic had two triangular pieces of material sewn into the sides to accommodate her developing breasts, the hem let down and a piece of navy cloth used to add a false hem. When the one white blouse that fitted her was in the wash her father's old white shirt was an excellent substitute. With a tuck in each sleeve and the school tie to cover the fact that it buttoned to the wrong side, no one would have guessed its origin. She was now a school prefect and captain of the school hockey team but decided that silence on her school news was essential. Then in desperation she said, "Damn, how am I going to explain the money I need for the prefect's badge." When Sarah demanded to know why she needed a badge Maggie told her that all the final year pupils had to get one. Lying came easily now. She got the money and the subject didn't surface again. The next week's news was the truth but it was more difficult to deal with. In the domestic science class the teacher set out the syllabus for the year and for the sewing part of the course they were told they'd have to make a blouse and skirt. From some there were grumbles that they hated sewing but Maggie would not admit to classmates that this news delighted her. It meant she'd have one outfit that wasn't a school uniform. Her heart was light and her step even lighter as she crossed the railway bridge and walked along the path towards home.

"Miss Bryson says we have to get material for a blouse and skirt and a sewing pattern."

"Did she say how much all this is going to cost? Where does she think I'm going to get the money for all that? Are you sure she said that or are you making it up just to get fancy clothes? I've told you before when you're earning you can buy all the fancy clothes you want but just remember I'm expecting you to help educate all the rest of them and…"

"La-de-da-de-dah," Maggie mouthed to herself, missing most of what followed except the phrase 'and him drinking' which sounded intermittently like a refrain. Frank's drinking had lessened considerably. It was confined to Friday and Saturday nights. Financially there was an improvement on the past few years. Frank had a regular wage, there was family allowance for the children and Robert was getting the old age pension though this made no difference to his status. Vegetables were grown in the large garden, there were eggs from the hens and the geese, and on Saturday evenings there was the best treat of all when Maggie and Louise were sent to town. All the stale bread in Hunter's Bakery was sold off cheap. A poor day for the bakery's sales was a good day for them as they eyed the shelves and said, "A shilling's worth of hard bread please." Depending on what was left they often came home with Paris buns, sugar topped baps, barmbrack and often a couple of loaves. A few minutes in the oven and they all had a treat. Sarah was often known to supplement Frank on a Saturday night with a ten bob note but money for this material was a major issue.

"I'll drop out of domestic science and tell the teacher we can't afford the material."

"You'll do no such thing. What would people think if that got out?" roared Sarah. So Maggie's first trip to Derry was arranged. Apart from being bussed to and from hockey pitches in other towns she had never been to another town on her own. Nervous tension gripped her as the bus reached the city fringes.

"Are we at Foyle Street yet?" she asked the conductor.

"I'll tell you when we get there." The Golden Teapot, first erected in 1870 in Waterloo Place was a famous landmark in the city and used to have steam coming out of its spout. So big was it that during World War II Lord Haw Haw said Germany would destroy it for the Admiralty was hiding under it. Neither Sarah nor Maggie knew anything of the history of the famous tea pot so following her mother's instructions Maggie expected to see this pot in a shop window. She stopped to gaze up at it, marveling at its size and wondering what Johnny Spin a Yarn would make of it. It brought to mind another teapot, the silver one with its matching milk jug and sugar bowl. She had seen it a few times when they were packing or unpacking and once Sarah told her that Frank bought it for her in a New York store. Then there was the silver eggcup and its small spoon with the crest of the RMS Athenia on the handle. With a proud smile she told Maggie that the captain of the ship had given it to her when she disembarked. When Sarah's spirits were high she would tell Maggie that these treasures would be hers when she grew up. Right now promised silver treasures would not get her any nearer to her immediate goal.

She walked on to the haberdasher's shop where the array of material dazzled her. She was like a swimmer doing the breaststroke, leaning forward with hands out to admire each roll then drawing back as her eyes read the price tags. After some sensible calculations that would meet her budget she emerged from the shop with a pattern, a piece of brown material for a skirt and a flimsy turquoise length for the blouse. The latter turned out to be a poor choice for it frayed easily and caused no end of problems. School now took over Maggie's life leaving her on a high she'd never known before. She even took it upon herself to coach the junior hockey players some evenings after school. That meant getting home much later than usual which was her real reason for doing it and not the extra lessons as she'd told her mother. The first blip to rock the boat came one winter's day when she arrived back from Ballycastle with a bandaged head.

"What happened to you?" Sarah asked.

"I got split with a hockey ball."

"Well that's it. No more hockey for you. If you can spend every Saturday away I can get you plenty to do around here."

"But I have to go for…" She was about to blurt out that she had to go for she was the team captain but decided to hold fire and think of something else.

"You've just had your last Saturday at that hockey. You're there to learn," Sarah said.

Doors slammed. The stairs shuddered. Maggie sat on the bed, teeth clenched and body rigid. "Damn, damn, I wish I had money." She confided in her best friend, Iris Black, and asked her to keep the hockey stick and boots in her house. Then she told her mother that the class teacher wanted them in every Saturday for extra lessons.

"Can they not learn you enough during the week?"

"It's just extra revision before the exams, but I don't have to go. I'll tell her I'm not allowed out on Saturdays," Maggie replied.

"Oh you can go then but I hope it's worth it." Maggie hadn't the slightest pang about lying. If there were consequences she'd deal with them when they arose. Near the end of term the school magazine was issued and Sarah met one of the parents when she was shopping.

"Well have you read it? It's a pity they lost that one match otherwise your Maggie would be holding the cup."

Sarah hadn't a clue what the woman was talking about and questioned Maggie when she got home. "Oh, the school magazine, you'll find all about it in there," and she produced the book from her bag. Sarah took some time to look at it.

"Why couldn't you have told me this at the start of the year? I could have bragged about it to that Fletcher lot."

Maggie looked her in the eye and said, "That's exactly why I didn't tell you for your boasting makes a laughing stock of yourself and all of us." That summer was blessed with glorious weather and awash with simmering tension as Maggie planned her final escape. As soon as school closed she called at Iris' house. She was going to send for application forms for jobs, nursing, banking, civil service, in fact any job that she saw advertised in the paper and she wanted to know if Mrs. Black would let her use her address. It was comforting to have her as a confidant. Practicalities like going for interviews never entered Sarah's head and Maggie knew that the suggestion of getting a simple outfit for such an occasion would be construed as wanting fancy clothes. Then there was the problem of getting her fare and the number of interviews she might have to attend before being offered a job. Transport took priority over an outfit. She had to earn some money. Mrs. Black spoke to the manager of one of the drapery shops and Maggie got her first job. For three days a week she was to sweep the store room, help to unpack cartons of goods and stack them in the appropriate shelves. She went home and unpicked the stitching on the prefect's badge and the braid on her tunic. In its plain state and with the white blouse worn over it she was all set for work.

"I've got a job, three days a week, starting on Monday," she said to Sarah.

"What! You can't even wait till you get the exam results. And what kind of job is it that you only work three days a week."

"It's working in the store room of a drapery shop and before you start ranting about me wanting to buy fancy clothes, I'm trying to earn some money for bus or train fares if I get called for interviews."

"Well try and not let people coming into the shop see you. What would they think of me if they saw you in a store room?" Maggie was silent as she decided that her mother's statement did not deserve an answer. When she got her wages she asked Mrs. Black if she would keep the money for her because her mother riffled through all her belongings but Mrs. Black had another idea. "Why not open a post office savings account, put your money in every week and I can keep the book for you." Maggie's job was a positive move in other ways. She got discount on wool to knit a cardigan and a piece of material in the sale was enough to make another skirt. It also got her out of the house and she had peace to examine the application forms as they arrived. Unless parents specifically stated what they wanted their offspring to study, the headmaster did not ask his pupils what they wanted to do after school. He told them what would be most suitable for them and got the appropriate application forms. Shortly after the exam results were issued Maggie got a letter inviting her to attend an interview at a teacher training college in Belfast.

"So when do you start there?" Sarah asked.

"I have to get through the interview first."

"And what does that mean?" Maggie told her it meant she had to go to Belfast, sit in front of a panel of people and answer umpteen questions. Then they would decide whether or not she'd get a scholarship. To herself she was saying, 'if she asks me one more question I'll go crazy'.

"What kind of questions do they ask?"

"Tell me, are you doing this to annoy me? I mean, how the hell do I know what they're going to ask?" Mrs. Black's niece had trained in the same college and with her help Maggie was well equipped with directions in getting to her destination. After the interview she checked the details on the application forms in Mrs. Black's house, put them in the appropriate envelopes and posted them. It gave her great satisfaction to know that any replies would not come to her home.

In the local paper there was an article about a group of people who were planning a trip to The Grand Canyon and when Maggie was on her own Sarah said, "When we were in America Frank was going to take me there but he couldn't get the day off work." Alarm bells began to ring in Maggie's head. She recalled her mother telling her that she and Frank used to walk out to the Statue of Liberty. Then she thought of her own fantasies in the last home they lived in. She had never spoken to anyone about them for she knew she had made them all up as a kind of comfort blanket in the midst of her frustrations. Her mother's ridiculous yarns began to disturb her. One day when the rest of the family were gathering firewood and Sarah and Ruth were in town shopping Maggie was left to make her father's tea.

"When you were in New York did you ever walk out to the Statue of Liberty?"

"Maggie, you couldn't walk to it. It's built on a wee island out in New YorkHarbour. If you wanted to get close to it you'd have to go out in a boat."

Father and daughter went on talking till tea was finished and Frank went out to help Robert and the boys drag the old broken branches of trees to the shed to be cut for firewood. Since the days when she was daddy's little girl, rocking to and fro on the swing, the sands of time had left them poles apart. Nevertheless there was still a bond between father and daughter even though it was reduced to a fragile thread. It would be the next generation who talked and debated freely, that found a way of dealing with this kind of behaviour. The postman delivered a fat letter offering Maggie a scholarship and with it a form of acceptance to be signed and returned but what sent Sarah into one of her raving fits was the long list of clothing Maggie was expected to bring with her. "There's no need to get in such a state about it. I don't need to go. I might as well tell you I've applied for other jobs." As Sarah started to deliver a barrage of questions Maggie took the clothing list and went to see Mrs. Black. There were two letters for her, one from a bank and one from the civil service. They sat and looked at the contents of the letters and then at the clothing list. "There's no way I could get all that stuff," Maggie said. "So it's another interview." They went to see Alice who smiled and said, "You don't need to bring all that stuff." She went through the list and ticked off what was really necessary which left the list about a fifth of its original length. "You know Maggie if you get a job with the bank or the civil service you're going to need money for lodgings right away but you have to decide what you want to do." Maggie viewed her options in a new light. The college residence provided free board, tuition was free and she'd get a grant. She thanked Alice for her advice saying, "You've lifted a weight off my shoulders this evening. I'll sign the acceptance form and post it tomorrow." They chatted over tea and biscuits and when Maggie got home Sarah and Frank were sitting in the kitchen. The atmosphere was tense for earlier Sarah had said, "She stomps out and doesn't say where she's going and how do we know who she's talking to?"

"Why can't you leave her alone? From she was wee you were never off her back." A row ensued and as Maggie went up stairs Sarah gave her a cold stare. Frank came to her bedroom door and asked her how much money it would take to get the stuff she needed. She was about to tell him the news she got while she was in town when Sarah appeared right behind him.

"Could I talk to you about it tomorrow?" When the morrow came it wasn't her lack of suitable clothing that was on her mind. In all the years she had lived under this family roof there had been no serious or constructive conversation between her and her father. Now with so little time before she left she felt an overwhelming urgency to tell him about her mother's strange and often destructive behaviour. Frank went to work and she sat in her room rewriting the revised list, trying to scale it down even more by calculating how many of these items she could make. They would look home made and amateurish but it didn't matter. Her mother came into the room.

"So are you going to this college or not?"

"Yes, I've decided to go."

"If it wasn't for him drinking so much I'd be able to get what you need but if I got some cloth in that shop where you work do you think you could make a coat?"

"No, I wouldn't attempt to make a coat but have you got an old blanket you could give me? One of those navy ones would be ideal." Maggie went into town to get two sewing patterns and on her return spent the afternoon planning how she could turn the blanket into a dressing gown. She kept an eye on the clock as she worked and then went to meet Frank before he reached the house.

"You asked me about how much money I needed for the clothes. There's no need to worry about that for I'm coping and anyway there will be lots of students that won't have everything on that list. What I want to say is something else. I don't know how to put it, in fact it might not be wise to mention it at all."

"Well tell me. Is it something your mother said?"

"It's a mixture of things, the way she treats Robert, the childish boasting stories and the way she wants to control everybody in the house. There must be something wrong. Could you not go to the doctor and see if there's some reason for it. What if she batters Robert on the head some day and he dies, how are you going to cope with a murder charge, or would you try to cover it up as an accident?" His face was haggard as he stood looking at the ground remembering the day years ago when he had a similar conversation with Sarah about seeing a doctor. "I knew it was a mistake to mention it but there's something else

I need to tell you." She blurted out her secret about the stash of papers and told him how the whole thing was getting on her nerves. Before either of them could say anything further Sarah came round the corner of the garden and approached them.

"What are you two talking about that you couldn't talk about in the house?" she demanded. Neither of them spoke but Sarah nagged on about them discussing things behind her back. "Have you forgotten what I told you last night?" Frank said. The frosty atmosphere lingered on for a few days. During that time Frank asked Maggie to help him carry some old rubbish from the shed to the big hole in the garden. They threw in cardboard boxes and a heap of old leather straps from the horse's harness. Frank poured paraffin oil on top of the heap and then pulled the tightly rolled papers from his pocket and handed Maggie the box of matches. "You light them," and as everything started to burn he said, "You know a clear conscience is one of the easiest things to carry." She nodded and watched the flames flicker and dart through the rubbish.

Day after day she was absorbed with her sewing as the blanket became a dressing gown and her old tunic a pair of shorts. The final results were anything but professional looking. Finally the day came for Maggie's departure. Frank slipped two crumpled pound notes into her hand. "It's not much but it might help," he said. As the train gathered speed its rhythmic clanking could be made to fit any words one wanted and Maggie's mind was saying, "I've got away, I've got away." She arrived in Belfast with a small bag of clothes and a huge bag of emotional baggage. Arriving at her student accommodation she found she had a room of her own with her name on the door. She went in, closed the door and sat on the chair. There was a bed, a small wardrobe, a desk and on the wall a bookcase.

This was a haven from the world she had left behind. For a few moments she sat with her elbows on the desk and her head resting in her hands as she listened to the chatter and laughter of other students arriving. Soon she'd have to leave this tiny sanctuary and go out and meet her new world.

Chapter 10

'What a wonderful world' was now Maggie's theme tune as she relished her new life of luxury, indoor toilets, baths with warm water and so many sports available that it was difficult to decide which ones to try. Apart from the books she had to buy, her first purchase was an umbrella and she planned to buy a raincoat in the January sales.

"For goodness sake why don't you wear your coat?" a fellow student said to her one cold October morning.

"Oh I don't feel the cold," Maggie replied, too embarrassed to tell her that she did not have a coat. With the umbrella and the wool cardigan that she had almost finished knitting, she should be able to hang on till the January sales. Sarah now turned her attention to Tommy. He could be the boss of the Electricity Company if only Frank would speak to someone influential. There were no openings in this field nor did Frank know anyone with that kind of clout so to get away from the constant requests he took to going out rabbit shooting with Bill Ferry. Bill lived alone in a small house nearby and in his youth had contracted polio and walked with a pronounced limp. He was an avid reader of books about travel and famous explorers and Frank found him a fascinating companion. He invited him home one evening for a cup of tea. Sarah wanted no outsiders to visit but knew she could not dictate to Frank on this matter like she did to the children. She was affable enough on his first visit but on hearing of their next shooting trip she was prepared. She made two apple tarts, one with normal cooking apples and sugar, the other with crab apples minus the sugar. While Frank ate a slice of the normal tart Bill sank his teeth into something as bitter as gall and spluttered the mouthful over the table. Frank was embarrassed. Sarah claimed that she had baked several tarts for the family and must have forgotten to put the sugar in that one. Bill continued to go shooting with Frank but declined the next invitation back for tea. Sarah, pleased with her efforts, laughingly told the children how she had put an end to the visits of that limping lump. About to enter the kitchen door, Frank stopped in his tracks as he listened to her confession. He reckoned there was no point in a confrontation. It always ended in a barrage of missiles, his drinking, his lunatic brother, the fact that she could have married half a dozen decent men and ended with the threat that she could still get a job and he could get who ever he liked to look after the weans.

He came into the kitchen and Sarah's laughter stopped. "I want you boys to give me a hand. I've a wee job to do out here," he said. They followed him outside and Sarah watched from the window as they sawed branches off the crab apple tree. She turned away, rehearsing the words she'd use when Frank brought up the subject of the apple tart. Shivering she glanced out again and saw the tree get smaller and the pile of branches get bigger. They used an axe to make a cut near the base of the trunk and soon the tree lay on the ground. Then they sawed the trunk into short lengths and split them into logs. As they piled the logs into the wheelbarrow Frank told them they'd have to wait till the sap dried out before using them for firewood. When they all came in for tea neither the tree nor the sour tart was mentioned. Frank spent more time than usual in Bill Ferry's company. After a shooting trip he went to Bill's house and over a cup of tea and a nip from their whisky flasks they spent many an hour discussing far away places Frank had never heard of. Sometimes he went for walks in the woods or along the river bank with only his memories for company. As he had done on other occasions, he yearned for a normal life, conversation and laughter and friends calling in. He remembered when he'd first fallen in love with Sarah she seemed so shy and naïve. True, she did not have the same prosperous background that he knew but surely, he thought, she had left her childhood behind her. But sometimes the veils put on in childhood are so well stuck that nothing can remove the glue that holds them. There were times he felt like giving up.

Maggie was in the second year of her course before she felt at ease with other girls. Having spent nothing on any social events, she and three other girls had managed to save what they considered a little nest egg from their grants. It gave them the idea for the great adventure, a spell in England staying in youth hostels. In early July they set off on bicycles and boarded the ferry for Liverpool. By thumbing they got a lift on a grain lorry all the way to Bristol. They cycled from one hostel to another, taking photographs of thatched cottages in Devon, eating cream teas and marveling at fire flies in the hedgerows at night. They toyed with the idea of going to Land's End but when they counted their money they reckoned that if they couldn't get a lift back to Liverpool they would have to go by train. Caution won and they went to Salisbury to spend a day around the cathedral. Tired but excited they made their way north again and after two more nights in hostels they got a train to Liverpool. Already they had the travel bug, planning and talking about the places they could visit the next year. And the years after that when they'd be earning wages, the world would be their oyster. They stepped off their magic carpet at the docks in Belfast and Maggie returned home bursting to tell everyone of her adventure. She was greeted with a mixture of hostility and indifference. Frank, who seldom talked much at the best of times said, "So you're back." Sarah said, "Well I hope you've saved enough to get you through next year. You didn't think about the rest of us trying to keep the bills paid while you were away enjoying yourself." Louise was the only one interested in her adventure. "Now wait till you hear my news. When I'm ready to go off to work I won't have to scrimp and save and make my own clothes like you. I'll have the silver tea service and I can sell it for a fortune. Mammy promised to give it to me when I start working."

"Don't bank on the fortune till you actually get it for not too long ago she said it would be mine when I grew up, but don't worry I won't do you out of your inheritance." They giggled and laughed as Louise said, "Maybe neither of us will get it."

One evening while watching a local football match in the field beside their garden a young man stopped and spoke to Maggie. Tom Blain, tall and fair like a Norwegian god, he was the most handsome being she had ever seen. During their conversation he asked her if she'd go with him on the summer excursion to Portrush. She readily agreed and so started what she thought was the romance of her life. He wanted to see her every evening and she couldn't wait to get out of the house every evening to meet him. He was an apprentice electrician who didn't earn much money and after her trip to England she had just about enough to pay her fare back to Belfast to start the new term. So they spent every evening like fairies in a woodland glen, capered around the rhododendron bushes in the driveway leading to the estate house and talked incessantly. On Friday nights when he got paid he took her to the cinema and bought her chocolate. She was a bit apprehensive about inviting him home, fearful that her mother would pass some cutting remark and drive him away. She decided she'd only ask him home when her father was there and she'd make sure that her mother did not make him tea. As it turned out they didn't want to be in the company of anyone else. They were in love, kissing and cuddling among the bushes and wandering along the country lanes. Laughing and talking and being on their own was all they wanted.

At home the nagging started, followed by the taunts. "Do you never think of staying in an odd evening to give me a hand? There's a pile of the boys' shirts to be ironed. You're making yourself cheap going out with him so often. I'd only go out once a week and I'd keep a man waiting an hour; he'd think more of me." These remarks were all delivered out of earshot of anyone else in the house. But Maggie didn't care. She didn't offer a reply, occasionally hummed a tune to show her indifference. Just before Christmas she was wearing a sparkling diamond ring. As soon as she finished her course in June they'd get married in July. Preparations for such an occasion never entered their heads for they were madly in love. A wiser owl could have seen it was mad infatuation. The younger fry of the family took little interest in the sparkling ring. To them Tom was like a big brother who came on his bicycle, waited at the top of the garden for Maggie and brought them chocolate. Louise was impressed but not for long. She was dealing with the same dilemma that had dogged Maggie for years, how to get through the next few years before she could get away to work. Sarah ignored the ring until Maggie was on her own.

"I hope you're not thinking of getting married for six or seven years."

"Oh I don't know, maybe someone will leave me a pile of money and I can throw the ring back at him and take off to some foreign land."

"What do you mean by that?" said Sarah.

"Ask your sister, she's good at explaining things." Sarah had no idea that her sister Letty, in the short time she'd looked after the children, had ever divulged anything of their early years. She didn't think that young children remembered anything from their childhood. Now she felt threatened.

"What exactly did she tell you?" and before any answer could be given continued, "Oh that one, do you know what she did when we were young?"

"No I don't, but I know what she did to us when you left us in her care and if I told you, you wouldn't believe me and she would deny it. Isn't that the way it goes? But I'm bigger and stronger than I was then and if she ever returns I'll finish her off next time I have a go at her."

Hard as Sarah had tried to build her castle of respectability there were times when she encountered signs of it crumbling. Whatever caused Maggie's burst of anger would be better kept under wraps for it might expose something she did not want to hear. She dropped the subject and concentrated on ways of ending this unwanted love affair. In the second term of Maggie's final year she was doing an extended period of teaching practice in the local school which meant seeing a lot more of Tom Blain. During the cold winter evenings her raincoat gave little warmth. He bought her a woollen skirt and jumper, mitts and a scarf. With an old raincoat below them and an umbrella above they'd lie huddled together on the earthy bank. The rhododendron bushes were now stark and disheveled. The leafless trees displayed their sculptured branches to a cold dark sky. Under the piles of decaying leaves they could hear faint shuffling sounds of night creatures foraging for food. Some nights Tom was in such highs of ecstasy that his mood was infectious and they giggled more than they talked. Then there were nights when he was quiet, in a world of his own. He told her of a work mate who gambled a lot and left his wife without house keeping money.

"Dear that's awful, you mean he gambled it all?" Maggie said. He claimed he took his unopened wage packed home to his mother and she gave him a weekly allowance. The perfect son thought Maggie, but it never crossed her mind where he got the money for her ring or the gifts he'd recently bought her. The first crack in her perfect man had appeared and she had missed even a glimpse of it. In their romantic relationship she was to him as a perfect doll is to a child. He was to her the man without a human flaw. One evening Tom said, "See that man that works with your father, well he told a mate of mine that he had sex with you dozens of times in the farmyard. Is it true?" Maggie was dumbfounded and looked at him in disbelief. "Well I've never had sex, never got the chance of talking to a man, let alone having sex with one. God knows what I might have done given the chancebut I'll tell you, I'd have picked someone cleaner, younger and better looking. For God's sake that ugly creep is not much younger than my father." That evening she quietly told her father the strange story that Tom had told her.

"Aye, that would be his style alright. There's hardly a girl in the area that he hasn't made the same claim about. Just leave it with me and I'll talk to him."

Next day Frank simply relayed the story to his work mate and without waiting for a reply went on, "Sure I'm not the only one that knows you'd have no interest in all them girls you talked to me about. I'm not much of a talker but I'm a bloody good listener and an even better watcher and I'd say you have no interest in any young lass, but somebody like young Blain or any young fella', well......you know you wouldn't believe what you see when you're out walking in them woods." What a barrage of protest and denial Frank listened to before he replied, "Well, I can tell you I wasn't seeing ghosts."

Doubts crept into Tom's mind. He suggested that if they had sex it would settle his doubts. For a while Maggie was against the idea, not because of some beautiful moral teaching, but more because in her young life she had gleaned from her mother's ravings that it was something disgusting and led to what Sarah called 'dirty auld diseases'. In those early years she never figured out where the watershed line kicked in but wherever it was she was about to cross it. Their first sexual union was like a research experiment where each went off to document their findings and make their conclusions. His conclusions were straightforward. To him there could be only one explanation; she must have had sex before. He would ask her again and if she admitted it to him he just might forgive her. The first flaw in his perfect doll had appeared and he wasn't so sure if he wanted to play dolls' houses with her anymore. When he did ask her she appeared not to understand, frowning and saying, "No, it's the first time I've done this." He didn't expect this answer. Surely she was a woman of the world as much as he was a man of the world. Did she really think he was stupid and gullible? So like big white chief who knows the answers to everything he explained it to her, a girl's maidenhead, you know, and went on to tell her he once had sex with a girl of fourteen so he should know.

"Fourteen," she said, without any expression and then went silent. He let her know that he had the experience of a man about town. He didn't notice her silence and went on to boast of his sexual prowess. She didn't hear him. For her the penny had dropped and not into any slot that would fit his theory. "Nearly fourteen," she said as though in a dream, then rose from the earthen bank and said, "I must go home."

"But wait a minute," he said.

She was already yards from him and dashing onwards, talking to herself. "This is my fault. Why didn't I tell Peggy Fletcher? She'd have taken me to the doctor. Instead I put myself through all the agony of pushing rolled up lint dipped in detol into my insides to clean away the pus, only to have it abscess again and again?" Her life of isolation had excluded all sensible sexual education and she felt humiliated and stupid. She decided that her mother could sort it out. It was getting dark as she went into the house. Sarah was in the bedroom putting laundry away. Maggie sat on the edge of the bed. She could not say, 'I've just had sex and there's something I want to ask you.' No, it would be a gentle lead up; the other could be introduced later.

"Remember when we lived at Aghanloo and you used to send me to the pub for Dad." Sarah, lifting her head as though she had just heard something outrageously unbeliev-able, looked at Maggie and said, "What do you mean, Frank never drank then? Who sent you to the pub?" Maggie stared at her in disbelief. Surely she couldn't have forgotten. "You must remember the night I came home bleeding," she said. Getting more and more agitated and screaming in a high pitched voice, Sarah's words tumbled out. "What do you mean? Frank never drank then. You were always a lying wee bitch from you were no age, always causing bother." Maggie opened her mouth but all that came out was, "You, you...."She was facing something that was impossible to deal with. She could understand forgetfulness but acting as though the past had never happened was unnerving. Then her anger surfaced as she thought of what would come next. The pattern was always the same; Sarah would either attack or snivel and tell everyone to leave her alone. Maggie flicked the door shut with her heel and vowed Sarah would stay in the room till she faced reality.

"If my father didn't drink how come one farm after another had to be sold for debt?"

"Tom had to get all the money to go to America and we had to work hard. We had to sell all the corn. He took everything."

"And what age were you when all this happened or is it any lie will do? You told me years ago that Uncle Tom joined the navy and was drowned."

Sarah sat fiddling with her apron. Maggie took a step towards her and suddenly there was hysterical screaming. "Don't touch me. Get away. Let me out." Still screaming, she bolted out of the room, through the kitchen and outside. When Robert appeared Maggie told him to stay in the shed till she got things under control. Now it was roles reversed. Maggie grabbed her mother by the shoulders and shook her, telling her to stop screaming. When that didn't work she involuntarily slapped her face which seemed to leave her like a limp rag. Inside Sarah sat shaking at the table while Maggie poured a cup of tea and got two aspirins. Without a word Sarah took the tablets and sipped the tea while Maggie watched. To herself she said, "If that was a dramatic performance she's a bloody good actor, but what if it wasn't?" She thought of all the times she'd heard her mother in trance like mutterings but had never seen her in a hysterical state like this. Sarah went to bed saying she had a splitting headache. As Maggie was making a fresh pot of tea Frank came in with a dead rabbit. He hung it on a nail on the pantry door and when they sat having tea she asked him what Robert's brother Tom was like.

"I don't remember much about him. I was only a lad when he went to America but he wrote home for I remember them talking about him working on a cattle ranch." They talked on about families that left home and how the next generation often lost touch with them. Frank went off to bed, rather gladdened that Maggie was engaging in conversation with him but Maggie's thoughts were on another matter, the state of her mother's mind. Then she realised that Robert was still in the shed. She brought him in to have a cup of tea and a sandwich. Like a well trained sheepdog he would have stayed in the shed till someone told him to come out. Three days later he was violently sick, vomiting and retching. Sarah had no sympathy. "Eats like a pig. If he didn't make a glutton of himself he wouldn't be sick." Maggie knew he didn't get the chance to overeat. She knew something needed to be done but if anyone confronted Sarah like Frank had done in the past or she had done so recently Robert suffered even more when they were all out of the house.

Seeing Tom Blain was the only respite Maggie got from life in her home. In his buoyant breezy moods he was the only one she had to talk to. Then he became insanely jealous. According to him she had sex with every man he could think of, the surgeon in a Belfast hospital where she recently had a knee operation, the college lecturers who came to assess her teaching practice. The list went on and on. Regardless of how outlandish his claims were he would always find a way of making them fit his theories. His violent outbursts always ended in the most profuse regrets and claims that it would never happen again and then a period of idyllic tranquility would follow. In her last term at college he gave her the fare to come home at the weekends. While she was away she kept thinking how Robert was faring, waiting every week to hear of some tragedy. Near the end of the term she found she was pregnant and miscarried almost before the news had fully sunk in. Tom rushed her to hospital on the bar of his bicycle and then vanished. On her discharge she was sent home by ambulance and as the driver drove along Catherine Street she saw Tom Blain hand in hand with a new girlfriend as they stood in the queue at the Regal Cinema. To anyone with normal feelings this would have been hurtful but Maggie's normal feelings had been crushed a long time ago.

She desperately needed to earn money and accepted a job in an isolated school where few young teachers would willingly go. It was in a hilly area quite a few miles from Limavady and she knew that in stormy weather she would have to take the bus to work rather than cycle. Her plan was to stay there till she saved enough money to get some decent clothes and then move further from home. Out of her monthly pay cheque she gave her mother a housekeeping allowance and kept enough for the inevitable bus fares. Most of what was left she put in her post office savings book and as before Mrs. Black kept it for her. As Sarah rifled through Maggie's papers she found details of her salary and with pencil and paper she totted up the gross amount, the deductions and net amount, giving her twice Maggie's salary. So what, she thought, was Maggie doing with all this money for she could find only a few shillings in the drawer. She thought it was time Maggie was thinking of buying a house for the family but the old patterns of the past continued. "What kept you till this time? Doesn't the school end at three o'clock? Were you talking to anybody?" Maggie did not tell her that some afternoons after work she sat in the library where it was warm and she could read in peace. Nor did she tell her that every Friday she bought the paper to scan it for jobs. Four months later she moved to a job just outside Belfast and her little nest egg that Mrs. Black kept for her came in very handy for the move.

A few years later Maggie agreed to marry a young man she had known only for a short time. There was no mad passion and no feelings of elation. All she wanted was pleasant companionship and he was easy to talk to, had no streaks of jealousy and treated her like a human being. As with Tom Blain, Frank got on well with this young man but Maggie did not want to get married from her old home. Frank was disappointed at this news so Maggie relented. Sarah made it clear she did not like him. On Scott Andrews' first visit Sarah made sure she got talking to him on his own. She quietly confided to him that she had terrible trouble rearing Maggie and couldn't keep her from hanging around pubs. "Many a time I took her to that pantry and gave her a good trouncing but it made no difference." Quite convinced she had scared him away she waited for the inevitable breakup.

"Your mother doesn't want you to marry me. In her own way she's telling me I'm not quite good enough," Scott confided to Maggie.

"My mother doesn't want me to marry anyone. To her I'm a possession who will work for the rest of my life to get her what she craves. I grew up chained to that particular anchor and if I turn out to be like her I'll expect you to divorce me. And if you turn out to be a drinker like my father I'll divorce you."

"You're not the only one who has parents that behave a bit like yours."

"Are you saying you've met this situation before?"

"Let's say I've seen a few upheavals in my time."

Scott had been transferred to Derry and while he and Maggie were preparing to move Sarah was arranging the wedding. She invited the Fletchers and a few of the neighbours. Maggie baked her own wedding cake and a neighbouriced it. Maggie and Louise were carrying the cake from the neighbour's house when one of the layers slid off the plinth and one side of it got squashed. They filled the gap with gelatin mixed in breadcrumbs and covered the offending area with light icing.

"See that pink rose, make sure nobody gets a piece from that part," said Louise. For the few guests that were coming, especially the Fletchers, Sarah was going to make sure that outsiders saw them in a good light. The famous chest with her treasures from America was opened. Out came cushion covers with moth holes in them, little glass dishes in bright gaudy colours, a chalk like Statue of Liberty and the silver tea service. A bed was covered in a white sheet and each item was placed beside a piece of paper bearing the name of one of the children. As guests and neighbours called they were shown the display of gifts. Nearing nightfall the treasures were lifted and the bed used for its usual purpose. On the day of the wedding Maggie was getting dressed and Frank was downstairs talking to the taxi driver who was taking Sarah and the younger ones to the church. The older ones had gone ahead on foot. Sarah came upstairs, poked her head round the door and said, "If this marriage doesn't work don't come back to this house for you won't be wanted." In the taxi with her father the words 'won't be wanted, won't be wanted' echoed in the car and she knew that she never was wanted and never would be.

When the clergyman said, "Who gives this woman in marriage" and Frank stepped forward Maggie did not see the man who had just escorted her up the aisle. He was the bedraggled drunk, with several days growth of beard, staggering forward and in slurred voice muttering, "takin' me home are ye, gone home ye feckin wee hoor ye." She felt herself reeling from head to toe and her dress was visibly shaking. She was sure she had wet herself. Only the firm arm at her side kept her from falling.

"I think I'm going to faint," she whispered.

"Just lean against me and it'll be all right," said the voice beside her.

She kept opening and closing her eyes. The service continued and she assumed she gave the right responses. What she heard was such a jumble. "Do you take this man….Frank doesn't drink…to be your…Frank doesn't drink…wedded what."

"Dear love her, it's weddin' nerves," whispered one woman.

Sarah, with a chiseled expression, muttered, "I knew it. I'll bet she's in the family way." The trip down the aisle was incident free, the confetti fell in the right places but when they got home the dog was drunk. He had overturned a crate of beer bottles that were on a shelf in the shed and lapped up the contents of those that broke when they fell. It was a source of amusement for the guests as they watched the dog stagger in circles round the yard. Scott's brother said, "There you are Maggie, he's the first to drink your health and wish you good luck." Maggie laughed and said, "Good dog Fido," and bending down to pat him whispered, "You're the only one in this house that will." The meal went reasonably well and Louise kept her eye on the icing beside the pink rose. After the meal Peggy and Helen Fletcher eyed each other as the guests tried without success to persuade Sarah to be included in the photographs they were taking.

"No change there, and if someone told you they'd seen that, you wouldn't believe them," Peggy said. Helen shook her head in disbelief. Peggy, holding her head high, strode to the hedge and said quite loudly, "Here's a good background for a shot. Maggie and you too Frank, over here, I'll be Mammy for a minute." They posed and smiled as the camera clicked. Peggy strode back to Helen's side and said, "Let's see what she makes of that." Peggy and Helen were taken to view the wedding presents and Peggy said, "Oh they are all beautiful and it's so good of you to give her the silver tea service. Maybe she'll be sensible and use the damn thing when she entertains her friends." When they joined the other guests Helen was inwardly shaking and pleaded with Peggy not to provoke Sarah. But Peggy was at the end of her tether. "Maybe it's time I reminded Sarah why she feels like this towards Maggie. Many years ago she admitted that when they were in America she could have left Frank. The only thing that kept her from leaving him was that she was expecting 'that one' as she called her. Helen wanted to make an excuse and leave. Peggy wanted to wait for any comment from Sarah but none came. With the wedding over Sarah gathered all the children's supposed gifts including the silver tea service and returned them to the chest. Louise looked at Maggie, mimicked the action of pouring tea and said quietly, "Any bets?"

Chapter 11

With rapidly failing health Frank lost his job. Their circumstances qualified them for accommodation in a housing estate but living in a housing estate was something Sarah was not prepared to do and getting out of Limavady was something she was determined to do. From a cousin Frank borrowed some money to buy a tiny house in Derry but there was a condition; the deeds of the house would have to be put in Sarah's name. He had seen Frank's life slide from a prosperous farmer to his present woeful state and his concern was the welfare of the young family. To keep the news of their intended move from as many people as possible Sarah waited till the Friday evening before telling the children that they would be moving on Monday.

In the new home there was one bedroom where Sarah and Frank slept. Robert slept at the back of the house in a cold damp annex which was a single brick building with a concrete floor and a tin roof. The rest of the family bedded down in the attic. After bumping their heads on the roof beams a few times they got used to standing to their full height only when they were in the center portion of the attic and they descended backwards on the narrow treads of the stairs. They missed the freedom of the countryside. There was no blackberry picking, no fishing on the banks of the River Roe and their jaunts to the woods to collect firewood were now looked upon with nostalgia. With a part time job Sarah started to save some money to pay off the loan. Although she was kept busy she was in her element. She owned the house and no longer needed to worry about Frank leaving them homeless. Robert was completely isolated. He missed the old shed where he used to sit and wash his feet in a basin of water or take the dog for a walk. When Sarah went to work he was left to wash the dishes, clean the kitchen floor and bring in the coal and always on her return there were complaints. Like in the past there were a few times when she resorted to beating him around the head, leaving him a virtual prisoner in a yard that he could not get out of.

One morning Robert did not get up at his usual time and when Frank went to investigate he found him in a coma. An ambulance took him to hospital and later that evening a policeman called with a message from the hospital. Robert was dangerously ill and for the first time in his life Frank felt terror creep over him. Only a week earlier he had a blazing row with Sarah. She reminded him that she was scrimping and saving and he was still spending money on drink and she'd be entitled to tell him and his brother to find somewhere else to live. He went to the hospital where a doctor spoke to him. "Your brother has a cerebral haemorrhage. That's a bleeding in the brain and he has developed pneumonia. I'm sorry but there is no hope of him surviving this. I'll take you along to the ward and you can sit with him." As he sat by the bedside of his unconscious half- brother he was overwhelmed with emotion. He had let him down so many times and now it was too late to say sorry. It seemed like the spirits of Robert's family were looking down on him. His mind was in a fog when the doctor put a hand on his shoulder and said, "It's all over. You'll want a few minutes with him. I'll be back shortly."

The doctor came back and took Frank to the office. "You'll need this to register the death and the undertaker can collect the body later on to day. Now is there any other help you need?"

"Yes. He'll be buried across the border in CountyDonegal and I have to go there to arrange to have the grave dug. Is it possible for the undertaker to collect the coffin on the day of the funeral?" The doctor assured him that was not a problem. Back home he quietly turned the key in the lock. All was still. He slipped into Robert's bed and tried to sleep. The morning noises from the kitchen told him the boys were up and getting ready for work and school. For a moment they were speechless when Frank came out of the annex and told them the news. Then one of them spoke. "What happened to him?"

"Pneumonia, that's what's on the form."

"Do you want any of us to go with you to the undertaker?" He shook his head. When they left he poured a cup of tea and made toast. Sarah appeared at the kitchen door and said, "Well how is he?"

"He's dead." There was silence as though a blanket had smothered all speech. She poured a cup of tea and sat down. The silence began to annoy her. Frank was thinking of his life when he was a lad and the friction that he could not understand. Somehow he had seldom got away from friction. Sarah's voice interrupted his thoughts. "Are you going to sit there and say nothing? There are things we have to arrange. Where are we going to put a coffin in this house? And there'll be people tramping in and out. I suppose all the work will be left to me as usual."

"There's no need for you to do anything. Robert never had a home or a day's peace since I took him away from Gleneely, so he'll be buried from the morgue." Frank dressed and left without saying another word. After calling with the undertaker he got a bus to Moville where a friend of long standing drove him to Gleneely. It was the custom for men from the village to dig a grave for a neighbour and when this was arranged the clergyman worked out a suitable time for the funeral. Frank's friend took him home for a meal during which they talked for a long time of their young days in Gleneely and the changes in the world since they both returned from America all those years ago.

Sarah sat in the empty house. She needed to find out what caused Robert's death. When it was time for Maggie to be home from work Sarah got a bus and called with her, telling her that Robert was taken into hospital. When Maggie told the ward sister that they'd come to visit Robert Fisher she informed her that he had died in the early hours of that morning. She assumed that these two women were not family relations of the dead man otherwise they would have known of his death. Maggie stood in shock. She thought of him dying alone with no one there but the hospital staff. Death must have been a relief to him. Sarah said nothing till they got to the car. "I thought you'd have asked what he died of." Maggie was silent as Sarah continued. "I don't know how much it will take to bury him but they say you can get a grant for that. And he'll have to be buried from the morgue for there's no room to bring people into the house for a wake. Anyway hardly anybody knew him." Maggie listened to her mother's reasoning and said to herself, "Yes, she's right. Hardly anybody knew him or any of the other Roberts of this world. They were shut away in asylums or kept in a house and hidden from public view as much as possible." When they got back the house was empty and Maggie had a gut instinct that there was something puzzling about this situation.

Where was her father and why was her mother making no effort to find him and give him the news?

Later that evening Maggie and her husband returned to the house. "When did you get the news?" she asked one of the boys.

"Dad told us this morning before we went to work. He was at the hospital when he died."

"This morning! I see," said Maggie. Robert was buried in Gleneely graveyard with his father and his little sister Rebecca. Maggie looked at the old marble headstone with its carvings and the words, 'Safe in the arms of Jesus' etched at the top of the stone. The subdued group left the graveyard, each deep in their own thoughts of the man they were leaving behind. Frank glanced back and gave a sigh. Maggie took a last look over the stone wall, remembering how he had protected her in the turbulent days of her childhood. "Oh God he was special and we all let him down," she whispered to herself. As for Frank any sparkle of life he had was draining from him as his health problems grew worse and like his father he died suddenly from a heart attack. He was buried in the same graveyard with his father. Surely now Sarah would be happy. Gone was the poor retarded man that she despised and taunted and gone was the husband who drank too much and caused her so much misery. As she settled down to life as a widow the old pattern of telling outrageous stories about friends and relations continued. When the family was young they listened as though they were bedtime stories but now they saw their mother's behaviour as an addiction that she needed just as their late father needed alcohol and they were not prepared to listen. Once when Colin came home unexpectedly he found his mother reading a letter he'd had from his girlfriend and he was furious. For him this was the last straw and he made plans to find his own accommodation.

After ten years of marriage and two children Maggie and Scott's marriage was heading for the rocks. Before they married he remembered Maggie saying that if he started drinking like her father she would divorce him. Now he had fallen in love and started drinking more and more. Instead of divorcing him Maggie was doing everything in her power to stop him drinking. His plan was not working so he made sure someone told her of his affair. She had married for companionship. He had married because Maggie was so like the woman who was the love of his life but being from different religions their families and the churches brought so much pressure to bear that they decided to elope and go to England. When the time came she went to England but he didn't have the bottle to leave home. When he returned from work that day he was expecting an unholy row but Maggie was sitting quietly at the kitchen table. "If you really love this woman you should be with her for I realise I married you for all the wrong reasons." They both realised it was a marriage that should never have taken place but to Sarah the news of their divorce was a disgrace to her family.

Maggie felt exhilarated as she planned her new life. However her siblings continued to battle with Sarah's malicious stories about each other as well as other relatives and acquaintances. Her constant demands to fulfill her dreams through her children and the achievements she attempted to force on them became increasingly intolerable and one by one the rest of Maggie's siblings left home. They held a family meeting to discuss what should be done about her increasingly erratic behaviour. Each in turn related how her actions and story-telling lies were affecting their lives. "She's a grown woman and yet she behaves like a child," one of them said. At the end of their meeting they jointly decided to confront her and let her know that they would no longer tolerate her disruptive behaviour. Sarah's response was, "After all I done for the whole lot of you, now you're telling me that I'm not wanted. Well I'm going to sell this house and move into a wee flat and I don't ever want to see any of you again until you apologise." She sold the house and moved into sheltered accommodation. Here a resident warden, who had nursing experience, was in charge of the complex. Each flat had a bedroom, a bathroom and a kitchen cum living room. The family encouraged the grandchildren to visit Sarah. That way they could find out if she was alright. When Maggie's children visited Sarah began to fill their heads with her stories. They listened as their grandmother subtly told them of Maggie begging to be sent to a posh school, the farm that had to be sold to pay for her education and each time they visited she'd add a bit more. They thought their grandmother was in her dotage and unlike children of a previous era they came home and repeated what they'd been told.

Maggie decided to go against Sarah's wishes and confront her at her new accommodation. "Mother I'm here to tell you that the way you brought up your children would not be accepted in to-day's world. Now unless you keep your lying tongue to yourself my children will not be visiting you anymore." Tauntingly, and with a smirk Sarah responded. "Well too bad about you, nobody ever wanted you. Even the man you married got rid of you and your weans told me they don't want to be around you either, so what are you going to do about it?"

Maggie felt she was back beside the range in the kitchen of their old home in Aghanloo once again fighting off one of her mother's attacks. A dark cloud descended as she lunged at Sarah, closing her fingers around her throat. It was only when

Sarah's moan penetrated her darkness did Maggie realise what she was doing. She released her hold and dashed out of the flat into the hall. She was approached by one of the other residents who asked, "Are you okay? You look terribly upset. What on earth is wrong?"

"I think I've hurt my mother. She's lying beside the range. Would you go in and see if she's alright?"

"But there aren't any ranges in these flats. We just have a small electric cooker." Hastily Maggie made her way out of the building. Later that evening she rang the warden's office to ask if her mother was okay. "She's fine," said the warden. "She's in the recreation room at the minute. We're having an evening of bingo."

A few days later, with nothing needing her immediate attention, Maggie sat over a cup of tea thinking about how she had nearly killed Sarah. Gradually her thoughts were interrupted by sounds coming through the open window, the twitter of a bird and the swish of tree branches making music in the wind. She had the sudden realisation that in her previously busy life she seldom had the time to sit and think or listen to the sounds around her. As she looked out the window she thought of all the places she'd like to visit and all the things she'd like to do but suddenly the black shapes of the past started creeping into the room and she again felt enveloped in darkness. "Why does this keep happening to me? All I ever wanted was to be normal." She gave her head an angry shake and poured another cup of tea. Had someone asked her what she was afraid of, or why in a sudden flash she saw herself in bursts of uncontrollable anger fighting some shapeless monster, she could not have given an answer. Why, she asked herself, was this happening now when she had nothing to be afraid of and was anticipating the endless possibilities of her future? Perhaps the wise thing to do was to seek answers. The next morning she made an appointment with her doctor. Three days later she sat in the surgery facing the doctor. "Well what can I do for you?" he asked. Her nerve was failing. She fiddled with her bag. "I think I've got athlete's foot again." He told her of a new cream that was giving very good results and started writing a prescription. She started to breathe heavily and thought of coming back another day. He passed the slip of paper to her but she remained seated.

"Is there something else?"

"Yes, I, it's that…" and in her spluttering she realised it was now or never. She took a deep breath and continued. "I think I'm going to kill my mother. To look at me you'd think I was all right but no one knows what's going on inside my head. I sometimes feel unable to cope when this dark mood comes over me. It's not that I want to kill my mother – it's just that I'm terrified that one day I will." Words continued to tumble from her mouth as the doctor tried to get her to relax. "All I know is that I don't want these dark moods and flashbacks to continue. Could I have some sort of brain disorder? I need to know why these things continue to happen."

"I can refer you to a psychologist. I think that would be best for now and when I get a report back we can take it from there." So began a series of meetings with the psychologist Sam Forbes. On her first visit she laid down her own ground rules; she would not agree to take any drugs or pills.

"I won't be giving you any drugs. What made you think I would?"

"Well some years ago, when I was trying to deal with my husband's drink problem, a doctor prescribed pills for severe headaches I was having. They helped the headaches but I was functioning like a zombie. Much later I discovered he had given me tranquilizers and when I slammed the bottle of pills on his desk and told him I was taking no more of them, he said I couldn't do that. I'd have to ease off them gradually. I refused. It turned out he was right. What angers me most is that people never tell me the truth. They assume I don't need to know and then make decisions for me as if I didn't have a brain of my own. It has left me that I trust no one so maybe I shouldn't be here." Calmly he listened and did not interrupt until her tirade was over.

"For our next meeting I'd like you to bring some photographs of your family. It helps me to put a face to the people you'll be talking about. And I want you to get a big writing pad and a pen. Think back to your first memory and write a short piece about it. I want you to include everything, warts and all, otherwise I can't help you." She looked at him and thought, 'A patronizing git who wants to treat me like a child, give me homework and thinks that's going to help.' But she agreed with his suggestion and made another appointment. She bought the writing pad and thought of her present colleagues and friends and recalled snippets of their chatter about their past. There seemed to be no warts in their lives. They were all such nice people. In many ways she was like them. It was the bloody awful flashbacks that came like a poisoned dart, leaving her feeling that she was in two places at the same time and leading two separate lives at one and the same time. That evening as she stood at the hob stirring food around in the pan she said aloud, "Photographs, where am I going to look for photographs?" There were few snapshots taken when she was young and she wasn't sentimental about them. She had always intended to put them in a proper album but they were crammed into a shoe box and she could not at that moment remember where she had put them. After she had eaten she took the pad and with pen in hand sat at the table and flicked over the front cover. The blank page stared up at her. She could not think of a single thing to write about. "Maybe if I stare at the wall something will come to me." Leaning forward, she concentrated, riveting her eyes on a stain on the paint. Nothing. "To hell with this. It's never going to work. I'll go to the next appointment and tell him I've changed my mind." She got up and put the kettle on, tapping her fingernails on the worktop as she waited for the water to boil. Between sips of tea she wrote any old word that came to mind. Half way down the page a memory of the collie dog they had when she was about three or four, formed itself into words. His shaggy hair, the smell of him when he got wet and the way he shook himself, sending sprays of water droplets out like a spiral was all so clear. She wrote the memory down. The next evening she began the search for the photos. In the spare room she got down on all fours and pulled out a variety of boxes from under the bed, one of which was the shoe box. "My God, would you look at all that fluff and dust. I must sweep it one of these days." She rummaged through the photographs and picked out four, all sepia coloured with ragged edges.

At their next meeting she showed Sam Forbes the photographs. "This one is of my parents taken in a studio in Brooklyn, New York." He took it from her and likewise the others, a snapshot of her father with three of his friends, taken on a grassy bank. They all looked young and carefree. The third was a snap of her mother feeding chickens. She passed the last one to him. It was one of Robert, sitting on a stool in the lean-to shed. She didn't need to look closely for she remembered the eyes, drained of all sparkle. When he took it from her she dug her nails into her palms until she felt they would cut through her flesh. In a faint voice she said, "This is my Uncle Robert." Then he looked at what she had written. She waited for some comment about the jumble of words but none came. He wanted her to talk about the dog. Inside she was shouting, "For God's sake, he was just a dog. What do you want me to say about him?" But her outer shell was much too polite to utter it. "We called him Flash and he died of distemper. It was horrible to see the foam coming from his nose and eyes. I wanted to run to him and stroke his hair but my father would not let me go near him." For some strange reason she felt exhausted. She wanted to go home and go to bed. In the next week the iceberg of memories began to melt onto the pages and at first she wrote like a robot, with no emotional distinction between pleasant and horrible memories.

Gradually she was looking again at every aspect of her past. It was like dredging a muddy river. Little nuggets stored in her subconscious mind began to emerge. There were times when pleasant memories floated to the surface and she'd smile and remark, "Heavens, I'd completely forgotten about that." At other times what spewed up like black lava was so treacherous that her anger was at boiling point. If this was what he meant by confronting her past, warts and all, in order to deal with it, somehow it was making her feel worse. Once she smashed a cup on the floor in sheer frustration and while writing about it the pen left a deep track on the paper. She said to Mr. Forbes, "If only I had done something or said something." He reminded her that in those days she was a child. No one would have believed her or listened. Present day facilities were non- existent all those years ago. In the evenings as she sat at the kitchen table writing her pieces, it dawned on her that this man's method made sense. For the first time in her life she was putting her trust in another human being and sometimes she could feel the tension slipping away from her shoulders. He was not after all a patronizing git. She had lived her life through a kind of tunnel vision and only now began to question situations on a broader scale, wondering what thoughts her siblings had and what the members of her wider family tree were like. So on the weekends when her children, Oliver and Rachael were not at home her house was empty, housework mostly ignored and the garden untended as she set off looking for information.

Her sister Ruth was unpacking a cardboard box. "Still unpacking! For goodness sake you've been here for nearly a year," said Maggie as Ruth peeled tissue paper from a silver teapot. "Ah, it's the famous tea service. Did you know I had that as a temporary wedding present?" She laughed and looking at Ruth's two children playing on the floor said, "Now any bets as to which of them will inherit the family heirloom?" Ruth was not amused. "Come on, can you not see the funny side? Every one of us was promised the same article, whatever it happened to be, and told to keep it a secret."

"There's nothing funny or secretive about this. When we lived in London I decided to have it valued. Can you imagine the utter humiliation when I was told it was the property of the Waldorf Astoria Hotel? I don't want it in this house a moment longer. I'll get Ian to get rid of it."

"Maybe this is not a good time to ask but I want to know if you have any particular childhood memories that stand out in your mind"

"If a particular memory is being forced to listen to my mother bad mouthing all of you and then warned what would happen if I told anyone, there you have it."

"Would some of those yarns be about me hanging around pubs after school and my father after a hard day's work setting out to bring me home? And best of all, the doctor told her I had a dirty auld sexual disease and had to get lots of injections to cure it. Never having heard of the Hippocratic Oath, anybody would be used to destroy the one who dared to confront her. My children used to laugh and say she was off her rocker."

"So I carried that load of garbage in my head for years. It was enough to sink an ocean liner and your children cast it off like jetsam."

"They are a different generation, free to question and challenge what they're told and isn't that progress?" Ruth was strangely quiet before she spoke. "I used to wonder what kind of woman would go to such lengths to destroy her own children."

"I'd say one with a very disturbed mind and years ago where was the medical help for that condition?" Maggie's expression changed and there was a glint in her eye as she donned a mantle of aristocratic superiority. "You mentioned an ocean liner. I might be the only person to possess a relic from a certain sunken liner. Do you remember the silver eggcup and spoon and mother's story of the captain presenting it to her as she was disembarking?"

"She told me the captain gave it to her when he invited her to dine at his table. How did you come to get it?"

"It was displayed as one of my wedding presents and when she was putting all her belongings back in the trunk she said I could keep it. By then it was tarnished, hadn't been cleaned for years. So I kept it. I might give it to a maritime museum. But think of it. If that German, Captain Fritz Lemp, had not given the order to torpedo the R.M.S.Athenia on the first day of WWII there might still be dozens of the ship's eggcups in existence. As it is there might only be one and I've got it."

Chapter 12

The rest of Maggie's siblings were her next contacts and here she had no success at all. It was either a blanking out of memories or a refusal to make any comments so she tried further a field. She knew that somewhere she had an aunt called Dora who used to knit jumpers for her cousin Amy. A visit to Peggy Fletcher was next on her list. Peggy was pleased to see her but reluctant to pass on Dora's address. "Peggy, you've known me since I was tiny and you know that my mother's behaviour was inclined to be a bit odd. All I want is to talk to as many of her family as I can. Is there something going on that I don't know about?"

"I think I should write to Dora, explain what you want and see what she says. If you leave me your address I'll enclose it in my letter." Maggie waited and waited and as time passed it seemed there was going to be no reply. She was on the verge of giving up hope when to her delight she got a letter inviting her to come and visit the Harrison family. Enclosed with the letter was a simple map of directions from Larne to Dora's home and after replying to the letter she set off early one Saturday morning. By the time she got to the top of The Glenshane Pass her early exuberance began to wane as doubts filled her mind. She pulled on to the hard shoulder to take some time to think. If this aunt was openly amiable like her mother and her Aunt Lettie but secretly out to trap her, how could she trust her? But then if she was like them surely she would have kept in touch with them. As she looked out over the mountain side and watched the early morning mist rise, leaving a clear picture of the scattered houses dotted over the quilt- like fields, she knew she would have to stop running away from challenges she feared to face. On reaching Larne she consulted her map again and as she drove into James Harrison's yard a door opened and a pleasant woman with a beaming smile and silvery hair came towards her with outstretched arms. She enveloped her in a hug which took Maggie by surprise for hugging was not a practice that she was used to.

"I heard the car. We've all been waiting for you," she said. Maggie stepped into an old farmhouse kitchen that was bubbling with excitement. Here were three adult cousins, Kate, Jane and Michael, that until this moment she never knew existed. "They have to get back to work. Jim couldn't get here for he works on the ferry, but you'll meet them again later on," explained Dora. Before they left they hugged her and said they'd be back straight after work. Maggie felt so overwhelmed that tears were not far away but old habits prevailed and she tensed her body and fought the urge to cry. At the solid wooden table she had tea with Dora and James. James talked about his sheep. He was entering two of them at the next Balmoral show. Dora talked about the scenic views on the drive to Larne and Maggie told her that she had not taken the scenic route. Then James went out the back door saying he had things to do. "He doesn't really have things to do. He's away to Michael's place to leave us on our own. Peggy tells me you want to pick my brains about your Mum's young days." Now that the moment had come Maggie didn't know what to say. She wondered what Peggy had written in her letter. "I feel awful, bothering you like this. I don't know where to begin."

"I'll pour another cup of tea and you just start anywhere."

"Well I've never had a normal relationship with my mother. It was one battle after another and now I don't know if I can ever be in her company again. I know she had a tough life with my father's drinking and when we were young she fed and clothed us in the best way she could but it was all the other stuff I found hard to cope with. Then when Dad died we thought all the arguments would stop but they got worse. It was almost as if he had been a restraining hand and after his death nobody could reason with her. I wondered if some terrible experience in her youth had left her mistrusting and hating everyone around her."

"Are you saying that a terrible experience would explain her behaviour."

"I really don't know what to think for there were other things like her intense hatred of her home village and everyone in it. I think she couldn't get away from it quickly enough. And her fantasy stories! When I was very young she would start talking, as though to some unseen figure and if I interrupted she would go wild. So I soon learned to be invisible. Then when we were adults she'd tell yarns that couldn't possibly be true and it seemed as though she herself believed them."

"Maybe you're looking for something that doesn't exist. Did it ever cross your mind that what you're searching for is all in your mother's head. There was nothing wrong with our village or the people in it. I never got on with Sarah or Letty but I don't feel any guilt about that."

"But how did you cope with them? I can understand people who indulge in a bit of idle gossip. If there's nothing interesting in their lives it could serve a purpose. I'm talking about deliberate lies and slander that's so destructive, but you were never in our home to know what it was like." Listening intently to what Maggie had just said, Dora thought she was seeing the rerun of an old film. Maggie's words, 'I don't know if I can ever be in her company again' took her back to her own youth. "You're right, I was never in your home but in a strange way I watched you grow up."

"Ah, would that be Peggy's letters?"

"Yes, there were times Peggy had real concerns for you all but she couldn't always intervene. I count myself lucky that I had someone who did. My father's first family had no one to intervene so he had free rein with his brutality. Did you ever try to keep a diary when you were young?" Thinking of how her mother used to rifle through everyone's letters, Maggie shrugged and said, "No I didn't and it wouldn't have survived if I had."

"Maggie, before you see any of the family relics we have, I need to tell you why I took so long to answer your letter. For reasons I won't go into now I did not want to meet any of Sarah or Letty's family. We read Peggy's letter several times and it was Kate who insisted that she wanted to meet you. She is very interested in our family tree and you belong to a branch of it that she knows nothing about. I tend to speak my mind so don't be offended by what I've just said. If you come here often enough you'll get used to me." She left the kitchen and returned with a cardboard box and set it on a chair. "You said if you had tried to keep a diary it wouldn't have survived. Well neither did Annie's early attempts." Looking directly at Maggie and then at the box she opened the flaps. "See these bundles of papers, they're Annie's writings that she started way back when she was a schoolgirl. Her father punished her for daring to write about what went on in the house, but it didn't keep her from noting the unjust actions she saw being carried out in her home. She wrote her little jottings at school and gave them to her cousin Charlotte for safekeeping. Somehow that arrangement became the norm and even years later everything she wrote was entrusted to her cousin. Then when Charlotte and her husband were planning to go to America Annie had to take the diaries back."

"I'm intrigued as to how you came to get them."

"Well, Annie gave them to Kate. Kate used to go on holiday to Annie's home and over the years they became very close. She'll be back before lunchtime for she's taking the afternoon off to show you her work on the family tree. But now I think we should go for a walk and get some fresh air." They ambled a little way along the lane looking at wild flowers and two rabbits hopping into the safety of the hedge. The conversation was light as they commented on their immediate surroundings. Then they sat on a bench which was made from a railway sleeper laid across three concrete blocks. "Maggie, how many of your mother's family do you really know and if you get any information while you're here what do you intend to do with it? I'd like you to be as open as you can with me." Maggie saw that she was being grilled and knew that Dora had a right to protect her own family. She had to trust this woman if she was to make any headway.

"Well I knew that Amy's mother was her half-sister and that she died when Amy was a baby. I never met Annie but I knew that she was the half-sister who reared her for she always talked about how harsh she was. I met Andy once when I was very young but never knew whether he was from the first family or the second. I knew her younger sister Lettie. I didn't like or trust her but I had good reasons not to. There were others she talked about but I never knew whether they were siblings or people from her home village and asking probing questions was not a wise move in our house. You want to know what I'll do with the information I gather. Right now I have no plans to do anything with it. I want to find out why she behaved in such an odd way and what drove her to carry out such vindictive acts. Surely it's natural for most people to want to know who they really are and what kind of background they came from. I know what I'm searching for is all in the past but I'm still curious."

"I can see that you and Kate are going to get on well. Now I think we should get back and I'll make a light lunch for we won't be having a meal till the others return."

While Maggie set the table and Dora made sandwiches and tea Kate drove into the yard. After lunch Dora said she needed to deal with the laundry. Looking at Kate she said, "Take Maggie upstairs for I know you're itching to show her what you do." Kate took the box of papers and Maggie followed her to a small room at the end of the landing. There was an easel, a desk and chair, a shelf holding folders and an old table with pens and brushes and a variety of paints.

"So you're an artist," Maggie said.

"Very amateurish. I don't do this for a living. I work in the local library but I've always been interested in painting and writing. What I write is not fictional. They're stories of people I know, especially in the family as you'll see when I show you some of my folders." She took a folder from the shelf and opened it at the first page. A young woman with brown hair, blue eyes and a hint of a smile looked up from the page. At the bottom corners pen drawings of a child's cradle and a coffin gave the dates of birth and death. "That's my grandmother.

She was your grandmother too and it's the first of these folders I did."

"Did you paint it from a photograph?"

"No, there were no photographs of her. I asked Aunt Annie to describe her and tell me what kind of person she was and when I came home I painted this and here on the opposite page I wrote Aunt Annie's description of her. You can see from this that she was a kind and gentle person. Now I'm going to show you something that is quite harrowing. This is about Aunt Annie's own mother and your grandfather's first family." The paper in the bundle Kate took from the box was faded and falling apart where it was folded. She had typed a copy of each one and put them in a folder. Passing the folder to Maggie she said, "Read this." Here was the charming John Cowper shown as a sadistic tyrant. He ordered his eldest son to collect poteen from a still in the bog and when he remained at home to tend his dying mother, his father gave him a merciless thrashing with a buckled belt and then alleged the injuries were caused by a group of hooligans who had accosted him. Then he threatened the rest of the family with the consequences they'd meet if any of them divulged the truth. This twelve year old lad, already suffering from tuberculosis, died three months after his mother. There were numerous times that he used the whip to punish the boys for disobedience. Maggie looked up at Kate. "This is horrendous."

"It is. Now turn over a few pages to where her father has remarried. It seems our grandmother took mastitis after Letty's birth and Annie and her sister Jane pleaded with him to send for a doctor. Instead he cut her breasts with a razor believing that would let out what he thought was pus and then he rubbed the area with poteen. Poteen was his cure for everything, external and internal. He was one of those men whose word was law in his own house."

"So she would have died of septicaemia."

"That wasn't the end of it. Her eldest brother was going to take him to court, for when he got the news of her death he asked the doctor what treatment she was given and discovered that the doctor had not been called to attend her. That's when old man Cowper claimed he had sent for the doctor and of course Annie knew he hadn't. In those days poor people didn't have the money for law suits and it was well known that a number of women died in childbirth. From what I've gathered from my mother it was the talk of the village for a long time."

"What age was Annie when she became mother to the second family?"

"She was thirteen but there is a twist in that story too. I want to show you a more recent letter. It was sent to my mother shortly after Annie and her husband settled in England." Maggie read the letter and said, "Good heavens! She was blackmailing her father over the death of her brother and her stepmother. And look at this bit. She gave him a day to decide either to give her complete control of the house, no more use of the whip or she'd join her sister in Glasgow and the children would be put in an orphanage and he would face two charges of manslaughter when she passed her evidence to the law. Well she was a plucky wee girl at thirteen. And what did your mother think when she got this letter?"

"She said she couldn't blame her. Then my father suggested that she should go and visit Annie so my aunt came to look after us and he went with her."

"All this has been an eye opener to me. It's a huge slice of history that could so easily be lost. I think what you're doing is fantastic." The whole idea enthralled Maggie. If she were to start her own family tree she could use cameras and record voices. As the idea was germinating in her mind there was the sound of a dog barking and voices in the yard. The family had returned. Soon the kitchen table was piled with fish and chips wrapped in newspaper. No ceremony here. Everyone was picking with fingers, joking, laughing and wiping greasy hands on yesterday's news. Maggie began to relax among these cousins. There were invitations to return, to go sailing with them and to take the ferry to Jim's place in Scotland and go hill walking. Amidst all the laughter and banter Maggie saw how different the upbringing of this family was compared to her own. She could not imagine any of them coming home and being questioned as though they were prisoners in the dock. So far this visit unearthed nothing that could redeem Sarah's behaviour but it left Maggie thinking about her own life. It's difficult to break away from habits and memories of one's past but she felt it was something well worth doing. When the evening's jollity ended she bade farewell to them and promised Kate she would return to look at more of her work on the family tree. She was given the bedroom next to Kate's den and after breakfast next morning she set off on her return journey, taking the scenic route as Dora suggested and promising to return for another visit.

The Antrim Coast Road provided a panorama of scenic beauty. Solid rugged rocks stood facing the elements. They were in turn, battered by the raging foam, baked by the sun, cooled by the wind and always a sure resting place for the seabirds. After driving for some miles she decided she'd like to get nearer to the water so she parked the car and wandered over rough grass till she came to a flat rock where she could sit down. It was a glorious day with the sun shining and a breeze blowing in from the sea. She sat on the rock looking at the water churning against the jagged rocks below and thought how it all resembled Kate's story of the family's life. Young lives flung about like rag dolls! She thought of Sam Forbes. Guilt, anger, frustration and even vengeance, she had claimed them all and he was showing her how to deal with them. She felt lucky. Yet, strong as she was becoming, life could still throw rocks at her vulnerability.

Some way off a man stood on a rock with a hawk perched on his arm. Suddenly the bird flapped its wings and took off, wheeling in a wide circle over the water. Slowly she turned her head as her eyes followed its path. "My God, it's beautiful," she said. Smiling, she thought of its every movement working in harmony to produce such a graceful display. The wing flapping changed speed as it came in to land. She watched it sit still on the man's arm. Even amidst the noise of the waves and the gulls this was a peaceful place to sit and think and get away from the hustle and bustle of life. "Yes, I'll come here again," she said and cupping her face in her hands she looked out to sea.

Jamie McKendron was in one of his dark moods. "Staring at me, insolent bitch!" He spat out the words as he put the hawk in the cage. With heavy steps he walked towards the rock where Maggie sat. She didn't see him approach or hear him come up behind her. He tapped her quite hard on the shoulder and turning her head she looked into a face, one side normal and the other scarred. "Maybe you'd like to have a closer look. You're not quite like the others. They glance and look away, but not you, you have to stare and stare." There was fury in his outburst. In the lash of a moment Maggie was whirled back in time, being accused and punished for things she did not do. But to take it from a stranger! She screeched at him. "What do you want from me? Sympathy? It's your face. You deal with it."

Shock hit him like a slap on the mouth. This was a reaction he did not expect and had never got in the past. He backed off and said, "I'm sorry, I thought you…."

"Never mind what you thought. Just piss off and take your bird with you." As soon as she'd uttered the words she regretted her harsh reaction but he had moved away and she didn't look round to see where he was. He was a little distance from her, alert and watching. He didn't know or care who she was or why she was there, but if she had some mental problem she might throw herself off the cliff edge. From bitter experience he remembered the anguish he'd caused his family when he tried something similar and he didn't want this situation on his conscience.

From the zenith to the nadir of his life he had dropped like a stone. Jeanie, beautiful, rich, the dancing party girl and Jamie, the handsome young pilot were the envy of all in town. He had no illusions about his flying sorties across the channel. Either he would survive the war and settle down with his beloved Jeanie or he'd be killed in action. Never did he think he would spend the rest of his life in this in-between state, neither dead nor fully alive. While he was in hospital Jeanie had visited, but only once. She could not bring herself to look at the terrible burns. At home she could not bear him to touch her. He remembered very little about the day his plane was shot down and wished that he had not been rescued. "It's shock. She'll accept it in time," they said. But they were mistaken. He felt like the Hunchback of Notre Dame. It was obvious that he repulsed her and two years after their fairytale wedding the marriage was shattered. She wanted a divorce but the reason she gave was the unkindest cut of all. The hawk seemed agitated and her squawk brought his attention to his present situation. This stupid woman now making her way to the road, had rekindled all his old hurts and he wanted to tell her so. He picked up the cage and strode towards his camper van. He opened the van door, put his bag and coat in and was about to lift the cage when she came along side and stopped.

"Excuse me, for what it's worth I apologise for screaming at you," she said.

"But not for staring at my ugly face."

"Look, let's get something straight here. I'll take the rap for anything I do or say but I'm damned if I'll take it for what I didn't do. I was watching your hawk make that brilliant flight. Do you imagine that from where I was sitting I could see the details of your face?"

"Now that you have seen it do you still think I should deal with it?" She looked straight at his eyes, her face tense and he sensed she was going to deliver another angry outburst. He was in the mood for a confrontation. Then her countenance softened and for a moment she was wrestling and grasping for words that would not take voice. "It's things. Things. They happen to all of us. It's the way we deal with them that matters. I…I'm only learning that myself. Look, I talk a lot of garbage at times so just ignore me."

"Maybe we should call a truce."

"Aye, good idea, and don't drive off without your hawk. You know it's an ugly looking specimen crouched in there, nothing like when it's in flight." She was moving off. Why then, did he want to detain her a little longer? She had irritated him, spoke her mind regardless of what offence it caused and she could be crude. After his accident he wanted to shout, to scream, to tell the world how he felt inside, but no one would let him. His family pandered to his every need, crept quietly around him in case a word or action would annoy him and agreed with him when he wanted to shut himself away from the world. Now a stranger had the cheek to snap back at his outburst. "Maybe that doctor was right. It's not my face I need to deal with." He snatched the road map from the dashboard and said, "I wonder could you tell me if there's a camp site near Limavady?"

"Limavady. I know it well." But she didn't know of any camp site. She suggested one of the local farmers might let him park on their land. As their conversation lost its earlier aggression he told her he had come from Scotland and planned to spend two days here. She told him she lived in Eglinton, a village at the other side of Limavady.

"There's a graveyard there where some airmen are buried. That's one of the places I want to visit."

"Well if you're only staying two days you're welcome to park at my place." He drove behind her car and parked beside her gable wall. "If you need some fresh water there's a tap in the back garden." He nodded and brought a kettle from the van while she unlocked the garden gate. When he filled the kettle she locked the gate and bade him goodnight. He was glad he did not have to search for a site to park the van. Once his mission was over he could get back home without meeting too many people. After a simple meal he checked the hawk, looked again at his map and went to bed.

Maggie looked in the fridge, sniffed and said, "I'll have to throw most of this out." Since her family had left home she could not get out of the habit of buying food in large quantities.

From the bits and pieces that were edible she made a meal and as she ate the camper van excited her. With a flicker of a smile she whispered, "Ah yes, I could." Peering out the gable window she looked at the van. The curtain was pulled across its side window so she didn't feel like a peeping tom. It was too big and she could not afford to keep a car and a van, but there might be a smaller version that would serve both purposes. Her trip to Larne had given her the travel bug like she remembered from her student days. This time she could do something about it so she found the only map of Ireland she had, spread it on the table and scanned the coastline. Apart from all the islands on the west coast there was GalwayBay, Dingle, Cork, Waterford, Dublin, The Ards Peninsula and RathlinIsland "That's just the coastline. There must be castles and places of interest all over the country and I haven't seen any of them." She sat looking at the map while softly singing, Among TheWicklow Hills. That night her head sank into the pillow as sweet melodies lulled her to sleep.

Chapter 13

On wakening Maggie's first thought was a cup of tea and a slice of toast but she found the bread stale and with mould on the edges. She drank a cup of tea, broke the bread into small bits and swirled them around the congealed fat in the frying pan. She was putting the contents of the pan on the bird table when Jamie looked through the rails of the garden gate. He thought if he could enlist her help in finding these places on the map, it would limit the number of people he'd have to meet. Pointing to the map he said, "Could you show me where this graveyard is?" He drove the van following her directions and parked beside the church. She showed him the row of headstones where several airmen were buried and asked him if he wanted to be alone for a while but he was freely chatting about the family of one of these men. They had worked on his father's estate and one of them asked him to take a photo of the grave if he was near the area. She was the quiet one, thinking of one particular evening when a group of locals stood watching the flames from a plane that plunged into BenevenaghMountain. There was the old woman who said, "Ugh, he'll make good fertiliser," and Bridie Brennan saying, "May God forgive you woman, that's a terrible thing to say," then cross herself as tears rolled down her face. The memory of that evening was clearer than the memory of what she'd done five minutes ago. Jamie had taken his photos and was ready to move on. She was so quiet that he wondered if she was related to any of these men but didn't ask in case it would upset her.

Back in the village she said, "Just drop me off here for I need to get some groceries." But he was willing to wait in the van. He needed a few items and maybe she could get them and he'd keep an eye on the hawk. She accepted his reasoning without a qualm and at home totted up how much he owed her and handed him the bag. He paid her and leaving extra money said, "I need to ring home. Could I possibly use your phone?" She directed him to the hall and closed the kitchen door.

"Alastair, it's Jamie here."

"Well how did you get on?"

"I found a place to park and took some shots of that graveyard in Eglinton and after I take Cas for a flight I'll go and see the mountain."

"That's good. Just remember, if you feel at all uneasy, ring me."

"I'll be fine. See you soon."

She was washing dishes when he came back to the kitchen. "I'll be moving on to-day and I want to thank you very much for all your help. I'll call in before I leave." She extended a hand and said, "In that case I'll bid you good bye now, for I have an appointment in town and I expect you'll be away before I get back." With a smile she added, "I'm sorry our first meeting was such a battle situation."

"And that, if I may say so, is the first time I've seen you smile."

"Well you're one up on me for I've never seen you smile."

The antagonists of the previous day parted politely and a little later he watched her drive off. In Sam Forbes' office she told him of her visit to an aunt and cousins she had never seen before and how after a short time, she felt she had known them all her life. She was planning to return and get to know her cousins with their outgoing and positive attitudes. The only thing she couldn't shake off was the terrible guilt she felt that she did nothing for Robert when she was adult enough to do something about his plight. She showed him her latest words. "See, I felt I was doing great. I'm happy, content, making plans for the future and then this morning it all went haywire. It was that bloody mountain that brought it all back." She told him how the incident in a graveyard made her think of Robert. After all these years his name was never put on his family's headstone. It was as if he never existed but her father's grave had a shiny black stone with gold coloured lettering. It seemed those who caused turmoil in their lifetime were still getting attention in their death. "If I could have a good cry it might help but tears never come. Instead I shout and thump things and leave myself exhausted."

He reasoned with her. "Your father and grandfather's grave has only recently had a headstone erected whereas at Robert's grave there is an existing headstone. It's simply that his name was never added. There may have been financial difficulties at the time or good intentions that were never carried out but I doubt that any malice was intended. A visit to the graves might help you see the situation in a different light."

"You're right. I can't keep on criticising others and do nothing myself. I'm on holiday right now and while this is on my mind I think I'll go to-morrow."

"You really have come a long way so look on this as a slight setback and for next time you could include some thoughts on your visit to the graves."

Jamie decided to take the hawk for a flight before driving to his next destination. He drove out of the village and took one of the side roads that took him to the wetlands along the River Foyle. He never tired of watching Cas wheel in circles. Over the last few years she was the only constant feature in his life. To his whistled command Cas returned and he tethered her on the ground while he sat on a mound of earth contemplating his next port of call, the aerodrome and that mountain. The stages of his life and everything he'd lost passed before him like falling dominoes. His brother Angus, destined to manage the estate, had joined the RAF and was killed when his plane crashed into BenevenaghMountain. The onus fell on him to step into his brother's shoes for the future running of the estate depended on him but he had no experience of managing such affairs. In the last year of the war when he was old enough he too was a pilot. Then the domino effect speeded up. His mind was racing, his plane shot down, Jeanie wanting a divorce because she claimed he was impotent after the accident and she dearly wanted a family. He looked over the river and shouted, "Lying bitch, you couldn't bear to come within a yard of me, let alone have sex with me, you bloody hypocrite. And the stupid words of the rest of you, 'It's God's will. It's a cross you have to bear.' Why couldn't you all let me deal with it in my own way? And the estate, in the hands of The National Trust, another failure chalked up to me. Well whoever rules the universe, you've taken it all. I don't even have an heir like my dead brother. How I've hated you Angus and I can't even face the mountain that killed you." He looked at the hawk scratching on the ground. "Only you and me now Cas!" He had been sitting on the ground for so long that his clothes were damp and he was so tired he could have slept where he sat. He couldn't drive to BenevenaghMountain and certainly not back to Larne in this state. There was only one solution. He'd ask that woman if he could stay one more night.

As soon as Maggie returned she made a pot of tea and opened her folder. The tick of the kitchen clock was the only sound as she wrote about the burden of guilt she felt about abandoning Robert in his terrible plight. She wrote about her weekend visit to Larne and how she discovered what a sacrifice her Aunt Annie had made for her siblings. A thought crossed her mind that her mother had inherited some kind of rogue gene and no matter what Sam Forbes said she blamed herself for not bringing it to light. She had married and walked away when she should have done something. The door bell rang and as she opened the door her phone rang. Jamie McKendron stood on the doorstep. She asked him to go through to the kitchen while she answered the call. He saw the open folder and noticed that it was written in longhand. When she returned he said, "Somebody's journal?" His words froze her like a statue. "Don't read that," she yelled and as she snatched the folder the loose pages took flight all over the kitchen floor. Like a mad thing she bent down to gather them, fuming and swearing. Then she squashed a handful of papers and throwing them from her roared, "Ugh, what's the point in trying?" She slumped in the chair and as though only then aware of his presence said, "Forgive me, I'm sorry about all this. Did you have a breakdown?" He didn't know what to say. He had just witnessed a stranger do what he desperately wanted to do many years ago, but his clergyman uncle and his refined mother would not allow him to behave like a common moron.

"I've upset you. Believe me I didn't read any of it. My van didn't break down but I think I did. I called to ask if I could park one more night. I'm not feeling too well but I'll leave first thing in the morning."

"I'm not upset. I'm steaming mad but it has nothing to do with you. I have issues in my life that I'm dealing with. Now if you're not well, of course you must stay. Driving when you're feeling ill is not safe. Can I get you a hot lemon drink?"

Dare he tell her what was tormenting him? A few times he had come close to confiding in a friend but clammed up at the last moment. "A lemon drink would be fine, but all the lemon drinks in the world wouldn't help." In that moment of desperation he had clasped her hand as he spoke. She didn't pull her hand away in revulsion as he expected her to and he continued. "These scars on my face are the result of war wounds and I still can't get used to people staring at me." But as on the other occasions he could not go on. As he released her hand she said, "Surely there are organizations that can help you deal with these feelings." She made the lemon drink and as he sipped it she made sandwiches and a salad. During lunch she was full of questions about the hawk and he was glad of the opportunity to talk about his nephew's falconry business for it took his mind off the mountain. After ringing home again he spent most of the afternoon in the garden with Cas and then asked her if he could treat her to a Chinese take away for all the help she'd given him. At the evening meal they talked of memories and how one memory triggered off another.

"That graveyard this morning made me think of BenevenaghMountain," she said.

"Were they horrible memories?"

"I'll say! We used to watch the flames and smoke rise in the air when a plane crashed. I used to feel glad it wasn't me and then feel so guilty. It got to the stage I'd go to bed and feel that the burning wreckage was sticking to me. I suppose I had no common sense."

"No common sense, why do you say that?"

"I pictured them alive and burning bit by bit when reality was that they were dead the moment they hit the rock, before the flames started, and they didn't feel any pain."

"But you have no guilt about it now." She smiled and shrugged.

"I think I'm a glutton for useless things. As soon as I get rid of one bit of guilt, another takes its place. That's why I'm going to see my uncle's grave to morrow."

"So you're off again to that Eglinton graveyard."

"No, this one's in Donegal."

They both laughed at the morbid topic they talked about. Inside he wasn't laughing. His only reason for coming here was to face this mountain and hope it would release him from the guilt he felt about hating his brother and rid him of the scars that he felt all over his body. She was thanking him for the meal. He had to keep alert and smiling for he wanted to see for himself why she was visiting a grave. "I've never been to Donegal. Would you mind if I came along too?" She agreed to let him come with her on her trip in the morning.

The drive to Gleneely graveyard was very pleasant as he admired the scenery and she told him of the wartime stories she'd heard the older people talk about. As agreed he stayed outside the graveyard and she went in. She assured him she would not be long. He watched her approach one grave and then move along the side of the church, presumably to another. He waited, walked along the road for a bit, came back and waited. Feeling irritated he went in the gate but couldn't see or hear anything. Then he saw her half clinging to an old stone. What on earth was wrong with her for she looked a mess? He lifted her up and held her close. He could feel her whole body throbbing but there was no sound of crying, just tears flowing.

How he had often longed to hold a woman in his arms again, but not like this and not this one. He didn't know what to say so he stroked her hair. It made no difference; the throb of her was like a drum beat.

When it eventually eased off she staggered away from him. He followed her. In a faint voice she said, "I'm very glad you're here. Had I been here in my car I couldn't have driven home on my own for ages." Her breathing was more regular now but he was angry, so angry. Everyone at home told him there were no major scars on his body but he felt them and still they wouldn't listen. Now this woman who spoke her mind and didn't give a fig for anyone's feelings had felt them too and couldn't get away from him quickly enough.

"I'll drive you home but what a pity my body is so repulsive to you."

"What are you talking about?"

"When I held you back there you must have felt the scars all over me and seen them too. Too terrible to look at, so you dashed away from me."

"How the bloody hell could I see scars on your body. You've got your clothes on, but if you say you have scars I'll take your word for it." He pulled off his coat, then his shirt. "Fine, strip your clothes off, streak round the graveyard if that's what makes you happy." He stood naked to the waist. She looked at him and roared. "What kind of game are you playing? You think I'm an idiot. I can see now why you were so keen to come here. There's not a mark on your body. You know it and I know it, but you thought you'd play a little prank, get this simpleton woman in a quiet place and let her think she's alone with a madman then go home and have a laugh with your tartan friends. Well go home and enjoy your little prank. I know people in this village. I'll get a lift home, but that's the last stunt you'll ever play on me."

He dropped to the ground and curled up like a hedgehog. At last he had the stark truth but it made him feel worse. His mind was more muddled than it had ever been. He needed help and she might walk away and leave him here. In a faltering begging voice he said, "Please don't leave me."

"If this is an attempt at an encore, forget it. There's no audience left." In a daze he got his keys and mumbling said, "You've got it wrong. Do one thing for me… number in the van…please ring Alastair." He looked so pathetic and lost as he held out the keys that she thought she might have misjudged him. But what the hell was wrong with him? She was scared. She felt like running away and got herself in a position between him and the gate. Taking the keys she said, "If you can make it to the van I'll drive home and ring from there." He put the shirt on and dragged the coat behind him. The drive home was silent for he was incapable of making conversation. He fidgeted, anxious that she ring the number. When she heard a voice she gave her name and asked to speak to Alastair. "Your uncle is here in my driveway and he seems to have suffered some kind of breakdown and I don't know what to do. Will I ring an ambulance?" She listened to the voice on the line – 'some kind of depression, believed he was covered in burn scars, wouldn't listen to the doctors'. Her head was reeling. Hadn't she seen monstrous black shapes squeezing the life out of her and when she described them to Sam Forbes he never shouted at her like she had just done to this man. The voice on the phone was saying, "Hello, hello, are you still there, can you hear me?" Sharply she shook her head. "Yes, I'm here, but tell me what to do." She listened to his advice and told him she would ring back as soon as she could. As she put the phone down she was sure that all this was her fault for she had provoked him in the graveyard. She went out and opened the passenger door, took both his hands in hers and said, "I said some terrible things to you. I suppose saying sorry is pointless."

"It's alright. When is Alastair coming?" he said in a faint voice.

"He'll be here as soon as he can. Why not come in for a while. You can bring the hawk in if you want to." Slowly he made his way into the house and went to the toilet. Then Maggie directed him to the living room where he flopped on to the couch. Quickly she put some warmed soup and bread on a tray and took it to him, telling him he'd feel better when he had something to eat. She went out to the van but could not find any of the tablets Alastair had mentioned. With as much courage as she could muster she wrapped her hand in an old towel and carried the hawk in its cage into the living room. He was eating but did not look up. When she looked in later the tray was on the floor and he was asleep. Sam Forbes' words made perfect sense to her now. If she could get rid of her guilt and anger and all the other negatives she would experience feelings of understanding and forgiveness. Now a stranger who needed help was in her home and she had just put the boot in. She rang Alastair again to report on progress and when Jamie woke the pallid complexion had gone and his voice was a little stronger.

"Your hawk, she didn't get a flight to day. Would you like to tether her in the garden?" He nodded, picked up the cage and tethered Cas in the garden while he sat on an old deck chair. At dinner Maggie told him of the arrangements. "Alastair and I agree that you need a good night's rest and to morrow I'll drive you to Larne in your van and he'll meet you there."

"But I can't put you to all that trouble. I'll be alright to drive myself."

"You know how anxious he'll be and besides you'd deprive me of a little trip. I have relations in Larne and they keep asking me to go sailing with them." After dinner he offered to trim her garden hedge and with each snip he knew nothing would keep him from going to that mountain yet he didn't want to go alone.

"Would seeing that mountain bring back those bad memories you talked about?"

"No, I've a bit more common sense these days. Anyway it's such a landmark that you can't help noticing it, but why do you ask?"

"Before going to Larne I want to go there and I'd like you to come with me." Next morning they set off and on the way she pointed out the old airfield site. She thought he only wanted to look at the mountain but he wanted to climb as near to the base as he could get. A silver sheet of mist draped itself over the peak and gentle rain began to fall. Unable to climb like he could she stayed some way off. He was a long time and she was getting soaked as the rain got heavier but she told herself to keep calm. If there was a scene like yesterday how would she get him down? At last he moved. He was coming down. With rain streaming down his face he said, "Good heavens, you're drenched."

"So are you." He looked odd. His whole countenance seemed to have changed. Was he even aware it was raining so heavily? As they began the descent he stopped and looked back. Her blurred brain cleared. "Did you lose someone close to you up there?"

"My brother Angus, but we're alright now." She thought it a strange thing to say and fell silent. As they continued the journey towards Larne he asked her how long she was going to stay with her relations and did she like sailing. She lied and told him what she thought he wanted to hear. Alastair was waiting anxiously for the ferry was due to sail very soon, so it was a quick introduction and a quick goodbye as he handed her an envelope. She sped off to catch the train to Derry.

Chapter 14

Maggie took a seat on the train and opening Alastair's envelope found some money and a note that read, 'I am very grateful for what you did for my uncle and thank you for your kindness to him. I hope that one day we will meet again. With best regards, Alastair Mc Kendron'. As she put the envelope in her bag she wondered what he'd think if he knew how nasty she had been to his uncle? On her next arranged visit to Larne the Harrison family was going sailing and invited her to join them. Once in the boat she had mixed feelings about this venture. The trepidation at each rise and dip of the boat mingled with the excitement of the surge through the water and the wind in her face. As she watched them pull on ropes it gave her a new slant on her one time fear of the sea. She made a firm decision that she would learn to swim and on her return home booked lessons for beginners.

Feeling that she had grown up enjoying very little and time was running out she wanted everything for her new life and she wanted it all at once. She turned her attention to clothes, remembering her longings to be dressed in beautiful creations. After trying on several outfits that the assistant said did wonderful things for her, she knew she would never be comfortable in clothes that said, 'elegantly dressed'. She raised her eyebrows and left the shop with nothing except a long felt yearning that she wanted to be painted pink at least a few times in her life. Maybe, she thought, this yearning for colour had nothing to do with clothes. In another shop she said to the assistant, "I'm looking for an outfit in deep pink, nothing fancy and not a dress." But nothing on the rails matched the picture she had in her head. In another shop and on another day she found a two piece outfit, pink, plain and classically cut. On her way home she sighed. "Don't know where I'll wear this but it's something I've always wanted." One evening Kate Harrison rang. "Isn't your next term break in two weeks time? We're going to Jim's place in Scotland so would you like to join us for some hill walking?"

"I'd love to give it a go but what would I need for a trip like that?"

"Just warm clothing, a sleeping bag and hiking boots or a stout pair of shoes. We'll be sleeping in tents but don't go buying a tent. We can sort that out." At the top of a high hill she was breathing in the bracing fresh air and filled with excitement at sharing binoculars with her cousins. This was the best possible way of seeing the countryside around her. Till now she had never noticed that there were so many colours in the hills and mountains. Sleeping in a tent gave her the best night's sleep she had ever had. On their last day they saw a group of men with birds and cages and Kate explained that there was a school of falconry further north. Looking through the binoculars Maggie was sure one of the men was Alastair McKendron. "Why don't you go and speak to him?" Kate said. She approached the group and found that it was Alastair. He greeted her with a broad smile and said, "Well I never expected to see you here."

"I'm here with some of my cousins. They do quite a lot of hill walking." She asked him about his work and how his uncle was. Pointing to the birds and the cages he said, "We give lessons on falconry and demonstrations at designated gatherings

and often give lectures in colleges." Taking her aside he continued in a quiet voice. "I've been trying to pluck up the courage
to ring you. Uncle Jamie is still very quiet and hasn't uttered a
word about what happened when he was in Ireland. So would
it be alright to ring you? My mother told me that after he was
wounded in the war he hasn't been anything like the man he
used to be." His companions were calling to him, obviously
keen to pack up and be on their way so their second meeting ended as quickly as the day they first met at the ferry. The
Harrison tents were dismantled, sleeping bags folded, camping
stove and food containers put into the haversacks and tired but
exhilarated the merry band set off to Jim's place to spend the
last night before returning home. That night Kate and Maggie
were deep in conversation about Kate's folders. "Now what's
your view on the gene pattern we all inherit? Are some of us
predisposed to certain nasty actions and carry them out come
what may?" Maggie asked.

"My mother would not agree with that. She believes we all
know the difference between right and wrong and we make our
choices. I believe we can inherit certain diseases but character
traits, I'm not so sure. I've known families brought up in the
same household and most of them are decent people but one or
two are really nasty. I can't make up my mind if they learn bad
behaviour or it's in their genes." Neither of them felt qualified
to make an absolute decision so they talked about the research
scientists did to find vaccines to cure diseases and wondered if
the day would come when they could isolate dangerous genes
and dismantle them. "Now getting away from this morbid topic,
when are you going to pay us another visit?" Kate continued.

"I'll be there as often as you'll have me for I'm fascinated
by the way you set out your work and I have heaps of questions

to ask you about searching for material. I'll make a list and bring it with me."

Back home Maggie felt the break had given her a new lease of life. She joined a Yoga class and the swimming lessons were coming on well. Then there was a call from Alastair. His uncle was quite well but they were concerned that he still did not want to talk about anything and certainly not his trip to Ireland. He wondered if she could shed any light as to what happened. Maggie saw that they were treating him like she had been treated, people making decisions for her behind her back. She had a momentary flash of anger but quickly composed herself. "Alastair, I need to give this some thought. Could I ring you back, let's say to-morrow?" This gave her time to think of what she would say to him. She sat at the table and tried to put her thoughts into words. After several attempts she had what she thought was a fair answer. Next day she rang him. "Alastair I've given your request a lot of thought. It seems to me that your uncle's situation should be a G.P. and patient relationship and it would be remiss of me to get involved. Besides I don't know anything about his problems so I hope you can understand why I can't talk about his visit." There was a long pause.

"Yes, I think I see what you mean and thank you for taking the time to ring me."

Alastair went immediately to his uncle's house to tell him yet again how worried they all were that he could not talk to them. "I don't want to see you end up like a hermit, talking to no one. What kind of life is that?"

"I'm perfectly alright. I just don't want to discuss my feelings."

"I might as well tell you that I rang that woman in Ireland to find out what happened when you were there and she refuses point blank to talk about you."

While Alastair was talking to his uncle Maggie was in a quiet thoughtful mood, thinking of Sam Forbes. She no longer needed consultations with him. The change he brought about in her life was nothing short of amazing. He had taken her mind with its one muddy window and transformed it into one with many clear windows that could look out in all directions. No doubt he was still doing the same thing for others and doing it without doses of medication. Suddenly the phone rang. It was Jamie McKendron.

"Alastair told me he rang you about my visit to your place."

"Yes that's right. I tried to explain why I couldn't give him any information. But I have something I need to say directly to you. That day in the graveyard I know that I was responsible for the breakdown or whatever it was you took. It was only after that first call to Alastair that I realised you had some kind of problem. When you wanted to drive to Larne on your own I lied to you when I said I was going to relations there. On the day I first met you on the Coast Road I was returning from my aunt's house in Larne and had no plans to return so soon. I am really sorry that I caused you so much misery while you were here."

"My miseries started a long time before I met you. I want to ask if you'd talk to me. It's true I have problems and I remember you saying you had issues to deal with. There is no way I can discuss my problems with my family. They're very supportive but confiding in them could create more problems. So please, if I came over early on a Saturday and left in the evening would you give me a little of your time?" Although Maggie knew nothing of his problems she could empathise with his plight and agreed to his request. On the appointed Saturday he arrived at her door without the van and without the hawk.

While having a cup of tea he asked her how she came up with the idea of writing about her problems.

"Oh that wasn't my idea." Without giving any details of her life, she explained how the psychologist that she was referred to got her to write about everything from as far back as she could remember.

"Did you feel that helped?"

"The writing was only a basis for his analysis; the real healing came through the many discussions we had. Some circumstances in people's lives can do strange things to their minds and that's where he helped. In my case you could say he performed a miracle. There were times when I'd slip into the old mould but when I thought of where I'd been and where I am now I'd get back on track pretty sharply." He put one hand on his forehead and tapped the table with the other as she continued. "A qualified psychologist can assess the problem and give advice. I don't know what else to say. You may feel that coming over here has been a waste of time but when you get back home and take some quiet time to think you'll come up with a solution." He took her hand in his, looked up with a glimmer of a smile and said, "I think I already have but may I write to you, nothing regular you know, just now and then to keep in touch?"

"No, I wouldn't mind at all." They had lunch and she drove him to the train station. He did find the kind of help he needed and occasionally wrote to tell her how he was getting on. She wrote to tell him about all the activities she had tried and those she had discarded. Very gradually a trust built up between them and they felt able to tell each other more and more about their lives. He wrote to tell her that the hawk had died and how much he was missing her. One evening he rang, sounding excited. Alastair and his business partner were booked to do a falconry exhibition in the north coast at the weekend. If he came with them could she come to Larne and spend the day with him? Amidst all the effort she had put into getting her new life going she had to admit that she was missing him more than she realised. Alastair introduced her to his companion and the two men, both wearing kilts, went off in the camper van to their venue.

"It feels strange seeing you without the hawk. Did you ever find out what happened?"

"Some kind of virus, the vet said. I felt devastated after she died but when the taxidermist brought her back I felt that she was still with me." He held up a paper bag. "Is there a quiet place where we can go? I've brought a picnic with me."

She drove a little way along the coast road and parked. "This will do. If it rains we can sit in the car and if the sun stays out we can sit down there by the water's edge." On a soft grassy patch in view of the water they sat down and ate the contents of the picnic bag. Their eyes met, not as young lovers mentally undressing each other but as two middle aged people, damaged by what life had thrown at them and lucky to be seeing light at the end of the tunnel. He was the first to speak. "I'm so glad you came. I thought all these new activities you're doing would change you into someone I didn't know." Gently he kissed her, knowing that the scars on his face would not repulse her. They lay, arms entwined, and touching cloth was the nearest they had so far come to loving. "I have changed," she said. She talked of all the activities she had tried in her grasping for the things of youth only to find that they were inappropriate. She laughed as she told him about buying the outfit that she might never wear. "Can you picture me at my age with a skipping rope and wearing a pink gingham dress? That's how I wanted to be dressed years ago."

"And what kind of outfit is it? Come on, I want to hear."

"It's a two piece creation in pink and nothing like the picture I used to have in my mind. There's something else I've discovered. Slowing down to observe my surroundings is not always a waste of time. Near where I live there's a place called The Ness Woods and one day I took a picnic and sat there watching the waterfall tumbling into the gorge and listened to the birds singing. Then as the evening wore on the sun, like a great orange ball, looked like it was easing itself below the horizon. Watching it slowly disappear from my view was an unbelievably beautiful sight. I had never taken time to do things like that before."

"And how are you faring with the water activities?"

"The sailing looks like too much hard work but I can do the breaststroke. A bit more practice and I'll be like a real frog."

"I'm much calmer now and more relaxed. I have no regrets about the life of grandeur I once lived and the formal balls I used to attend."

"But they must have been wonderful, floating on a dance floor to all that music."

"There was nothing wonderful about them. They were hollow and false. Nothing about that life was genuine. Now I'm free of it I want to meet real people."

"You want to meet my Aunt Dora, she's as real as you can get, decides what's right for her, discards the negatives and has no guilt about it. You know it's only a ten minute drive from here and I told her I would call after I left you at the ferry."

"Maybe I should meet this real woman but before we go I want to ask you if you'd spend a few days with me in Scotland?

I could meet you at Stranraer," and leaning closer his tongue licked her neck as he whispered, "Say you'll come and maybe we could…"

"Aye, I'd like that," and she ran her fingers through his hair. They walked for a while along the sand, skimming stones into the water and then went to the Harrison home. At the sound of a car Dora came out to the yard. "Ah, you're early. I thought you weren't coming till later." She swept Maggie into her arms in the now familiar hug. "And you brought your friend, Jamie, isn't it?" He expected a formal shake of the hand but he got a warm hug and before he had time to think he was in the old kitchen. "You two arrived just when we could be doing with your help. James is trying to get some sheep in the pen and a couple of them broke away. I keep telling him to get rid of the sheep and rest himself but he never listens." All this was said as they followed her out to the meadow. If Jamie wanted to meet real people doing real jobs he got a speedy introduction into their world. He was running around helping to guide unwilling sheep into a pen that they didn't want to enter. "Good man your self! They can be a bit thran at times," James said as the job was completed and they all returned to the kitchen. Dora dished out steaming Irish stew and dessert plates of rhubarb and custard. After saying goodbye Maggie drove to the ferry terminal where they waited for Alastair and his companion.

"When does your summer break start?" he asked.

"Three more weeks and next time we meet I might see you in a kilt." With a devilish twinkle in his eye he said, "I might surprise you, might even bring the bagpipes." She waved as the camper van disappeared on to the ferry and three weeks later she was the one on the ferry. When it docked Jamie was waiting. As she got into the van she noticed a kilt hanging on a peg. She laughed as she said, "Oh you really do have a kilt."

"That's Alastair's but I do have a kilt of my own, same tartan but better looking."

They drove out of Stranraer, listening to music cassettes and singing along with them. He turned off the main road and parked near a sheltered cove. He had planned a picnic by the shore before driving to his home further north. As they ate he talked of how he saw his life changing, the peace of mind he felt and the ease with which he could now talk to friends and neighbours. She told him she had stopped dashing around doing everything in a mad rush. "I read more and join in village activities. I listen to music and even dance round the kitchen. I always wanted to dance but when I was young I never got to a dance or any kind of social event. I used to envy girls in my class who talked about being at a barn dance. Scott tried to teach me the steps and I thought I was enjoying it but I was stiff and awkward. It wasn't flowing the way I saw it in my head."

"So you're going to take lessons on this flow kind of dancing," he teased.

"Stop laughing at me. I don't mean any kind of formal dancing. I mean soaking up the music and letting it move me. I'll show you what I mean." She took her shoes off and singing a jaunty tune she glided over the sand, a fluttering butterfly then a spinning top, round and round, her coloured scarf wheeling above her head. He watched her. She was like a crazy woman and he wanted some of this crazy colour in his life. Shoes cast aside he joined her, swaying, whirling and twirling in a hypnotic musical ecstasy.

"Jakers you can dance," she shouted.

"Years of practice," he shouted back. Their feet threw up splashes of water but they didn't appear to notice. Then a freak wave knocked her off balance and as Jamie bent to steady her, a second wave completely drenched them and left them lying in the wet sand. As they got to their feet he said, "Go into the water and strip off. That'll get rid of the sand. I'll go to the van for a couple of towels." He sped off and returned with a bucket. "Have you not been in the water yet?"

"Have you taken leave of your senses? I'm not in a bloody nudist camp." He shrugged, set the bucket down and raced into the water. It was then that she noticed the towels in the bucket and his mad behaviour began to make sense. She watched as he took off each item of clothing and bobbed the lot up and down in the water. Deciding there was no other way of getting rid of the sand that stuck to her she followed him into the foaming waves. Holding a bundle of wet clothing in front of them they headed for the bucket. "Here, you can have the big towel," he said, as he put the other towel round his waist and put the wet clothes in the bucket. Outside the door of the van he waved his arms around letting the warm sun dry his skin. Inside the van Maggie sat on the edge of the camp bed struggling to dry herself. He came in and sat down beside her. "You know there's nobody but me to see you and you're making a dog's dinner of getting dried." He inched closer and under the old rug they were in tune with the waves. When they were still she said, "Do you think the tide will come up this far?"

"Heavens woman, what a time to be thinking of the tide! We're well above the tide line." They lay still till he gave a soft chuckle. "I wonder what your Aunt Dora would say if she saw us now."

"She'd probably use one of her well known phrases; throw out the negatives and have no guilt."

"That's just what we'll do. But right now we'll get dressed."

His home was pleasant, orderly and in secluded surroundings. He showed her a small laundry room where she rinsed the wet clothes and hung them up. She joined him in the kitchen where he had started to cook dinner. They chatted about food while he stirred a saucepan and she set the table. He opened a bottle of wine. "Red all right," he said. As he set the bottle and two glasses on the table, a sharp tingle ran through her and she shuddered. "I don't really drink. Half a glass will be fine." She took a deep breath and the tinge was gone. "This is really tasty. I can see you're a dab hand at the cooking." The evening was a success, an enjoyable meal and a stroll through the park to the local village. In his bedroom he showed her the immaculate kilt, jacket and socks. "This is the surprise I planned, you in a nice dress, a quiet dinner and a few dances in a little club near here. I thought we might go to morrow evening."

"I've only got my pink creation. I never buy dresses." Patting the bedcover, he motioned her to sit beside him. His eyes went from her to the bed and he saw the momentary flinch and a slight quiver on her lips.

"Maggie, sit down for a minute. I want to talk to you. If you're not careful you're going to slide back to the old dark days. Do you think I didn't notice when I put the wine and glasses on the table? I could see where that was coming from. Now the dress! You didn't say, 'I don't like dresses', you spat out, 'I never buy dresses'. Talk to me. Where is it coming from? Come on, you know we can tell each other anything."

"I told you what my upbringing was like. There was always money for whisky but why would anybody want me to have a dress? I know that may not have been the real reason but things like that stick in the mind."

"Good, you've got that out. Now the bed! You're either saying you have regrets about today at the beach or there's something about a bed."

"No, it's not regrets. I could make love to you on a bed of bluebells or on a bed of dead leaves in a forest."

"Well if I were a young man I might consider driving round the countryside looking for a bed of bluebells, but dead leaves, I'd have to wait till the autumn and the humour would be off me by then." They both laughed. "Maggie, you know all about my time with the counselor so are you a slow learner or a poor listener? I think you don't want to let go of that anchor that was holding you down. That way you don't have to face the world and anything it throws at you."

She took some time before she spoke. "My divorce was a family disgrace. It was a case of, 'you made your bed, now you can lie in it'. And I did lie in a bed I had no right to be in when I married a man I didn't love and one who didn't love me. It felt like the worst kind of adultery."

"That wasn't too hard to talk about. I'd say you have a lot of respect for your Aunt Dora. What puzzles me is why you don't take a leaf out of her book."

Supper talk was about ideas for the future, now that each of them was an unchained melody. She wanted to travel, not short holidays here and there but into the lives and cultures of other peoples. He wanted to study photography. The birds and animals of his native Scotland would be a starting point. In the bedroom she took off her dressing gown and slid between the sheets. As he hung his dressing gown on the peg on the door he looked at her and said, "I'm too tired to go looking for handfuls of bluebells." She grinned and said, "Crocuses would do just as well."

"Move over, you crazy woman." For them the whole world was outside until the morning dawned. They wakened to bird song and a world not fully awake. "Breakfast, boiled eggs?" She nodded her answer. He put the eggs in a saucepan of water and she set the table. She went to him and put a hand on each side of his face. He held her like a soft pillow. "I've had an idea," she said. Smiling and looking into her eyes he said, "Let me guess, it's now daffodils or tulips."

"No, this is a serious idea. It's a way of capitalizing on your face as a means of bringing attention to ecology. Look at oil slicks that are reported in newspapers and in the media. After a few days how many of us, apart from those directly involved, give them a second thought." There was a spluttering on the hob as the water boiled over. They pulled apart. "Cracked eggs it is," he said as he scooped their contents into two cups. At the table he said, "You know you have a point but it's how to develop it."

"I see a series of books for school children entitled, 'The Two Sides Of ….where you draw or paint, say a penguin or a seagull, and disfigure one side of it. The photography side should not present too many problems but what angle to present the writing would take a bit of thought. Children are the future and it's amazing how they can latch on to new information provided they are not overwhelmed with too much at one time. I'd say keep it simple and eye-catching." They tossed ideas about as they ate and then planned the second day of her trip. They strolled to the village to have lunch. "And what relaxing activities are you planning for the future?" she asked.

"I have big plans to dig up half the garden and plant bluebells."

"I'm never going to live this down, am I?"

"I'd say you have no chance." He spent Christmas with her. She spent Easter with him. He started his course on photography. As well as work she went swimming once a week and to her Yoga class. As before letters and phone calls kept them in touch and in the summer she was back in Scotland looking at the dozens of photos he'd taken. He made three attempts to write his first book, The Two Sides of The Otter, but was not happy with the results. "It was a good idea, but maybe I'm rushing it or writing isn't my forte."

"Never mind, you'll know when it feels right and you know the old saying – success is just failure that decided to have another go."

Their gentle teasing and laughter, interspersed with deep meaningful conversations about things that were important to them, became the pattern of their relationship. They touched base whenever they could. Redundancy brought her career to an end earlier than expected and she saw it as an opportunity to start her travels. One day Jamie rang bursting with excitement. He got his first book, The Two Sides of the Hawk, published and was offered a photographic commission in Norway where a group was making a documentary film. When he asked her about her travel plans she told him she'd start with a trip to visit her son in Canada.

"Great, take lots of notes and don't forget your camera." They made plans about keeping in touch while they were on two different continents and she set off on the first leg of her journey, a flight from Belfast to Heathrow.

Chapter 15

How do you become an instant- walking snowman? You alight from a plane at Fort McMurray Airport in a snow blizzard. Maggie was not dressed for these weather conditions. Minus 26 degrees with the chill factor, exacerbated by the whipping wind, her nose was feeling numb. The icy coldness made it difficult to breathe. There were no hugs of greeting from her son Oliver, for the priority was to get off the tarmac, out of the small airport and into the car as quickly as possible. Vehicles impacted snow to the road leaving it hard and unyielding. The snow plough heaped the recently fallen snow into grey curtains at the sides of the road. The windscreen wipers laboured against the fast falling flakes. It took a long time to drive through this hazy tunnel. Maggie's memories of snow at home were of soft white flakes, falling gently to carpet the ground and children laughing as they threw snowballs and built snowmen. This snow was at war. With its ally, the cold wind, it pelted everything below it into submission.

For centuries this was the land of the Native Indian Cree Nation where hunting and fishing were their main activities. FortMackay remained very much as it had been for years but Fort McMurray became a town known all over Canada. Finding that oil could be extracted from the surface of the land brought a sudden and drastic change to the lives of these people. The area, known as the Tar Sands of Northern Alberta, was so rich a source of oil that developers quickly rushed in. Soon there was a population explosion as people from high unemployment areas flocked there, tempted by the high wages. Services that every town needs mushroomed. A pipeline and a wide road were laid along the 250 miles to Edmonton. Developers cleared tree strewn areas to provide housing for the hundreds of workers who came. Oliver was one of these workers. One morning as Maggie and some of the residents were talking her young grandson shouted, "Look, a big bear." From the window they saw a huge brown bear standing on its hind legs and its front paws leaning on the fence. "What do the authorities do when a bear gets as close as this?" Maggie asked, seeing at first hand one of the dangers of this northern climate.

"The rangers shoot a dose of anesthetic into it and put it into a metal cage. No doubt they'll starve it for a few days before airlifting it two or three hundred miles north of here," said one of the women. The vast majority of people were blow- ins who wanted to make as much money as possible and get out again. Plans did not always follow this pattern. Some got so used to the affluent lifestyle that they were reluctant to relinquish it. They settled here, dipping annually into the outside world for exotic holidays. Others could not handle the excess of money. The credits and debits of their bank accounts were like shallow flowing streams. They could not afford to leave. Some left but when work prospects dried up they reluctantly returned. On Oliver's arrival in Canada he worked on the east coast before making his way westward. Having seen quite a bit of the country his ambition was to settle in British Columbia and he was at this time looking for a job there. People socialized in each other's flats and one of the callers was a preacher. He was quite charming and welcomed her to his group. When he voiced some of his beliefs Maggie was appalled. (Young children should be strictly disciplined with physical punishments to teach them right from wrong. Women should be completely subservient to their husbands. AIDS was a curse. As soon as every last victim was dead the world would be cleansed of it.) Those who disagreed with his opinions left the group, leaving the vulnerable, who were easily brainwashed. Most of them had drug or alcohol problems or came from families where these twin menaces had traumatized their lives. Others were refugees or recently arrived immigrants.

Outwardly Maggie avoided confrontation and simmered inwardly. She hated herself for this cowardice for her silence gave the impression that she was in agreement. "When am I going to stand up and state what I feel and what I believe?" she asked herself. Already her mind was looking for excuses. This man was a guest in her son's home and she did not want to rock the boat. Sometimes he wanted to talk about the political situation in Northern Ireland. Maggie didn't.

"How would a preacher like me be accepted if I came to your country?"

"You'd be booted out of town."

"So with all the years of fighting they haven't come very far."

"Oh, I don't know, we may not have come all that far, but I'd say we've come a lot farther than you." She had taken the first tentative step, but using sarcasm was not the answer she wanted. He asked her further questions about religion and politics in her homeland and before she got an answer formed it was obvious he was trying to tie her in knots or impress her with his perceived higher intelligence. She recalled an old friend's advice, 'never let them see they've angered you, for that way they've won'. That advice was welcome now. "You know some people who've lived through the ravages of wars don't want to talk to outsiders about their thoughts, and I think I'm one of those people," Maggie replied. He was now advocating that the families of his sect should have their children educated at home or in groups set up by his church. It would keep them away from the evil doctrines taught in secular schools. Whether or not he was aware of it, he had just insulted her profession. Maggie was becoming a lone voice or no voice at all. His hypnotic power and overbearing attitude could easily alienate her from her family.

One day while shopping in the mall a woman approached her and said, "By your accent I'd say you're from Northern Ireland." She was Carol Simmons from Belfast, an extrovert who was a refreshing breath of fresh air. She took Maggie under her wing and turned out to be a really good friend. Through her Maggie met some of the older Native Indian women. They were pleasantly unaffected and unrushed, like people who could sit and appreciate a sunset. "Do many of them work at the refinery?" Maggie asked.

"Huh, you kidding! The best job they can get is sweeping the floors of the mall." Carol, who did quite a bit of voluntary work, took her to an old people's home where she introduced her to an old man in a wheelchair. He had worked for years at a depot up north where the road ended and goods were transferred to sleds. One evening he got drunk and exposure to the cold left him with frost bitten feet and he had to have his toes amputated. From books and television he followed world affairs, sport and nature programmes and being a great fan of Edmonton ice hockey team Carol jokingly told him her greatest wish before she died was to see Calgary win the cup. Quick as a flash he said, "In that case you'll live forever." Once when going for a coffee Carol approached a dark skinned man who was sweeping the street and with a form of sign language and a few words of English she talked to him. When he moved away she explained that he and his wife and two sons had fled from Nicaragua. She had some trousers her boys had grown out of and his lads could have them.

"Why did they have to flee?" asked Maggie. Carol shrugged. "He spoke out against some injustice and staying was not a wise move. He's desperately trying to earn enough money to get the rest of his family out, but if he stays in the clutches of preacher man it'll never happen."

"I take it you know all about him."

"I keep my ear to the ground. Nobody in that group ever sees the financial statements but they're asked to fork out plenty. He's anti every church in the town. Even your Oliver is a changed man since he met him."

Maggie bought a small car which gave her the freedom to explore more of her surroundings. Mostly the town was like a grey blanket with the only colour coming from the neon lights and artificial displays in shop windows. But on the shore of LakeAthabasca the starkness and vastness of this northern landscape had a beauty that was inspiring. With the ice floes, the water and the land around them in white and grey it felt like it was drawing the watcher thousands of years back into the mists of a time long gone. She wished that she had a pair of binoculars. Spring came and she was amazed at how quickly the rush of new foliage covered the ground. In early summer Oliver finally got a new job and the whole family was excited about getting to the other side of the Rockies. Some of Carol's predictions were becoming reality. Maggie watched as preacher man furnished the family with an address where they could find an identical religious group when they moved. She was watching a control freak take over the mind of a child she had reared and there was nothing she could do about it. The usual pattern was on the menu again as she was ousted from a family group where she did not fit in. She knew that everyone had hurdles in their lives from time to time. How did they deal with them? Did they jump over them, bore through them or skirt around them? What if these hurdles were ghosts that she could not see? The removal truck came and took all the furniture and household stuff. Apart from a few cases and bags, lined up on the living room floor, the flat was empty. In Maggie's case there was a towel, toilet bag and two changes of clothes. Her camera, a vacuum flask and a Tupperware jar with some biscuits in it were in a cardboard box. Passport and money were in her handbag. Oliver and Maria planned to have a short break somewhere on the route west. Maggie was not invited but Oliver gave her a simple sketch showing directions to get out of Edmonton and on to the highway. On the back of the paper was the address of a motel in BC. She put her case on the back seat of the car, the cardboard box on the floor in front of the passenger seat and slung her bag on her shoulder. She drove to Carol's house, her heart as numb as her nose had been on the day she arrived. Oliver had changed from the witty fun loving son he'd been to a stranger who couldn't talk to her. Maria had changed too. That twinkling eyed young woman, laughing and excited, was now someone else. She was quiet as though looking at a vision no one else could see. Maggie confided her thoughts to Carol. "How could a preacher bring about such changes in people? It beggars belief." She got no sympathy from Carol. Carol didn't do sympathy nor did she have a vindictive streak. She said what she felt, up front and in your face. "The preacher! This has nothing to do with the preacher."

"Well I can't see any other reason for it." Maggie sat at the kitchen table, furious and dreading this journey she'd have to make on her own. Carol poured two mugs of tea, took the lid of the biscuit tin, flicked it on to the worktop and put the tin on the table. She sat down opposite Maggie.

"So, things are not going too well."

"You're right, they're not. It's like the air is laden with unsaid words. In many ways I wish I hadn't come on this trip."

"You're seeing only what's in front of your face. The real problem is over your shoulder. Did it ever strike you that you might be the selfish one, expecting him to do what you wouldn't want to do yourself?" Maggie frowned. Was there another side to this woman she thought she knew so well? Before her jumbled thoughts could come out in words Carol launched into a monologue, not stopping to let her interrupt. "I've known Oliver for a long time. He works with my husband Joe. Maria has two brothers and two sisters, all younger than she is, but you already know that. Do you know anything at all about the Phillippines? The one that has a job or gets out of the country to work helps the others. That's their culture. Oh, I've heard them called lazy bastards, out for all they can get. My brother was in the merchant navy and he could tell you another story, a country stripped of its resources and I don't need to tell you where the wealth goes. He took this photograph when he was there."

She took a photograph from the shelf and set it on the table. Maggie picked it up and stared at two adults and six children, so thin they looked almost emaciated. "Oliver and Maria know they don't earn enough to bring all her family over here, but how do you explain that to a family who has seen the wealth of the west and think we all have fat purses. You sit here aggrieved at your treatment. No doubt you left Ireland looking for a quiet life. We could all get a quiet life, but it's often at someone else's expense. Oliver is giving you a way out. He doesn't want you embroiled in his problems and I'm sure neither of them knew the pressure they'd face when they married."

"I had no idea what they were facing, and there I was, blaming the preacher." All the aggression had gone out of her voice. She was drained.

"Of course you had no idea. That's the trouble with us, we don't dig deep enough and the big boys at the top don't dig at all. They toss money at problems and hope they'll go away and then throw their hands up in despair when folk aren't grateful to them. I'd say until we look at the roots of problems like corruption these cankers will never go away." Maggie felt she had a few roots of her own to look at, for Carol's words sent her spinning back to her childhood. She sat speechless. "Listen Maggie, if you're offended by anything I've said, I'm not going to apologise. I meant every word. You're free to make your own decisions. The people in that photo don't have the freedom we take for granted." There was a rattle at the door and Carol looked up. "Oh, it's Joe. In the name of God how did you get in such a mess?"

"It's that car we're working on. I need the other spanners. Any tea going?"

"You're not coming into the kitchen dripping oil over the place. Stay out in the yard and I'll bring you out a cup." Maggie joined Joe on the wooden bench.

"So you're off on the long drive," he said.

"Aye, and I'm not looking forward to it for I don't know what to expect." Carol joined them with three mugs of tea on a tray. Joe told her of the straight boring road to Edmonton, advising her to stop and give a lift to anyone on the road.

"Would I not drive to the nearest house to phone for them? I mean, with me on my own, is it safe to pick up strangers?" They both roared with laughter.

"Here it's an unwritten rule for there's not a bloody house between here and the gas station and it's not too far from Edmonton. If it was winter they'd freeze to death in a short time and in summer they'd die of thirst or sunstroke," said Carol.

This news put the fear of God in Maggie. When Joe left with the tools he needed, Carol suggested that she stay another day with her and rest before the trip. She took Carol's advice and next day was on her way out of Fort McMurray. The road was as Joe described it, monotonously straight, and in places skinny trees tried to grow in marshy ground. Maria's family would not leave her mind. They probably saw everyone in the west as billionaires and thought Maria should get them there and look after them. What a selfish attitude, she thought and then some of Carol's words came to her like an echo. And that photo! She could still see the acceptance of despair on their faces. "I suppose if I had as little going for me as they have, I'd try anything, use anybody, to get myself out of such a dire state." She imagined the family in the photo coming to the west, not speaking the language, no work skills, two of them schoolchildren and the shock of another culture where money did not grow on trees. What would she do if it was happening to her own brothers and sisters? "Oh God, there's got to be another way."

Driving alone on this road was hypnotic, mile after mile of the same greyness. The sole of her right foot ached for her car did not have cruise control. Finally she came to the lone station on this dreary road, hot coffee and biscuits at a high counter and toilets at the back. The tank filled and her needs satisfied, she went outside and walked around a while to stretch her legs. Then she took the sketch from her bag and tried to visualize the landmark in Edmonton where she had to make a right turn. When she got to the Yellowhead Highway she was not overly impressed with the mountains. No one told her these were merely the low foothills. They assumed she knew just how far and how high she'd have to go. The further she drove the higher they got, monumental rugged towers tapering into the sky. At the side of the road was the Mt.RobsonMonument. She stopped to take a photo of it and then tried to take a snap of one of the peaks but it was useless. Maybe from some miles away and with a zoom lens she could capture the top and bottom of a peak but not from where she stood. There was a sign marked, 'run away lane' for trucks to get off the highway when their brakes failed. Looking back at the road she had climbed she realised how high she was and wondered how much higher it got. So far she had turned off the highway twice to get gas. Before leaving Fort McMurray she planned to spend the night in a B&B somewhere on route. Darkness fell quickly, so quickly that she was terrified to leave the road.

"What if I can't find a B&B, or there are none or I get lost and end up driving north. I could find myself in Dawson Creek." As her fear grew, reason flew out of the window. It was safer to stay on the highway so she drove on and on into the darkness. Her thoughts came back to her family situation. She could go back home and put this trip down to experience. At least she had experienced something of the bitter cold of winter in Northern Alberta and the heat and mosquitoes of its summer. She had talked to some of its older native inhabitants and marveled at their sense of peace with the simple things of life. The quiet peaceful life she had often yearned for could mean living in a cocoon and any feelings of inquisitiveness she had might fade away and never return. She was free, so why go to that motel address in BC? Her mind was in a whirling tornado but her body was telling her it needed to rest. When she came to a lay by she pulled in and stopped. Suddenly she needed to go to the toilet. She heard blackness creeping nearer and nearer, coming to crush her. There could be a bear in the vicinity. There might be a bear nearby. Soon she was convinced that outside there was a bear. Her black shapes were returning with sharp claws and loud growls. Checking that the windows were closed, she took the biscuits out of the Tupperware jar and peed in it. Then she snapped the lid on and putting her coat around her shoulders she tried to sleep.

In that moment when the black blackness of night gives way to the grey streaks of early dawn she awoke. She felt stiff and every muscle ached. Through the back window tiny glints of the sun were coming up on the horizon. She got out of the car, timorously looked around and stretched her arms and legs. These mountains were a truly awesome sight and there was no one here but her. It felt like she had slept for a short time on the top of the world. From the cardboard box she took two biscuits and the flask of tea. After the simple breakfast she felt better even though the tea was lukewarm. She was unaware that she was about to make the deepest decent of this mountain highway.

"Brake, brake, you're going too fast. Change to a lower gear," her voice kept telling her. There was an odd sound from outside then a feeling that her ears were going to burst. Sweat from her fear, dampened her face. She was rigid. The car started going in jumps. Her right leg was trembling. "Please God, get me to the bottom." She thought the car was going to topple over on to its roof. Then she remembered this feeling in her ears. Yes, it was when the plane was losing height to make the landing at Edmonton airport. Her trembling leg was causing her to make jerky movements on the accelerator. She took deep breaths to calm herself. When she got to the bottom the road leveled out for almost a mile. She stopped again and sat quietly as the waves of her recent fear subsided.

"My life has been filled with fears; fear of what was happening, fear of what could happen, fear of staying and fear of running away. Well, I'm sick of it." She got out of the car, took the Tupperware jar and without a pang of guilt, emptied the contents at the base of a tree. "I'm sick of it," she shouted and her voice got louder and louder as she shouted, "I'm sick of it. Do you hear me mountain, I'm sick of it?" Her words hit the mountain and bounced back to her….sick of it…sick of it. She looked up at the mountaintop and said, "So you want to get acquainted. Helloah, helloah, yodel lade oh, yodel lade ah." And the mountain answered.

At a bend on the road was a truck with two men in the cab. "Did you hear a noise?" said one of them. The other shook his head. When they got closer they saw Maggie. "I told you I heard a noise. Look at that woman shouting her head off. Do you think we should stop?"

"Na, they're waitin' for this load in Kamloops. Let some other sucker deal with it." They drove on and ignored her. She went to the car and threw the Tupperware jar on the floor, saying, "I doubt if you'll ever hold biscuits again." The morning sun was rising and she felt its warmth on her bare arms.

She looked up at the mountains and sensed the stillness of the place. Then she looked at the road ahead. There was a movement from behind that made her turn round sharply. "Dear God! That must be an eagle." Every fearful thought of the past hours was wiped from her mind as she watched this amazing spectacle. It swooped down the side of the mountain, wings still and outspread and then just as quickly their powerful flapping took it up into the sky. Suddenly it wheeled in a circle and came back. Instinctively she bent her knees and dropped her shoulders as she heard the mighty rush of wind as it swooped barely a yard above the roof of the car. "Bloody heck, look at that wing span." In those few seconds she had gazed at the underside of a huge eagle. Her heart was thumping and her whole body tingled with excitement. "Cor, that's a moment I'll never forget." As the eagle flew higher and higher she watched till it was out of sight. For a few moments she gazed upward at these truly majestic mountains. "A quiet peaceful life! Who wants it when there's so much of the world to see?" She got into the car and drove off. It was still very early in the morning when she turned off the highway into Hope. The streets of the town were quiet but she found a gas station and an all night café. Then it was back on the highway heading for Vancouver. On her left she could see early morning traffic crossing The Lion's GateBridge and straight ahead brought her to HorseshoeBay ferry terminal. Across a ten mile stretch of water and she was on The Sunshine Coast and a short distance from the motel.

After a long sleep, she woke next morning, had a shower, a cup of tea and collected her mail. She found a charming little restaurant overlooking the water where she watched brightly painted boats leave the marina and skim over the water. From the travel guides and tourist leaflets on display were pictures of Vancouver's StanleyPark with Canada geese, dolphins, killer whales and the tall carved totem poles. Further along the SunshineCoast were pictures of bald eagles and killer whales competing for the plentiful supply of salmon. She read Jamie's letters as she ate. They were full of the highs and lows of his trip but he was home again taking a well earned rest. Suddenly her thoughts went to her cousin Kate as she recalled a conversation they once had about her work with her family tree. Kate had pointed out how difficult it was to persuade people that the simple stories of their lives was real history that should be preserved. She said that often snippets came out in whispers like a light breeze blowing through aspen willows. As she ate and took in the scenery she resolved to start her own family tree when she got home.

The owner gave her a warm welcome as she came every day for her meals and through him she found the roadside market, overflowing with mouthwatering fruit and vegetables, produce from the Okanagan Valley. She had to have some of it and when Oliver and Maria arrived there were bags of peaches, melons, cherries, apples and pears. "You're lucky, coming to live in a place where you can get such fresh farm produce. I know I'll be dreaming of fruit like this when I get home."

A long sleep after the long flight did nothing for Maggie's spirits. Jamie said, "I can tell there's something bothering you." They sat at the table and it all spilled out.

"I remember Kate telling me that the stories she heard people whispering were the really interesting ones she wanted to write about. What's on my mind is nothing I'd like to whisper about. I feel like screaming and shouting about it." She told him about the photograph Carol had shown her. "But what can I do about the greed and corruption in the world. Dozens of very able people have addressed the problem and it doesn't make a blind bit of difference."

"Maggie it's alright to be angry but staying angry isn't the answer. Do you remember when you had the idea for my series of books? Could you start thinking along those lines? We could do this together. You could use the exact words of a starving child and weave them into a simple story that one child would tell another. I could do the pictures." Jamie spent a lot of time going into schools and clubs to tell children how to look after their pets. Maggie joined him, at first as an observer and listener. Then she asked the children to tell her what they thought the injured animal was feeling. Soon it led to them writing snippets about their own fears. One day a very talkative child came to Jamie and whispered, "See my friend in the back row, she wants to tell Maggie something but she's too scared."

"Do you think she'd tell you and then you could tell Maggie?"

"I'll ask her." Jamie went to the chair where Maggie was sitting and with one hand over his mouth said, "We might have a breakthrough here." Maggie looked at the child in the back row and in her she saw herself as a small child in the midst of a turbulent household. Jamie's idea was right for she had just witnessed two small children, one trying to help the other. That evening she wrote down as many words as she could remember that the children had used and Jamie started drawing animated figures trying to get the faces to match the emotions the words had thrown up. In the weeks that followed most of their time was taken up with planning their first book. It was small enough to fit in a child's pocket and showed two children talking to each other. Using simple words and simple drawings with the emphasis on the faces, they called it, "Just whisper, I'm scared." When it was published they were already working on the second book, "Just whisper, I'm hungry." As each day passed their commitment to the project got stronger and both of themrealised it was taking over their lives. There was no time for her own family tree but she'd leave that to Kate. She knew Kate would understand that had they started their books earlier Robert would have gone to heaven as a bruised angel.

About the Author

Margaret Mary Lena Kane was born in Brooklyn, New York in 1930, the daughter of Irish immigrants. She returned to Ireland as an infant and apart from a short period in Western Canada, remained living in the Emerald Isle until her passing in 2017.

She married David Lyle and raised five children all of whom left Ireland in their twenties and settled overseas. During her 30 year tenure as a highly regarded Primary School teacher, Lena visited her children in England, Australia, Canada and Hong Kong. Her worldly experience and fierce independence, combined with an ever ready dry wit and a refusal to ever suffer fools gladly, gave her a uniquely insightful perspective on life in general.

She first dipped her toes in the waters of published works in 1998 with the formation of "The Maiden City Writers Group" and their collection of poems and short stories entitled "She Steps Out". This was later followed by "Summer Days and Tossed Salads". "Whispering Trees" is her only novel.

Made in the USA
San Bernardino, CA
25 July 2018